LIQUID, FRAGILE, PERISHABLE

LIQUID, FRAGILE, PERISHABLE

a novel

CAROLYN KUEBLER

MELVILLE HOUSE
BROOKLYN · LONDON

Liquid, Fragile, Perishable

First published in 2024 by Melville House

Copyright © 2023 by Carolyn Kuebler

First Melville House Printing: March 2024

Melville House Publishing

46 John Street

Brooklyn, NY 11201

and

Melville House UK

Suite 2000

16/18 Woodford Road

London E7 0HA

mhpbooks.com

@melvillehouse

ISBN: 978-1-68589-109-1

ISBN: 978-1-68589-110-7 (eBook)

Library of Congress Control Number: 2023951839

Designed by Sofia Demopolos

Author photograph by Karen Pike

Printed in the United States of America

1 3 5 7 9 10 8 6 4 2

A catalog record for this book is available from the Library of Congress

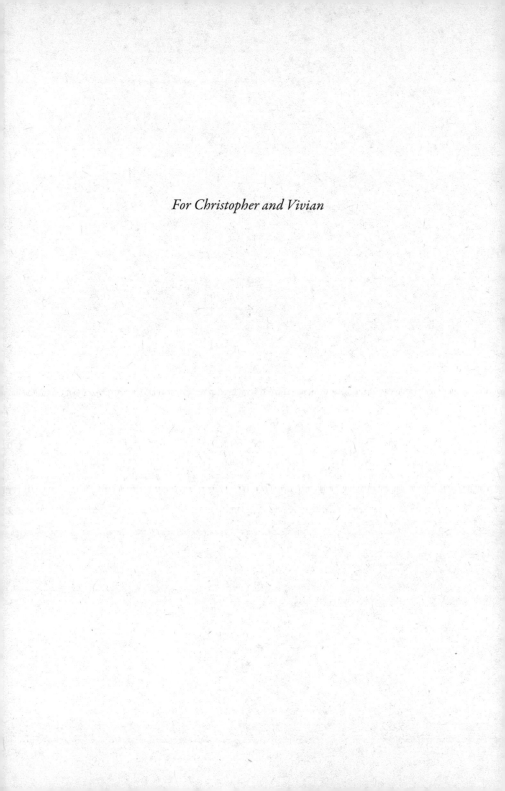

For Christopher and Vivian

one minute a slender pine indistinguishable from the others
the next its trunk horizontal still green the jagged stump
a nest for flickers
                          one minute high wind and rain the skies
lit up the next a few bright winking stars the lashing of the brook

—Ellen Bryant Voigt, "Storm"

Roaring Clyde, you roar so loud
Your streams are wondrous strong
Make me a wreck as I come back
Spare me as I'm going

—From Child Ballad 216, Traditional

1

If she can walk to the supermarket and back, three miles down, three miles up, then she can do without the car.

Nell stops to rest where the trail meets the road, where the road curves from the mountain into town.

The old house is still there by the river. She's looking at it from the other side now, at the yard, the porch, the place she used to live.

The back porch is bare but for a blue recycling bin, upside down.

A pair of mallards sleeps in a patch of sun on the bank. Heads tucked into feathers, unmoving.

It's spring now, and all the rivers are rushing. Brown with white caps, foam and branches swirling beneath the bridge.

The rivers are rushing, but not Nell. No reason to hurry.

She will sit here a while, on a rock in the sun.

The car can stay up at her place until she decides to fix it. Seven hundred and change is more than it's worth to her now.

Another spring without a job, and now she'll do without a car too.

See, I am doing this, walking to the supermarket. Resting in the sun, on a rock, by the river.

Of course everything is easier with a little sun. With the smell of mud, warming and rising.

What's possible in May is more than you can expect for January, even a warm January, like this year. The year before that too.

She looks out to the old house now, its backyard stretching from the porch to the riverbank.

It was too close to the river, Dad always said, but they lived there anyway. All six of them, for so many years, until one by one they left.

She'd stand there on the bank with the binoculars, after Mom died. See that, Nell? he'd say, do you see them?

The green herons were the most difficult to find, their squat bodies, their ugly sounds. Not like a heron at all, she'd say.

She did the best she could for him, though. Scanning the reeds and treetops, closing her eyes to listen.

And later she knew what he needed before he asked.

A heating pad, a cup of tea.

But he's gone now too. Dead and gone. Some words toll like bells.

Like the bells on the hour that always rang, that still ring, if you stop in the town long enough to listen.

She didn't think she'd live more than a minute without Laura, and yet here she is.

Thirty years later. Thirty years longer.

Her sister Laura who was first at everything, afraid of nothing, till they found her, broken, on the rocks below.

Even now, Laura precedes every moment.

Or is Nell exaggerating?

Certainly she goes for hours, days even, without thinking of her. Thirty years now. Thirty-one if you count that first year.

She doesn't count that first year. She can't count what she doesn't remember.

The winter was long and gray, but Nell can breathe in the smell of spring now, the smell of wet, which is the smell of life, which just keeps going.

A fisherman steps into the river, all in brown.

So quiet, like a deer coming out for a drink.

Nell is like a deer today, too, coming out of the woods by the river. Quiet, disturbing nothing, in need of nobody.

If she could disappear back into the woods again like that, she would.

But there's a small list in her pocket of everything she needs.

Flour. Canned food to last. It will be heavy.

She still has applesauce from last fall. A ten-pound block of cheese getting smaller.

Little by little she's finding what she can do without.

The fisherman steps in deeper, and out goes a ribbon of line.

The shadow of a cloud lifts from the grass across the river. The fishing line swoops and glitters.

She could stay here forever, with the sunshine pressing through her hair, the cool of the rock through her jeans.

But how long will it be, really?

A half hour maybe. Then the sun will shift and she'll get going.

It's all she has to do today, to get back before dark, three miles down, three miles up.

A duck lifts its head and shakes its neck, its wings. Both the ducks now, flapping in the sun.

Nell will get moving too.

Across the bridge, through town, and out on the highway to Shaw's. She'll walk along the shoulder. It's not so far.

She can carry her pack. Her legs are strong and she has more time than she needs.

*

You can't open a plate-glass window, so Jeanne props the door.

Ah, if only they'd call a holiday on the first real day of sun! They have holidays for everything else around here.

The sun is nearly hot and yet it's just the start of May.

It's a treat, such a gift—free heat for everyone! Even for people who never pay their bills.

From the look of things, LeBeau's not paying. You can barely fit another thing in his box. Another final notice.

Nothing's ever quite final for the LeBeaus, though. They've been here forever, and forever they'll stay.

Not even Jeanne can keep track of their whereabouts, those endless cousins and sons.

Today Jeanne is standing at the counter. It's better than sitting, they say. Sitting is the new smoking.

Jeanne never smoked. Not cigarettes, anyway.

It was the seventies back then—what do you expect? Yes, she used to be quite a peach, smoking grass in her hippie skirts, hair down to there.

They don't call it grass anymore, though, do they? The kids. Smoking a blunt, her sons would say.

Not that her sons ever really went in for that stuff.

Jeanne opens *Summer's Parade* just below the counter. It's always a game of will they do it, or won't they, in these books.

Or more like when, because it always works out in the end. The characters are always so young, so good-looking.

Don would tease her. What, you don't get enough at home?

He'd tell her to read something better. You're smart, he'd say. You could get a degree.

When did he stop saying that?

Both of them too tired now from working all these years. Raising kids. The whole nine yards.

Their boys both have degrees now. Kevin and Danny with their jobs up in Kingsbury. Jobs and wives.

Yes, Jeanne did okay by her boys. Didn't need a degree for that.

No reason she can't just read whatever she wants now. Though it's taking its sweet time, this book.

People are really coming out of the woodwork today. The young ones already in T-shirts and shorts.

Jeanne doesn't know the little ones anymore. Now she mostly knows the old-timers.

Of course she knows Nell Castleton. Walking by with an old metal-frame backpack. God knows where she must've dug that thing up from.

Everyone knows the Castleton family. One of them went to Harvard.

Maybe Yale? One of them died in a hiking accident out west.

No, Jeanne doesn't really know them. She can count on her fingers the people she really knows anymore.

Apart from the mail they get. One for you, one for you. Day after day the bills that come, the cards and letters less and less.

Such a waste to be at work on a day like this! She could be home cleaning out the garage at least.

All those old baby clothes. The kids' art projects from way back when.

Sometimes it's like she's saving all this junk just for the mice to nest in.

Well, mice have families too. They have to sleep somewhere.

With the door open like this, Jeanne can't help but look up every time a car goes by. A truck now, grinding its gears at the stoplight.

A heavy bass thumps from a car with the windows down. Since time immemorial kids in cars blast their music.

Jeanne used to blast music.

Still does, now and then, back on Chubb Road with no one around but the deer and the skunks.

There's always that sudden quiet when she turns off the ignition. "Silence descends."

She must've read that in her book, though really she should be reading the new regulations.

She read them once but has forgotten. Who can remember stuff like that?

If only she hadn't eaten her lunch so early.

She shifts from one foot to the other. Standing is no better than sitting if you lean like this.

Give me a break, she says. I'm old.

A breeze comes in from the door and she closes her eyes.

But not really. I'm not old when I close my eyes. Not when it's May.

*

Two class periods to go and Eli was out of there! Just walked out the back and nobody to stop him.

And now here he is behind the trees, the barn doors wide open in front of him.

And there she is—a girl named Honey, like the bees. Ha! Like the bee-yards where she lives.

He used to know this girl. He knew all kinds of girls, playing in the woods, hide-and-seek with his sister.

Not anymore, though.

Amber's not even much of a sister anymore.

Cousins barely see him either. Jeff and the gang. Hey, we're supposed to be family!

Doors open all over town for LeBeaus. That's what they say.

Girls, too, opening up for them.

But not Eli. He hasn't got the charm.

He's not smart either, not like his brother Cyrus. And not big like Jeff. No football for me, no sir.

He knows what they say. Eli's not a real LeBeau.

You're the runt of the family, Dad always says. And you know what farmers do with the runts.

Ha ha. Dad's always so fucking funny!

A runt, though, can see things other people don't see, know things other people don't know. Sticking his nose in.

Like today. Like now. Already he's making inroads. Collecting evidence, adding it up.

First you're just walking out the door, then you find a girl like this.

All mine, Eli says. Mine to watch. Mine to mind.

He doesn't need his sister to play out here anymore.

He stands behind the trees where nobody can see him. Not that anyone would.

She opens a box of jars and sticks labels on them, one at a time. One after the other. Lining them up.

Eli crouches on his heels, she pushes her hair back. Bees buzzing around.

She reaches up under her T-shirt to scratch.

A little scratch up under the shirt—just for Eli!

The girl's not even wearing a bra. Put that in your pipe and smoke it!

If you take just a little at a time nobody notices.

Just a couple hours off school. One scratch, one jar of honey, a beef stick or two near the register.

She puts the empty jars into a box, adds it to the pile of other boxes. So many of them already.

She must do this every day. Slave labor, and no school. Evidence of what?

She yawns. Eli yawns too.

He and Amber used to come here in the old days. Just kids, playing games.

Same old house, same old barns, and still all those bees. Stacks and stacks of them.

Don't go near the damn bees. Same as it ever was.

Don't hide in the barn either, or her mom will come out and yell at everyone.

Yes, he remembers this place. Ready or not here I come!

Then nobody would come for him. He'd wait and wait until he knew the game was over and he heard them laughing.

They all thought it was so funny.

Amber and her friends, way back when. Back here. Back exactly here with the girls and the bees.

He's not falling for that now, though.

He knows things now. Saves things, takes things, hides things. Mr. Invisibility Cloak is what he is.

He can come here every day. He'll stand here and wait for her. Getting closer and closer.

He'll stand here and watch.

Waiting for what, he doesn't know. Won't know till it happens.

*

Tra la, tra la . . . how does that song go? That blissful month, that lusty month, when everything goes astray.

She can't quite get the words, but the old tunes just show up in her brain like that and she wants to sing.

It's the weather. So amazing today. And hormones, too, probably. It all comes down to hormones when you're in high school.

That's what they tell you in health class anyway.

Something about lads being cads. She could remember every verse if she really tried.

But she needs to pay better attention to Madame Micou, conjugating on the whiteboard.

Isn't conjugal something to do with marriage? They were conjugating. They are conjugating. They have always been conjugating.

Or maybe it's congregating.

Amber's congregating with other kids now, with the theater kids. Not with me.

Honey has her bees and her Baptist congregation. She has her Honey in the Rock. That leaves Sophie with what, with whom?

With *lundi, mardi, mercredi*. And every day listening to music alone.

The three of them used to have such fun, used to be such good friends! Singing songs from musicals. Dancing around like lunatics.

Seems like forever ago now, though.

Sophie still has those best-friend necklaces somewhere. All those bracelets they used to make.

Sophie Amber Honey. Honey Amber Sophie. The only girls in their grade all the way up to middle school.

Amber's in choir last period. Sophie could've been in choir right now too. Maybe she shouldn't have quit choir.

She loves to sing more than anyone, but she couldn't stand the songs. The songs they picked were terrible. *Terr-eeb!*

So she is taking French. She thought maybe French.

Je suis heureux de faire votre connaissance. The teacher says it again. Now you try. Last exercise of the day.

But there's nobody here whose acquaintance she is pleased to make.

She used to think maybe Luke. But everyone thought maybe Luke, and he went out with Amber for five minutes.

Sophie turns to Erin next to her. *Es tu heureux?*

Erin is all right. But Erin smiles and says things like "That party was a rager," trying to sound like she has the most fun.

Everyone knows she's just a try-hard like Sophie. And like Amber too. Or at least Amber used to be.

Erin overdoes the accent. She says to Sophie that she is happy to make her acquaintance and she doesn't mean it.

Nobody ever means it. They've known each other too long by now.

Honey would have taken French, but instead she's homeschooling, which means praying, basically.

Homeschooling is for zealots, Dad said when they took Honey out of ninth grade last year.

She'll just call and ask them. Why not? See if they want to go up to the river, up to Circle Current.

Maybe Amber will come if she doesn't have play practice or whatever.

Honey will do anything if her parents let her out of their sight. Not that Sophie asks her much anymore.

And if Mom doesn't make her set tables. Please, she'll say—please, Mom, it's the first perfect day of the year, don't make me set tables.

She has so little time to herself anymore.

It's just school and work and worry and the wedding parties starting again.

Dad said it last night. Summer is hell around here, get used to it. He said it loud because he'd just taken off the headphones.

But summer can't be hell for Sophie. Without a good summer, she'll die.

Erin slaps her book shut and shoves it into her bag. "*Bon soir*, dudes," she says to nobody.

Sophie finishes the page, puts it in the folder with the worksheet. Finally, three o'clock on *vendredi*, and she is free!

*

They arrived last night in rain and darkness, but today is bright and clear, everything washed clean. The smell of fresh paint inside, the smell of wet earth out.

There's nothing for Sarah to do but wander the empty rooms, admiring the new appliances, opening all the windows.

She and Jim will have the front room facing the sky, Willoughby has his own in the back, nestled in the trees.

And they finally have a third bedroom, that guest room they could never have in New York.

You have to have a guest room when you live in the middle of nowhere. Not that they expect many visitors.

It's so good to finally have some space and fresh air. No more sirens from Bellevue. No more crashing grates and trucks from the tunnel.

Even up on the tenth floor she could always feel the whole city around her. Traffic on the FDR.

Will she miss it?

She will. A little. But for now the summer lies open in front of them, with no real plans, no obligations.

Soon she'll set up her floor loom and get to work on something—anything—but for now the empty house is perfect.

She breathes it in deeply. It's so good just to breathe. Easy to forget that the planet is on fire when you're up here, looking out over the treetops.

Will is out on the deck, eyes closed, a book propped open on his belly.

Good. Let him relax. Let him just breathe in the fresh air and get ready for whatever comes next.

It's time for him to find his own way.

And what better place to do that than here in Glenville, the mountains and rivers all around them?

Sarah has always loved it up here, ever since she was a kid and would come up with Dad for weekends at his hunting camp.

Dad gave them the apartment in Murray Hill when Will was born, and he left her the hunting camp when he died.

He certainly wouldn't approve of their moving here for good, though. Just like he never really approved of Jim.

Your husband the tree hugger, Dad liked to say back when Jim first started to write about the environment.

Jim has already gone into town to check things out. Open a P.O. box and get some supplies for dinner.

You two are peas in a pod, he said, and he laughed, when he saw Sarah and Will on the deck on his way out, stretched out in the sun with their books.

It always makes Sarah happy when he says that, but she can't help notice a little note of jealousy. Resentment maybe?

Will doesn't have his father's hustle, or his ease in the world. He's more like Sarah: shy, self-conscious, content to be home with his D&D friends on a Friday night.

When Jim comes back from town they'll have their first dinner in the new house, sitting on the floor like a picnic.

But for now, nothing they have to do, just absorb this sunshine, inhale the scent of new cedar from the deck.

Everything is good when the sun is out. Streaming through the trees and spinning the dials of the meter, their very own off-the-grid electricity.

Jim keeps checking the kilowatt-hours, racking up today in the sun. Another fifty already! he says. Like a child with a new toy.

Hard to believe the old camp is completely gone now, furniture and all.

The whole place was falling apart when they took it down finally, hauled it away in a dumpster.

Even the antlers that Dad was so proud of, hanging over the fireplace.

Sarah always hated those antlers, couldn't help picturing the deer hung from a tree by its legs, a slit down the front where the heart and guts spilled out.

She loved to come up here, but she'd never join Dad for the hunt. Not here or on any of his trips in search of more exotic prey.

It was like a religion to him. His only way to be at one with nature was to stalk and kill it.

If she'd been a son there would have been more of an attempt on his part. As it was, he just shook his head. Suit yourself, he'd say.

The same with art school. He never expected a girl to accomplish much anyway.

The trees shake again, and raindrops fall down. Cold on Sarah's bare arm. Cold through her hair.

Willoughby opens his eyes and looks up into the treetops.

Her son will come to love it here, too, now that they've finally come to stay. How could he not?

"I think I'll go for a walk," he says and stretches his long limbs. Willoughby has grown handsome this past year, grown into himself. Nearly ready to go out into the world.

But not yet. First they have one more summer.

The screen door closes quietly behind him in its brand-new frame. Not like the screen door on the old camp that shut with a bang.

When Will comes out he looks ready enough. Running shoes and his backpack from school.

"Stay on the trail with the white blazes," Sarah says, "and you won't get lost. And you should always carry some kind of ID. Just in case."

"Okay, Mom. And I'll bring my MetroCard too. Just in case."

He's laughing at her. That's okay. Because there he goes, strong and free toward the trail.

She can be alone now in the quiet, as the sunlight warms the new cedar and a breeze shakes the trees. It's the best kind of music, the best perfume.

*

Jeanne still counts the hours as dollars. She wishes it were five and she could close, but she can't wish away the dollars.

When, oh when, will Summer get her parade?

With the door propped the customers startle her every time. No tinkling bell. Only sometimes a hello, the slap of a mailbox door.

It used to be a parade in here on Fridays. I should bring chips and dip, she used to say. Everyone coming for their paychecks, stopping to talk.

Now it's just auto-pay, auto-response, auto-deposit, and her job on the line. Nobody wants to pay a clerk to just stand around.

The young moms come in sometimes. She remembers those years. Just to have a little adult conversation was enough. Even if it's just the same old Jeanne, with no degree.

Someone opened a new box today at least. One of the big ones, and paid cash for the whole first year.

We're expecting some packages, he said. No electric bills, though. Going off the grid!

Well, good for you, she wanted to say, if you can afford it.

Though he seemed friendly enough, not like some of the others who come up here thinking they know better how to live.

You don't want to be the town gossip, Don will say when she tells him about the Calper family, paying cash, here to stay now.

Like when she tells him about the final notices and the *Soldier of*

Fortune subscriptions. The heavy packages for Cyrus LeBeau stamped PERISHABLE. LIQUID.

She sees what she sees, there's nothing you can do about it. Just don't talk so much, Don says.

But when Len comes in Jeanne can't help herself.

"Leonard Larocque," she says, same way as she always does. "How's the day treating you, sir?"

Len is always good for a smile. He comes up to the counter with his envelopes, his catalogues, and she catches a whiff of Tide and river both. You could bottle that up and call it bachelor cologne.

"Can't complain," he says. "Day like this is worth a year of Saturdays."

"Everyone's out today," Jeanne says. "Or should be."

That's the conversation here these days. In, out, weather, hello, a smile if she's lucky.

Jeanne reaches around her mind for something to say, but it's like an empty closet in there.

"Fishing good today?"

Jeanne doesn't care about fishing. But it's talk and it moves from fish to Don to the weather again. Nell Castleton out walking on the road with a pack.

"Like a hobo," Jeanne says. Though she knows the Castletons always had doctors in the family.

"She hasn't had a delivery all winter, come to think of it," Len says. "Though Rudy LeBeau's been burning double."

People who deliver propane know things too. You can't help but know things. In a town like this someone's always looking out for you.

Or talking smack about you, is how her sons would say it, is why they both moved up to Kingsbury as soon as they had a chance.

"Well, have a good rest of your day, Jeannie. Don't forget to tell Don about the brook trout up there. They're fat and could use some exercise!"

She promises she will, and Don will love hearing about the trout, though Jeanne would really rather talk about people.

Now it's just quiet again, with the sun slanting through the plate-glass.

Twenty-two dollars for two more of her hours. Take away the tax and it's less.

Taxes pay your salary, though, Jeanne reminds herself. Comes around and goes around. As long as you end with more than you started with.

More money, more education. Or maybe just more time to organize all the stuff you've saved.

If Leonard would just trim his beard once in a while, he could be a good catch for someone. He could be a good-looking man.

Don was always a good-looking man. She saw people looking at him. At both of them, back when they first came up here.

Up from New Jersey to get some land of their own. Cheap land around Glenville. Good for raising goats and raising babies.

They lived off those big blocks of government cheese while they tried to piece it together. Never any money. Never any time.

You wouldn't catch her standing around for twenty bucks back then. No, two hours were more precious than that.

Minus the taxes of course. Paying for other people's cheese.

Why would someone with money like that be walking around with an old backpack?

Crazy is all. Women at this age. If it's not one thing it's another.

I'd worry about Nell if she worried about someone else once in a while. Plus, she's got a sister up in Kingsbury. Christine. And a brother moved away long ago.

Now the kids are passing by in knapsacks. Must be after three. You can tell time by the sudden appearance of kids, the sound of their voices, shouting, why is it kids are always shouting?

Still, they cheer her up, these things that don't change. A school bus at the stoplight heads out to Route 11. Out to the high school and then the middle school and all the kids go home.

Used to be like a parade in here. Everyone getting paid.

She'll tell Don what Len said about the fishing if she can remember.

She won't mention the packages for Cyrus LeBeau. Calper and the new box. Won't even mention the Castleton woman walking by.

Such a crime to be indoors on a day like this. In another minute the tulips will open up, but the mice will still be in her garage.

*

Yes, please get me out of here! Honey said when Sophie called after school. If I see another crate of jars I'm going to die.

And Amber said, sure, why not? Nothing else going on. And then she showed up in flip-flops and is taking forever just to walk up the trail.

With the sun nearly down already, you'd think she could hurry a little. Sophie tries to be patient, but Honey has already raced on ahead without them.

The lusty month of May's not so lusty when the sun's nearly down and your friends have nothing to say.

They all need to get back into the sun before this turns into a bad idea and they'll never want to hang out with Sophie again.

Finally she can see the water sparkling through the trees, and the falls are loud and crashing into the river below.

They just have to come here this summer, every day, as often as possible! It won't matter anymore how long they've been apart. They'll catch up soon enough, won't they?

Honey's already got her shoes and socks off, and she's claimed the best flat rock, wide enough for the three of them. The sun is just high enough to peek over the trees.

"We have the whole place to ourselves today," Sophie says. She tucks her socks into her sneakers, dips a toe in, pulls it back out. "It's freezing!"

She looks at the other two, who don't say anything in response.

Honey's just sitting on the rock edge, knees folded up and staring into the water, and Amber's taking off her sweatshirt.

Now she's tucked it under her head like a pillow, eyes closed, as if nobody else is even there.

What was Sophie thinking? With these two. They have nothing to say anymore.

Or maybe it's just that the falls are so loud you have to shout.

She takes the tiny bottles of nail polish out of her pack and lines up them up on the rock: Emerald City. Goody Two Shoes. Kiss Me Catherine Deneuve.

Isn't that what girlfriends do, give each other pedicures? Megan left her the supplies. She used to do this with her friends all the time before she left for college.

"Who wants to go first?" Sophie says. With her own nails so short it's hard to really care, but Amber looks like she could use a touch-up.

Still, nobody responds. Nobody's listening.

Honey rolls up her jeans, puts her feet in. She slides off the rock and stands in the water all the way up to her knees.

"Honey, what are you doing, you're crazy!" Amber shouts.

At least she's paying attention now, sitting up. She's laughing too.

Now Honey's in up to her thighs. What is she doing?

Her jeans are soaked and she's holding her arms up out of the freezing water, wading toward another rock.

This is not how Sophie planned it. They're supposed to be warm in the sun, talking and together, not wandering into the freezing cold water.

They didn't come to swim, not in May.

Honey climbs onto another rock, with the river rushing between them. She's wet up to her waist and waving to them, shouting, "Come on, come over here!"

"No fucking way," Amber says, sitting back down. "She's totally lost it. All that Jesus stuff's gone straight to her head."

But Sophie needs at least to try. If this is what they're doing today, she will try, just a little at a time.

But the water is so cold, it bites. It takes your breath away.

And then Honey screams and slips and she's gone, carried off by the water, sliding down the rocks like they do in summer.

What is she doing? She'll die of the cold! Or she'll get pulled downriver and smashed on the rocks.

It's spring, and the water is twice as fast and twice as cold. Sophie didn't think Honey could be so stupid!

She's shouting and waving again, on another rock now, but you can't hear what she's saying.

"Honey, come back here! It's freezing out there!" Amber shouts. But Amber's impressed. She might want to be Honey's friend after all.

Maybe homeschool makes you crazy but in a good way.

Honey just stands there, smiling and shivering, with her long hair dripping and her shirt stuck to her skin.

Why couldn't Sophie have done that? Brave and wild and standing on a rock in the sun, dripping.

Instead she has her bottles of nail polish, which she only brought to please them.

Pathetic, the little pouch of cotton balls and Q-tips. Pathetic socks tucked into shoes.

Sophie is quiet and forgotten and Honey, who is homeschooled, is triumphant.

It was Sophie's idea to come here. She's the one who called them, who asked them to come out.

But now it's all about Honey, freezing and sparkling in the sun.

*

Will is in exile but his summer has a purpose now.

She didn't say much, but she didn't have to. Standing on that rock, wet hair streaming down.

He would have saved her, but she saved herself first. Climbed out of the water and into the trees where he stood waiting.

"Hey," another girl said. "Hey, who are you?"

He was just walking in the woods, following the sound of the waterfall.

And now he has met a girl. Three girls, actually. Locals, by a river, in the woods.

He didn't stay long. He said he had to hurry.

But that moment she stood up from the water, dripping with river and sunshine. Did she see him in that moment too?

Will didn't want to come here. He never liked the old camp, those weekends in the damp and dark.

But the new house is bright and clean, and Mom is so happy. And Dad, too, even though he's always just about to leave.

They say it's his chance to get to know the place, and now maybe he will.

Now there's that girl.

She came out of the river the second he came out of the woods, the timing perfect, everything about her perfect too.

2

Nell awoke to warmth and birdsong, but the moment she stepped outside her door the peace of the morning dissolved.

She's picking her way up and up now through the trees, on a mission.

Nell has to find that smell and make it stop.

It will go away, she's said each morning this week, closing the windows. But it has only gotten worse.

How a morning that began with so much birdsong has turned to this.

Stalking. Creeping. Just follow your nose.

The smell is weaker then strong again on the cool wet air.

The *scrip scrip scrip* of a cardinal all that's left of the morning now. A crow in the distance, cawing its warning.

You're too sensitive, Christine tells her. Thicken your skin.

But even her younger sister, so sensible, so pragmatic, would not ignore the lingering smell of sewage.

Nell did her best to tune out the banging on the new house on the ridge all winter, the trucks rumbling up the mountain with their sheets of glass, but she can't ignore this.

She steps through the leaf litter, the fiddleheads unfurling, picking her way up through the trees.

There's a strand of Dutchman's britches—she nearly crushed them—the tiny white blossoms hanging from a line.

How they used to spend hours looking for flowers like that—the trout lilies first, then the trillium—every day when finally it was spring.

Or maybe it wasn't hours, days. Maybe it was really just that once, she and Laura, after school with nothing else to do.

The spring woods are so fragile. Her own equilibrium, too, seems to get more fragile.

Another headache is coming on already, though it's only been a few weeks since the last.

It's just glistening on the edges now, but it's coming. The stench is getting stronger as she goes too.

The smell of sulfur and shit and something else, wet and stagnant.

It's not coming from the old sugar shack, which marks the beginning of the LeBeau land. Posted and private.

It's not coming from the pile of metal and glass, two old cars rusted into one.

Her heart beats fast with exertion from the climb. With fear too. She has always tried to avoid these people, bearded men with their loud machines. Women who don't look up.

She makes her way toward the little house covered in moss. A light in the window. The smell is powerful now.

Branches high above scrape together in the breeze. There's a creaking.

A rustling sound as something approaches. A person?

But no, just an acorn, tumbling through the overstory to the ground. Then another.

She doesn't want to bother anyone. She doesn't want to cause them any trouble.

But this smell. They have no right! Being human comes with certain responsibilities and cleaning up your own waste is one of them.

There are two cars by the house, one new and one nearly rusted out. A stroller on the porch. And at the edge of the woods a PVC pipe and a puddle.

A septic in overflow. She's found it, just like that, and now she has to do something about it. But what?

She'll call the town clerk. The state police maybe. Who do you call about a septic violation?

It's the last house on Tower Road, with the moss on the roof, she'll say. You know the one. She won't need to mention the name.

The little house that was empty for years, not much more than a trailer. She thought it had been given over to mice by now. Birds, maybe, in the chimney.

She feels eyes on her back now. Feels the hair on her neck rise too.

She'd run if she could, but you have to be careful in the spring woods, all that tender new growth and mud.

Even when she stops, out of sight now, her heart pounds loudly in the quiet.

There's the rustle of a chipmunk in dead leaves. A bird maybe, gathering materials for a house.

And Nell's footsteps, one then the other, snapping the branches dead from winter.

Is someone hiding in that sugar shack? Was someone watching her from that dirty window?

She's back on her own land now, but the smell lingers. Maybe even stronger now.

This land is my land. That land is your land.

What about the air, though? You can't post the air, no trespassing, no hunting. Signs in bright orange and black.

She'll go back inside and close the windows. She'll make a call and then she'll lie down and wait. This headache will only get worse before it gets better.

*

Jim's drive to the airport took fifty-five minutes. More than twice the distance but less time than it would have taken him from Manhattan to JFK on the subway.

Two-lane roads and farms on either side, then forest, then finally some traffic lights as he got closer. He wants to tell someone, to take a picture. Can you believe this is my trip to the airport?

Jim's going to fly less now and make the most of every flight. He'll give the conference keynote in Denver, but also tack on a trip to see his parents in the suburbs.

Not that it's much of a consolation, once you figure the gallon-per-second of fuel the plane burns.

But you can't change everything all at once.

He finds a seat in a rocking chair by the windows near his gate. It's not comfortable but that's probably not the point. It's just part of the branding. *Hey, you're in Vermont, relax!*

There's nearly an hour till boarding, so he might as well settle in, get some work done.

He plugs in the laptop, and already he's got more than thirty new emails since yesterday.

Going without internet at home has been harder than expected. It'll only be a few weeks before they get everything set up, but he's been stopping at the library every day.

He feels like he's cheating somehow. Cheating on Sarah. She keeps saying how this is a break for him, to do without for a few weeks. Stay a while, be with me.

But it's hard! And there are messages he really can't miss, like the one from the conference asking him to do an extra session the next morning.

He feels like an imposter, signing up for half hour sessions in the library with the teenagers in their hoodies, the young mothers jostling their babies. But he also feels good about it.

He likes to be out in the world, to get to know people.

He's already on a first-name basis with the clerk at the post office. Jeanne. Who has two grown sons, and her husband works as an appliance repairman and something else. Electrician?

Three of the emails are from his agent, and they're all about bees. She's taken an interest in hooking him up with a new project.

This is going to be big, she says. The bees are losing their way, and nobody knows why. In Europe, Brazil, California.

And look at this—the largest apiary in the county, right down the road from your new house!

Jim clicks through to the site: Honey in the Rock. Or he tries to. It gets stuck loading, loading—even at the airport the internet is so slow.

He needs to learn to be patient. He finished up the big book about sea-level rise, coastlines disappearing, and they finally got the new house ready to move into.

Now's the time to take a break. He promised her that he would. Maybe this summer they'll find a way back to meditating together, like they did before Will.

But he misses it already. The small planes to the islands. The interpreters, so eager to please.

So relieved that someone out there was noticing.

It was nearly a year ago now he took his last trip to Tuvalu. On a puddle jumper just like that one out there on the tarmac.

In ten years he'll do a follow-up if the book does well enough. In ten years those islands will be under water. Whole communities, gone.

But for now he's trying to find something closer to home, something that feels just as urgent.

When the site finally opens, his screen fills with bees, crawling on a comb.

There's a picture of the beekeeping family—Mom, Dad, and daughter, two blond braids running down her shoulders, the epitome of wholesome country living.

But what's with the Bible verses? He should have guessed with a name like Honey in the Rock.

But I would feed you with the finest of the wheat, and with honey from the rock I would satisfy you.

Jim has worked with religious people before, people who see the wrath of God everywhere, or who think they can do what they want because it's in God's name.

He didn't expect them in Vermont, though, despite all the pretty little churches in the pretty little towns.

When he asked Sarah on the drive up, what do you think they use all those churches for, she said, for God stuff, of course.

People in small towns need to believe in something bigger. You can't expect them all to be enlightened atheists like us.

When did she get so bitter? She gave him that look again when he left this morning.

It's not fair to leave me with the unpacking, the setting up, she said. Do you really have to go already?

But she knew this trip was coming. It's been on the calendar even longer than the date with the movers.

Plus, he's doing this all for her. She's the one who always wanted to live up here.

It will be good for Will, too, she said, to have a whole summer to make it his new home.

For Sarah it always comes back to what's best for Will. That boy hangs the moon for her, even on his bad days.

Jim used to hang the moon for Sarah too. He knows he did.

Vermont will make it better. After all that time planning the house, the move, they can finally live it, and they can focus back on each other too.

That's the plan anyway. If not, well, he'll give it a year, maybe two.

When he gets back he'll go down to Honey in the Rock and see about the bees. First, though, he has to revive the old PowerPoint for this evening. Alternative energy for the home.

His passion for all that is lukewarm by now, but at least they pay him for it. He's not Al Gore but he does all right.

*

Cyrus can see Mom's daffodils coming up by the side of the road already, dozens of them, like every year.

Even in Upper Glenville it's like spring already. Not a trace of snow even in the darkest woods.

Not that there was much to begin with. All those days at 35 degrees, or 40, even in the dead of winter.

He didn't get a single shift at the Ski Bowl.

Not a single day at the chair, helping the pretty girls on and off. No smoke breaks behind the equipment shed with the mountains spread out before him.

Just every day at Shaw's and nights at the Maplefields. Everyone in town passing through and Cyrus just standing there.

He's just got a few more bags to load into the trunk, then he's out of here. Redemption center opens at 9:00, P.O. at 10:00.

He steps around the bright green shoots that poke through the leaves. There must be hundreds of them.

Jenny Rose and her damn daffodils, Dad says when he sees them. Your mother always spent money like she had it.

He says it like he was lucky she left him all those years ago. Like her leaving Dad here with Cyrus was exactly what he wanted.

I made it easy for you, Mom likes to remind him. Taking Eli and Amber when they were still in diapers. Cyrus was in school, so he was easy.

Besides, Uncle Rudy was just a stone's throw. He and Aunt Stacy had enough boys for their own basketball team. Cyrus could play with them. Have dinner with them too.

He was nothing more than a benchwarmer, though, with Jeff and the guys. But still, it was better than being home alone with Dad.

Mom just likes things nicer than Dad could ever make them.

She'd probably like that new house up on the ridge. He can see the top of it from here, where it hovers over the trees.

Lots of new places up near Kingsbury, but this is the only new one up here in a while.

Cyrus wouldn't mind living in a place like that. Fresh new cedar on the outside. Solar on the roof.

Pretty much the opposite of anything Uncle Rudy ever built. That shitty place he's letting Jeff use, now that he's back from the city.

Brought a couple friends this time, too, and a baby.

They're either up to something, or they're running from something. It's always one or the other with Jeff LeBeau.

Not Cyrus, though. Cyrus is onto something better. He's got to be. He's smarter than Jeff. Harder working. And he has an idea.

Today he'll see if his packages have come in.

He'll be making something of his own soon. He's cleaned the empties out of the old sugar shack and is ready to get to work.

This product is something people want, something they'll pay for, and it's strictly legal, unlike Jeff's deal.

Z8, it's called, for the eight ingredients you put in it. Scent, because they say it smells like incense. Like cigarettes, with a bonus.

That's what it said on the internet. Nothing a halfway decent chemistry major can't make with a few commercially available materials.

And Cyrus was more than halfway decent.

If he hadn't been so set on making money back then he might've been able to keep up with the other kids on the college track.

He still did better at school than Eli is doing.

Better than any of his cousins, which isn't saying much.

In high school Dad said to take automotive but Cyrus took chemistry and passed it no problem.

A long time ago now, though, taking any kind of classes. That time is over.

The time for working at Shaw's is over too. He's done with that for good this time. I'm onto other things now, he tells people, if they bother to ask. You'll see.

Mom won't say it, but he'll see it on her face. Sure, that's what you all say, all you losers. All you LeBeaus.

As if she was never one of them. Mom, who has everything all figured out, working with the rich people at the inn all summer. Weekdays in the office at the school.

He's just got to get out of Dad's house. He's had it up to here with this house.

It's nearly 10:00 on Saturday morning and Dad is still sleeping like the dead.

Cyrus has already cleaned up last night's dishes, got all the cans and bottles ready to go.

He's even picked up the chip bags from the woods from when the trash got knocked over in the wind.

Just leave it for the raccoons, Dad said. It'll blow away eventually. But no way Cyrus was leaving all the trash in the woods like that.

He's not a slob. And he has a good idea.

At the redemption center Cyrus will get enough to buy some new trash bags, just to start all over again.

But this time it'll be different. A few commercially available materials, making something legal people will want.

He can do this. He's more than halfway decent.

And then he'll move on to something even better. A real job, maybe even a real business, and a place of his own.

When you come from nothing, Mom says, you step forward however you can. For her, LeBeaus were a step up. It just wasn't up enough for her.

*

The movers came, they left, and now Sarah is alone, setting up her old floor loom.

She'll unpack the rest when Jim gets back from Denver. She's finished doing all the housework without him.

It's been nearly eighteen years in storage, but she could once work this loom with her eyes closed. She'd weave for hours at a time, loud music thrashing in the background.

Now she'd rather just hear the sound of the wind in the trees. Church bells, if they can be heard all the way up here.

She'll make something simple while she learns what she has forgotten. Just a table runner or a shawl, something soft to wrap around herself at the end of the day.

Look at all that yarn! Jim used say when he saw her finished work, twisted and hanging from the ceiling, covering the walls.

But it must have seemed romantic to him once, before it seemed like a waste. My wife, the artist, with her fibers, woven, crocheted, braided.

When she set it up in the living room this morning, Will said it looked like a clothes-drying rack. He'd never even seen it before.

Good luck! he said when he saw all the parts spread across the table. Then he was out the door again.

Sarah has just begun to count the bobbins and lay them out when a shadow crosses the windows.

Was that a knock on the door?

Sarah has to answer, of course. But she is surprised, she didn't count on neighbors coming by.

"Amber LeBeau," the girl says. She sticks out her hand and Sarah takes it. The name rings a distant bell, and not a pleasant one.

"Is Will here?"

She tells her Will is not here, but she doesn't ask what she wants to ask: How do you even know him?

Before she has a chance to say anything more the girl steps inside, her flip-flops flapping across the floor.

Is this what people do in Vermont, just barge in and start talking?

The girl's eyes take everything in. Small light eyes and long brownish hair.

"Wow, what's this?" She touches the loom, running a finger across the heddles. Will Sarah have to explain now?

No. She won't. She offers tea instead, not because she wants to, but at least she can be polite.

"I have some green tea iced. Or I could make some fresh, if you prefer it hot."

The girl says yes. She says thank you. She moves away from the loom, but Sarah doesn't really want her in the kitchen either, covering the whole room with her gaze.

"Sorry about the mess," Sarah says. There are so many boxes piled on the floor that it's hard to get around. "We just moved in."

The girl sits. Her chair scrapes across the new oak floor but she doesn't seem to notice. She chatters about the weather while Sarah gets the iced tea.

"It's not sweetened," she says, pouring it into a glass. She notices its yellowish color, so unappealing. "Would you like some agave syrup?"

The girl takes a sip and Sarah can see on her face that it's bitter. "Here," she says. She hands over the bottle, but the girl adds only a drop.

"You live around here, you say?"

"My dad and my oldest brother Cyrus do, and sometimes I stay with them in the summer. My cousins are here too," Amber says. "But mostly I live in town with my mom and my other brother, Eli."

"That must be nice, having a big family like that," Sarah says. "Having a place to go in the summer." Though maybe it's not nice at all. What does she know?

Amber drinks the tea quickly and, standing, reaches into jeans pockets, with some effort—even up here girls insist on wearing things so tight. She pulls out a folded piece of paper.

"Here's my number," she says. And she hands it to Sarah, soft and warm from her pocket. "For Will," she says. And, "Thanks for the tea."

Sarah sits in the chair where Amber sat and looks at the room. Copper-bottom pots on a rack. The chandelier over the table, which is too modern, too bright. She'll have to change it out.

But of course the girl wasn't judging that. She was only looking for Will.

She just showed up at the door, she will tell him when he gets back. Long brown hair and tight cutoffs. How do you know this girl, this Amber LeBeau?

She remembers now, the old man who used to thaw the pipes and stock firewood for her father. The man in the wool cap who'd come out of the woods, taking Sarah by surprise.

He'd look at her, with those strange light eyes, like a husky's, as if to say, what's a girl like you doing at a hunting camp?

Rudy LeBeau. He talked to her father but never to her. He was missing several teeth.

Maybe Amber is some relation, a granddaughter. All Sarah really knows is that she was looking for Will, that she lives in town but stays up here in summer sometimes. That's what she said.

Sarah should know these people, should remember their names. But she always forgot about them as soon as they went back where they came from.

They were never part of the picture when she thought of her new life here.

If only Jim had been here, if he hadn't insisted on doing that trip to Denver before they even set up their bedroom, it would have gotten off to a better start.

He would've asked questions, made her laugh, and maybe even figured out why she showed up looking for Will. And he would've made sure the girl took more sweetener.

This green tea of yours is so bitter, he always says. What's wrong with a little sugar?

*

Monday morning and the boys will be here soon. When David sees their trucks at the lower end of the drive it's time to go.

Today they're checking the hives farthest out first. Way out past the airport before they circle back closer to home.

David gets up before dawn on these long days in spring. Nearly sixteen hours of light and more than sixteen hours of work. That's spring for you.

He's up before even Ruth and Honey, who will be schooling today. Just another couple weeks till that's over—and not a moment too soon.

Not that he's ungrateful. Ruth is a whiz with math, and she has Honey reading good books, none of that garbage they feed them in school.

But when he comes in for lunch, sometimes he hears them shouting. Books slamming down on the desk, doors slamming too. He didn't know either of them could shout like that.

If it were up to him he'd send Honey back to school. Ruth's got too much to do as it is, and now she hardly has time for her own prayer group.

And anyone who knows Ruth knows she needs to boss a prayer group. She probably would've been a preacher herself if girls were doing that back when she was young.

Now she's up to her ears in bookkeeping for the church, bookkeeping for Honey in the Rock. And all this schooling.

Ruth insists, though. She always does. It's better this way, keeping our daughter out of the fray. Keeping her away from all the goings on at the high school. You know what they get up to, she says.

And he does. He was a high school kid himself once. Nearly lost his way in the goings-on, and that was even before the internet. Before the twenty-four-hour access to sex, drugs, and the rest of it.

Well, summer's coming soon enough. They'll lay off the books, give Ruth a little break. Give everyone a little break.

Mr. Coffee gives one last gurgle, and David fills a mug and a thermos. Spoons some of Ruth's pink applesauce into a Tupperware bowl. Some bread and ham from the fridge and he won't need to come in till dark.

He picks up the messages Ruth left for him on the table. Two emails printed out from the weekend and some notes in her perfect handwriting.

"Jim Calper. Journalist asking about colony collapse. Time for an interview and tour?"

In other words, the journalist wants an answer for what's happening out in California. In Europe. Not here, though. It's not happening at Honey in the Rock, he's glad to say.

Colony Collapse Disorder, they're calling it. And it's pretty much all they can talk about these days in the bulletins. So many bees losing their way, everyone wondering why, worried it'll happen to them next.

Pesticides, hormones, mites. It could be any of that, all of that. Sure. But it's no mystery, he'll tell this Jim Calper. It's no mystery why the bees are dying, he'll say. It's sin.

Let's face it, God is pissed off.

And not just about one sin or the other, like some people think, blaming it on homosexuals or whatever. No, it's sin of all kinds. Greediness, mostly. And we're all to blame.

As soon as we get something good we want more. People always wanting too much and wanting it to be easy. That's the root of all sin.

The guy will give him a look when he says it. Don't you believe in science? They always say that. Like you can't believe in both God and science.

And David will say that science is great. He loves science. He also knows that at some point science ends and God calls the shots.

Vermont has its sinners, sure it does, he'll say. But we've got nothing on California. Los Angeles, Silicon Valley, and the rest of it.

"Tell Calper evenings after seven or Sunday afternoons," he writes. His own handwriting's nothing more than a scrawl anymore, but Ruth can read it even better than he can.

Honey will be free at those hours, too, and he'll ask her to come along. She can help lead the tour.

Maybe this summer she can lead all the tours. Now that's an idea. Give her something to do to keep out of trouble.

Used to be she could just play all day—neighbor kids out in the woods, out in the barn. But not anymore. Somehow that just ended, and they haven't found a way to replace it.

Ruth says no to her working with him and the team. No to Bible camp, too, since what happened last time.

And she says they need to stop calling her Honey and call her by her baptized name. She's not a little girl anymore, let's not treat her like one.

Dorothy is a good name. People think *Wizard of Oz*, but to David and Ruth it means gift from God.

Still, it will be hard to change. "Honey" just seems right. Sweet girl, with that head of blond hair—ever since the moment she was born.

She's like a cuckoo bird, Ruth says. Such a beautiful child and come so late. They'd nearly given up, and then there she was. A miracle.

For David it's always the best things that come late. Beekeeping and the church besides. All the cornerstones of his life.

He reads the note again. "Dorothy can help with the tour," he adds, and tucks the paper back under the fruit bowl where Ruth will find it when she comes down.

He takes one last gulp and leaves the mug in the sink. He can see Aidan's truck now through the trees, down at the end of the driveway.

Aidan sure has come around. Showing up on time, training the other guys to do the same. Aidan's on the right path, for now anyway.

David still mourns for the ones that got away, though. Jeff LeBeau was one of the worst of them. Not enough to just quit. Had to knock down a dozen hives on his way out.

Word has it that Jeff is back up on the ridge now, come crawling back to the bosom of the family after who knows what kind of trouble.

Aidan could've gone the same way, but here he is, up with the dawn.

First pollen is out, and with May coming so bright they need to hurry if they're going to catch up on testing and repairs.

3

Jeanne always used to wait till Memorial Day to put in the garden, but not anymore. Winters just aren't so long these days.

Wait till the end of May to plant your starts and you miss another dozen cucumbers.

Now it's cold, though, of course. Cold and rainy. She opens the door. She closes it. You can't tell what the weather will do from one day to the next around here.

No more frost, though. Maybe in Upper Glenville they'll still get some. Two months' extra winter up there.

Jeanne has no interest in any extra winter, though she knows they need it. World's heating up, they say. Soon the snakes'll be moving up north. Stink bugs are already here to stay.

But for now she wouldn't mind a little heat. Once you get a taste of it it's painful going back. Rain in the forecast the rest of the week.

D'Angelos are getting ready, though. She could see them hosing off the awning, unstacking the picnic tables out front of the place. A fresh coat of yellow paint.

How her kids used to love opening day. Somehow the D'Angelos made it a town holiday: opening day at the Country Creemee! Balloons tied to the sandwich board, bobbing on the chain-link around the back.

Jeanne flips through the new regs as a way to prolong the anticipation for *Summer's Parade.* It's finally picking up. She can feel it coming, the big scene.

Don says he can feel it too. He doesn't mind much when she gets in the mood, even if it's just these silly books helping things along. Whatever it takes, he says.

The two of them walking around naked now that the kids have gone. Two old birds, too old to bother with pajamas once the house heats up.

The door jingles and it's Leila Pierce, heels clicking across the floor. Leila must be the only woman in Glenville to wear shoes with any kind of heel anymore.

Except Jenny Rose LeBeau in her cowboy boots.

Why she didn't ditch the name the moment she escaped that godawful compound on the ridge—that's anyone's guess. Divorced for how many years now?

Divorced and still looking. Always in those cowboy boots and skirts, cowboy boots and short shorts. She won't give those up till she's in orthotics for good.

Jeanne has never had much patience with shoes that make such a racket.

But Leila, she's a classy one. Has to be, if she wants to do business with the out-of-towners who stay at the inn.

And it's a good thing she does. Glenville needs as many rich people coming through as it can get. Got to benefit somehow from all those new mansions cluttering up old Route 11.

Used to be when people moved up here they'd try to blend in a little, get some chickens, do like the locals do. Now they're just trying to bring the suburbs with them.

"Last one of the year," Leila says, putting the package down on the desk. "And I need to send it overnight. Megan'll be home next week."

"I guess that's a relief to you," Jeanne says. "First year of college, that's a big one."

"I've missed her even more than I thought I would. I can hardly stand it!"

Leila laughs, a little embarrassed for herself maybe, but Jeanne understands. She felt the same when Kevin first left, and he only went up the road twenty miles.

"What are you sending this time? Little Sophie bake her some more cookies?"

"No, Megan's sworn off cookies. All that butter. Just some energy bars, to get her through two more exams. And some barrettes I picked up at the farmer's market."

"Farmers making barrettes now, are they?"

Jeanne has always gotten along well with Leila. She laughs when Jeanne means to be funny. Tells her more than she needs to know.

"She coming home for the summer then?"

"We're letting her waitress. She's been bugging for years. Of course Sophie won't like it, but she can make some tips bussing. Not as much, of course."

"You've got good girls, helping you out. You and Steve are lucky to have such good girls. Not that it's all luck."

"Oh, I know. Though sometimes I wish they'd be less good. Always doing the right thing, it catches up with you."

"Be careful what you wish. You never know!"

But Jeanne knows. She knows about good kids. Her oldest nearly worried himself into knots when he was that age. Anything other than an A and he'd threaten to drop college altogether.

Jeanne weighs the box, tapping out the postage. "Fifteen twenty-five," she says. "Overnight sure has gone up!"

"I know. And it's not like she can't buy these at the grocery store herself."

"Well, it's how we do things," Jeanne says. "For our kids." Though she'd never be caught dead sending candy bars in overnight mail.

"Looks like they're getting ready to open the Country Creemee," Leila says, watching the little transaction machine run her card. The machine always keeps people for a while at least. You can't hurry the machine.

"Rain or shine, they've got to open for Memorial Day," Jeanne says. "Must be a busy weekend for you all at Birches."

"First wedding of the season on Saturday. I expect a few hundred more phone calls from the mother of the bride before then."

"Some people like to do it all up," Jeanne says. Her own kids kept it simple. Receptions at the VFW. An iPod for a DJ. "But good for them, if that's how they like it."

"It pays the bills," Leila says. "Speaking of which, I hope they're not still talking about closing this branch."

"Oh, they're talking. But things are picking up with those new people up on the ridge. Lots of mail for Jim and Sarah Calper—they must be pretty important!"

"They've been coming around here forever, though it used to be just weekends up at their camp. They eat at the inn pretty regularly," Leila says.

"They have a kid named after Lake Willoughby, did you know that? Who names a kid after a lake?"

"Apparently they met up there, at some kind of meditation retreat.

They're nice people anyway. Fresh from New York City is all. Finally decided to stay."

"Yep, I know the type. Came from New Jersey myself, you know," Jeanne says. "Way back when."

But the transaction has cleared, and she knows Leila doesn't have time for more talk. She's got the mother of the bride calling.

They work hard, that Pierce family. Jeanne can't deny it. Weddings in the summer, skiers in the winter. Though of course there wasn't much for skiing this year.

The whole place will fall to pieces if they don't get a good winter next year, though Jeanne sure wouldn't mind a little heat right now.

She follows Leila out the front door, the bells tinkling behind her. She breathes it all in.

Rain still coming, though hopefully it'll be done in time for that wedding. Not warm enough today to prop the door.

That's okay. She has her book. Summer's just about to get with her tawny man. Jeanne has waited a long time for this.

*

Sophie is walking home. Walking a straight line down the sidewalk. Under streetlights.

Bats swoop under the lights, swooping and whirling. Sophie likes bats.

And Sophie is not weaving. Is she?

She is only a little bit drunk. I am only just a tiny bit drunk, she says.

Not like Amber. Not like Honey. The two of them laughing like hyenas. Stuck to that sticky table all night.

A-gaaaaa-vay, Amber said.

She told the story so many times. Would you like some of this *a-gaaaaa-vay*? I'm afraid the tea's quite bitter.

What, is his mother British or something?

Sophie said that. She said other things too. Like, Why would she be trying to impress *you*?

Sophie didn't mean to sound mean.

I wasn't talking about just you, Amber! she said. I'm the local riffraff too.

But Amber got sulky. I'm sure she just took my number and threw it away. That's why he never called.

Let's have a toast to the local riffraff! Honey said. Honey was just trying to make it better.

Why was it so funny, then, when she knocked Amber's purse on the ground? Change and pens and tampons under the table, in the dirt.

They laughed and laughed and Sophie wanted to laugh too but it wasn't funny. It wasn't funny when Honey picked up the dirty Popsicle stick either.

Is this yours? She was on her knees under the table. Is this yours? And Amber couldn't stop laughing.

Sophie might be a little bit drunk but not like those two.

If she hadn't been late getting there. If she'd been there on time maybe she might've been part of the fun too.

But she was late. I had to practice first, or my parents wouldn't let me go, she told them.

The fact is she got caught up and forgot the time. Her parents are too busy to notice if she practices her guitar.

She only wanted her friends to forgive her being late. Poor Sophie, whose parents make her practice.

But Amber said, I bet Taylor Swift doesn't have to practice! And Honey said, Who's Taylor Swift?

And they went on like that, the funniest girls in the world. Sophie didn't even matter. Her guitar and her lateness and everything about her didn't even matter.

We've already had ice cream, but get us all some more ginger ale, Amber said when Sophie got there. You'll see why!

Honey held up her cup. Creemees are good, but this is even better, she said.

Sophie drank just enough to blur the edges. Vodka and ginger ale. She's pretty sure her parents won't even notice.

Her sneakers make no sound on the sidewalk. She's walking straight as straight can be.

A car slows down, then passes, on its way up Mountain Road.

Bats whirl in and out of the trees. They whirl and swoop.

I'm a girl who likes bats, Sophie says. Who wouldn't love a girl who likes bats?

Willoughby will . . . Willoughby would. Will must love a girl who likes bats. A girl who plays the guitar.

I will show him the bats and play the guitar for him.

Oh my god, my mom will think she died and went to heaven when I bring him home! Amber said. Oh my god, she'll totally be thinking *jackpot*!

How Amber ruins everything. How Amber thinks everything is funny. A party.

We'll show him where the parties are, is what she said. As if a kid from New York City would care about their parties.

We *are* the party! Honey said.

And that was funny, too, at least, but not as funny as the Popsicle stick or the agave syrup.

Amber said that Will was looking at Honey, poor Honey, all wet and shivering. And not at your beautiful hair either, she said.

Honey looked down at her own chest like she was surprised to see the breasts there. Looking down like, Who, me?

She can be such a dope. Those chocolate sprinkles on her chin, her knees dirty from crawling on the ground.

Willoughby wasn't there, though Sophie kept scanning the line. Older kids, kids from school, people she didn't know.

He didn't show up, but why would he? He wouldn't know that everyone goes out on opening night, every year when the balloons go up.

Sophie goes every year and this year she is a little bit drunk. But not as drunk as Amber, who's lucky to live so close. Who's probably home already.

Not as drunk as Honey, who lives a lot farther. My mother's going to kill me! she kept saying, as if that was funny too.

Sophie will go straight to her room. Her parents will say good night, sleep tight. Nobody will know the difference.

But what will Honey's parents say?

Honey is on Chubb Road by now probably. There are no streetlights on Chubb Road, or all the way up that long drive to the bee houses.

How could she not think of this till now?

Honey out walking. Honey out weaving. With no streetlights. She was supposed to have been home hours ago, she said when they left.

Sophie walks faster now. I'll get Mom to go out and find her, to give Honey a ride.

And Mom would do it. She would do anything, if she thought it would keep someone safe.

But then they'll all three be in trouble for certain. And it will be Sophie's fault for making a big deal of it.

Please, Honey, please just walk safely, Sophie says.

She will get home okay, won't she? If she doesn't, it will be Sophie's fault for not stopping her.

I'm the kind of girl who drinks vodka and likes bats, Sophie says. And who lets her best friend walk home alone, drunk on a dark road.

She could have insisted they call her mom. Could have insisted on walking with her, but she didn't.

What kind of a girl is that?

Sophie just worries too much, even her own mother says so.

No, we're all going home and we're all going to be fine.

It's not like drivers' ed where everyone drinks and everyone dies. Nobody's even driving.

I am walking home. Walking a straight line. I just have to go straight to my room.

*

The moon is shining on the big white tent and it looks like the weather will be fine tomorrow. A week of rain but now everything is clear.

"It bodes well for the season," Leila says. She has taken her place in the wicker chair, feet up on the hassock.

"A season in hell," Steve says, raising his glass. He refuses to go along with it, with what he calls her relentless cheerfulness.

Though the fact is, this was all his idea. She's been thinking about this lately, how the inn, the restaurant, even their marriage—it was all his idea.

Steve swirls the gin, thick from the freezer. He turns up the music. In other words, let's not talk about it.

Leila doesn't want to talk anyway. She's tired too.

Steve is making his way through the French impressionists, he says. Satie, Debussy, Ravel. They're not as soothing as you'd think.

Stereo speakers out on the screen porch were his idea, too, of course. And she'd been happy to go along with it, despite the expense.

Has she always been blinded by love, or just blind?

Back when they first came to Birches, it was just supposed to be a weekend, a friend's wedding, like so many others.

And how happy she was that morning when the idea first came to them! Nursing Megan on the porch while Steve settled the bill.

Old Mr. Dupree, standing there at the front desk, the same old oak desk they use now. He said they were planning to retire. You looking to buy?

And that was it. Off to the races. All the way back to Boston, it was all they could talk about.

You looking to buy? and Steve's smile. That was all it took.

Well, it took a hell of a lot more than that to actually buy the place. To get it up and running, keep it up and running. But still. How quickly someone else's wedding turned into a lifetime.

24/7, 365 days of the year, but on the other side of the desk now.

They never really get a break, so this is their break. Steve with his ice-cold gin. Leila with her glass of wine. More likely two.

They can do this now. The girls are older, and they have good staff. Caleb's got the kitchen. Randy will close up the bar.

And here they are in their own quarters, the porch of the carriage house. It's all very picturesque. The music, the wicker, the flagstone path to the inn.

Steve seems about done with it, though. Steve seems like he's had enough of Birches. Enough of everything.

Except the gin. She wishes he'd at least leave the bottle inside.

Leila already has enough else to worry about. Megan always needing something. Sophie seeming to need so little.

It's too bad Sophie hasn't made new friends in high school. Friends with some ambition, with some plans for where they'll go next.

Amber LeBeau, though, she must have at least some kind of ambition, if her mother has any say in the matter. Jenny Rose's chubby daughter, whom they've known since she was five.

Leila really wouldn't mind if Jenny Rose would quit. She wouldn't mind firing her either for that matter.

No, thank you, she'd say when she showed up one day for work. We don't need you anymore.

Jenny Rose LeBeau, who thinks she's part of the family. Who thinks she's indispensable.

She *is* indispensable, Steve would say. Ten years and she knows this place almost as well as we do.

What can Leila say? She can't fire someone just because she seems to take more than her fair share of the tips. Just because she makes the younger waitresses do the side work.

You just *don't* like her, Steve says. And he's right about that too.

How she touches Steve's arm when she asks him something. How she lifts her head higher when he comes into the room.

Oh, Steve, can you give me a hand with this?

But summer hasn't even begun. They can't be tired of it already. The first rehearsal dinner is over, but it's every weekend now through October.

Still, there are these moments. The breeze on the screen porch. Steve's music, which is beautiful, when she can just close her eyes and listen. How lucky they are to be here.

Steve's eyes are closed, and then they're not. "What time did we tell Soph to be home tonight?"

"Ten, I think."

And just then there she is. Sophie, coming up the path from the street, as if Steve had summoned her.

A quick wave to each of them and in the door she goes. All motion. All escape. She never hugs them anymore, won't accept a kiss good night.

"Have a nice time, Pumpkin?" Steve says, but the screen door is already closed behind her.

"It was fine," she says from inside. "G'night!" And they hear her footsteps, taking the stairs two at a time.

"Damn," Steve says, "how do they grow up so fast?" He sighs and reaches for his glass, nearly empty now.

"Soon, *we'll* be the parents at a wedding," he says. "Complaining about the ice sculptures, because they melt."

"Criticizing the flowers because they wilt," Leila adds.

"Unsure about the choice of husband."

Leila can't even begin to think about that part of the arrangement. How does one ever choose the right husband?

Maybe she should go in and check on Sophie now. She raced by them so fast. Was there a whiff of something on her clothes?

She was just out getting creemees with her old friends, the same old Honey and Amber. A few minutes late, but Leila will not worry. Not tonight.

She'll have enough to worry about tomorrow. The wedding of an only child and plenty of money to spend on it.

They didn't order any ice sculptures, at least.

Still, she knows these people will find something to displease them. Something that doesn't match their vision of a perfect day.

In the morning she'll confirm with Phoebe's again about the flowers. Remind them, there absolutely must be peonies.

*

Nell lets her eyes close again. You can't will a headache away but you can just float in it, try not to fight it.

And it has faded now. It's just a slight knocking over her left ear, not that vise, squeezing from both sides.

Headaches come on so fast now, so often. Used to be monthly, predictable. Now it's how often?

It hardly matters when there's no job to go to. The luxury of emptiness and loneliness. Nobody she has to call and say I'm sorry, I can't come in today.

Nobody to say, you should do something about that. Can't you take some kind of medication for that?

They were just trying to help. They also didn't like being short-staffed.

All those greenhouses heating up in the spring. In winter, the shop untended.

It's okay, they'd say. There was always a touch of pity for the single woman, the childless one, not quite right in the head. They'd find a way to do without her.

But it wasn't okay with Nell, calling in like that, needing the favor of a few days off.

Now she leaves nobody in the lurch. She can go for days without eating, just drinking some water, honey dissolved in a cup.

Just me and the trees up here. Me and the birds, and birds don't mind if I do nothing, say nothing, for days at a time.

She's nearly better now, though. Almost ready to get up and resume her routine, such as it is. Bread on Saturday, laundry on Sunday.

It's almost time to go back outside, breathe the air, open her eyes to the light.

Though of course there's that smell. She nearly forgot about it, these days with the curtains closed. It might still be out there.

We'll look into it, the town clerk said. Nearly a week ago now. Nell has no idea what looking into it might mean.

She needs to get up. It's time now. Hungry as a bear in spring and ready to face it all. The garden full of weeds.

And just in time too because there's a sound, and it's not in her dream, it's in her driveway. Tires on gravel.

A car door slamming. She sits up, very much awake now, alert, and sets the afghan aside.

She slides open the curtains on her kitchen door and there's a man there, familiar looking. He waves, then steps back from the door as she opens it.

"Pardon me, Ms. Castleton. I was just passing by and thought I'd see if you might need a delivery this week."

Yes, she knows this man. Leonard Larocque, who comes by with the propane and plow.

"Gauge says you're nearly out, and I'll be up next week, delivering to the Judds. To Ernie at the general store."

She straightens her shirt, creased with sweat. It's the headaches, she wants to say. I'm not lazy, sleeping in the afternoon, really, I'm not.

Instead she says, "No, but thank you for the offer." She steps out onto the porch in bare feet and closes the door. "I thought I'd wait till fall."

"You sure? Prices always go up in fall, and you don't need it but twice a year, the way you operate."

"Thanks for checking. But really, I'm fine. I can wait." She smiles back at him. Relieved it's not some angry neighbors from up the road. Relieved her head's not throbbing.

And the air, it seems fresher. No sewage. Not yet.

Just sunlight filtering through the trees and the sound of machinery, grinding and rumbling in the distance. The new house again, maybe.

"There's an excavator up there," he says, pointing up to the trees. "New septic going in at the old LeBeau place."

Was it because of Nell's call? Could it be that simple?

"Neighbors called to complain, and it's a good thing they did before the well went bad."

She nods. Still bleary. The last few days. Now this, a person, a conversation.

"Must cost a fortune," she says, "using machines like that."

"Oh yeah. But old Rudy LeBeau does what he can for those sons of his. Ne'er-do-wells, every last one of them. Didn't hurt that the new people offered to pay half."

Then he points to her roof. "You got a leak there?"

Nell steps off the porch and looks to where he's pointing. The tarp is fraying after the winter. "Just a little one, yes," she says.

"No such thing as a little leak," he says. "Tarp won't keep it dry forever."

The tarp ripples in the breeze, bright blue and shredded around the edge. No wonder the water came through with the spring rain.

"Call McClean," he says. "Don't call Collins. McClean'll fix it right, and fast. Collins will sell you a new roof. Nothing but a new roof will work for Collins."

"Right. Thanks. McClean, I'll call him," she says. She hopes that will be enough to send Leonard on his way.

She has known this man since high school, maybe longer, and this may be the first conversation they've ever had. Certainly the longest.

But he gestures to her car now, backed behind the woodshed, the windshield covered in leaves.

"You doing without that now too?"

"I am, actually," she says. "Doing without it." Is he laughing at her? Is that smile his way of laughing at her?

"It's a long way into town," he says. He seems to be considering it. Not laughing so much as considering.

"Just three miles down, three miles back, if you take the trail," she says. "Longer on the road."

"What about the winter, though? Could get tough in the winter."

Nell only nods. She's already thought of this, but she's only beginning to make her plans.

"Of course, there's that bus to the Ski Bowl comes by here in winter. Or you could hitch," he says. "Plenty of people happy to give you a ride."

"We'll see."

"I admire that, though. Doing without the propane. Doing without the car. Good for the environment," he says. "Good for you."

He gets back into the truck and rolls down the window. A German shepherd sits in the passenger seat, looking out.

"But call McClean," he says, waving out the window as the engine roars. "McClean books up fast."

His big black truck backs away now, tires crunching over the gravel and onto Glenbrook Road.

New people on the ridge called, he said. Nobody's blaming Nell for it. All will be well. All is forgiven.

Now she just needs to fix her roof.

She won't be calling any McClean about that though. She doesn't have an old man Rudy to bail her out.

She has the money her father left behind, but only just enough for the barest of day after day.

Though Christine would help, if it came to that. Taking care of her older sister again. See, I told you it was time to move into town.

Nell can't let it come to that. It's okay to live life her own way, but only if it doesn't cost others.

She'll get some shingles and do it herself. She can do it this week. How hard can it be?

Yes, she'll get a book from the library to tell her how, then she'll get some shingles and she'll nail them down.

*

"Here's the extractor," she says, "and here's the barrel for the wax." Honey is showing them around, just as David asked her to. A few bees hover around the door, but it's clean in here now, still months till the harvest.

See, Ruth, he wants to say. We've got a good kid here. She'll make mistakes now and then but she's a good kid.

"This is a piece of comb. Here, you can touch it," Honey says. The son takes it from her hand and looks quickly, handing it to his father.

She is doing so well. David is proud. David can stand back and watch now, just like Honey used to. She even knows all the numbers: eight hundred hives, twenty-two locations, sixty thousand pounds in a good season.

This morning Ruth wanted to cancel. Look at this child. She's in no condition.

But that's the thing about children. They recover quickly. He doesn't know what she was drinking last night with Amber LeBeau, but it taught her a lesson, that's for sure.

Hopefully it was lesson enough, being sick all morning. A beautiful spring morning like today's, wasted.

She's doing great. Jim Calper is taking notes on a little pad and his son follows behind, taking pictures on a fancy-looking camera.

David just hangs back, keeping his mouth shut. It's hard not to jump in but so far he hasn't had to. She's got it covered. He'll wait till they get to the field to take over.

The best part is when they go out to the field. When they get to perform their magic tricks, as he likes to say.

When the inside tour is done, Honey offers them each a zip-up suit from the rack, shows them how to tuck everything in to keep the bees from crawling up their sleeves.

She just puts on hat and veil herself.

"I'm used to the stings, but I don't like the bees getting in my hair," she says. She takes a good long time tucking it all in, too, while they watch her. No wonder Ruth's been harping on her to cut it.

"Let's go see some bees," David says.

It's still plenty light out in the field at 7:00 p.m., and the bees have mostly returned for the day. You can see them hovering around the hive entrances, waiting their turn.

"Smoke it just a little around here," he tells Honey. And she comes around like a priest with the incense, puffing smoke into the hive entrance, puffing some more around the top.

Everyone gets nervous around bees, and David can see Jim and his son hanging back as he pries the hive open. Lifts the rack from the frame.

He never wears gloves or a veil anymore. Ruth says that doing it barehanded makes him feel like Moses parting the sea, and she might be right.

"We're looking for the queen," he tells them.

He holds up the first rack, just a few bees working it, and Jim comes closer, taking notes and asking questions.

Which David is happy to answer. It's much easier when they have questions.

David removes the frames one at a time, slowly and calmly. He has to be so patient. That's the hardest part for him, the slowness of it.

"We're getting close to the queen," he says. "We don't want to squish her. You can see here, where she's laid some eggs."

He doesn't find her till the next super down, as expected. "Here she is, you see her? She's the big one. I marked her with a green pen."

He feels some thrill with the miracle of it every time. The way the queen struts around among her minions, the way their antennae are constantly moving, the larvae constantly hatching, constantly working, making wax, making honey.

"The others are licking her, see? They're licking her pheromones. Got to keep loyal to the scent," he says.

He lifts her up by the wings and shows them. "She'll lay more than a thousand eggs in a day."

"How can you tell which are the workers, which are the drones?" Jim asks.

"Most of the bees you see here, these workers, are all females," he says. "The drones' only job is to mate with the queen, then they laze around until the workers kick them out."

People like this story. All those hardworking females, the lazy guys getting their due. And Jim chuckles on cue.

"A nice life while it lasts," David says. Though he knows it won't be long till the drones end up dead on the ground.

The hives in this pasture do well, despite disruptions like this one. Only May and already they've capped off some nectar.

"So far no problems with colony collapse, with the bees not coming home?" Jim asks again.

"So far, so good," David says. "We keep it natural at Honey in the Rock. As long as the farms nearby keep it on the up and up, the bees will be fine."

"And as long as there's not too much sin," Jim says.

"That's right," David says. He's not sure Jim believes him, but at least he's not scoffing, not too much, anyway.

The bees are crawling up David's arms now, buzzing around his head. Some crawl through his hair.

"I should be wearing gloves, but I like to feel everything," he says. "I've been stung so many times I barely notice anymore. They're used to me too."

After he reassembles the hive, so slowly, so patiently, he can tell Jim still wants more.

"Why don't you take off that suit and I'll show you around," he says.

He takes Jim around the pasture. The solar-powered electric fence—"strictly for the bears," he says—and twenty hives in all.

The thing about bees is, they do all the work for you. There's not really that much to see. You just set up a house, set up some protection, and steal their honey.

"Quite a bit of labor in from April to November," he says, "but winters are free for my other work."

"What's your other work?" Jim asks. Which just may be David's favorite question of all. It's not often he gets a chance to talk about it, not during bee tours.

And when he tells Jim about his missions in Haiti, in the Sudan, he can tell that he really wants to know.

Ruth always says he needs to rein this stuff in, though he can't see how anyone wouldn't want to hear about other parts of the world, their struggles, the things they do right.

It scares away the non-Christians, she says. They assume he just goes around converting people, bribing them with promises of running water and roads and things. Which isn't true at all.

Jim seems to get it, though. He seems to get that there's more to it. And he has his own stories to tell, his own service trips, of a sort.

It's great to talk when you have someone who knows, someone who cares. And this guy has been around. He's seen some things too.

The two of them could go on forever. Flood zones and hurricanes, destruction and intervention.

Plus he wants to know about David's crew of outlaws, as he likes to call them, the guys he takes with him in the field, and sometimes on the missions too.

"Nothing better than labor to help people kick their bad habits," David tells him, "to kick their addictions." And Jim seems interested in that too.

The kids, of course, have lost interest long ago. Gone back to the barn, it seems.

But that's fine. David doesn't get this kind of conversation every day. The crew sure doesn't want to hear about it. All his preaching, his tales of mercy.

And the light is just right this time of day. The sun is on the horizon and the world has a kind of peaceful glow.

Yes, with bee work his winters are free. It keeps him sane, he always says. Satisfies his wanderlust.

"It's good to get out and make a difference in the world," Jim says.

"True," David says. "But it's not good to eat too much honey, nor is it glorious to seek one's own glory." And they both laugh.

"Proverbs," David says.

"Fair enough," Jim says. David really can get along with people, even a guy like this.

"In the end it's really not about you or me," David adds, "but about what God sees fit to have us do. I learned that the hard way."

Jim is nodding, taking down notes. Then he closes the notebook, shades his eyes to the sun on the horizon to get a bigger view of the place.

"I guess I lost Will. Probably taking pictures somewhere," he says. "If you give that kid a camera you never know where he'll end up."

"I probably scared him off," David says. "Honey says I always do too much preaching. Stick with the bees, Dad, she says."

"No, no, it's good for him to hear about other ways of doing things. Other ways of looking at things."

"Well, I hope we've given you enough to work with here. You can come back any time if you want to try opening up the hive yourself. You and your son are welcome back any time."

*

He knows for sure now she's the reason.

The reason for all this—for Vermont, for summer, for finally leaving the city behind. The reason for his existence even, on the earth, in the universe.

With the wind blowing through the car windows on the way back up the mountain, he's like a different person than the one who came down.

It was her, he couldn't believe it. The girl from the falls, his elf-maiden, his Arwen.

It's too strange. Too coincidental. To see her twice already, and for her to see him too. I recognized you right away, she said

They didn't say much else. Did they say anything at all?

He followed her back to the barn. The light wrapped around the corner.

She watched him slip out of the big white suit and hang it back on the rack next to her hat and veil.

He asked if he could take pictures of the place—the jars all lined up, the huge empty vats. He mostly took pictures of her.

Her brown eyes and blond hair like nobody he's ever seen before. Living in a way he's never imagined, unreal, like from another time.

He has her number though she told him not to call. Her parents wouldn't like it. I'll call you, she said.

His phone only works in certain spots, but Dad told him where to find them.

He'll go there every day and check until she calls.

And she will. He knows she will. There's so much more they need to say to each other. So much more they need to do.

4

Bingo—yes! This is it. This is what Cyrus has been up to. Cleaning out that sugar shack. Sneaking back there when he thinks no one's looking.

Eli knows what's what. You can't hide anything from Eli anymore.

It's lucky he brought his stuff up to Dad's this weekend. About time, kiddo! Dad said. You already missed the Fourth of July.

Dad says he always has a place here. Always a place for you on the couch, kiddo.

Not much space in the old bedroom, though. Cyrus moving to the top bunk, like he's top dog, as soon as Eli comes back for the summer.

Or for as long as he feels like it. Mom's, Dad's, whatever. He's neither here nor there, coming and going, like a cat. It's how he finds things. It's how he knows things.

What Cyrus has been up to besides keeping house. His big secret. You'll never catch Eli keeping house. Not for Dad, not for anyone.

At least when he stays at Dad's he's left alone. Mom always on him. Clean your own damn dishes! Amber too. Just like Mom. I'm not your maid, she says. As if.

Just one from each box, ×1, ×2, ×3. One little cigarette, hand-rolled like a joint but not a joint. Not exactly.

Not sure yet what these are except good. Except—holy shit!—also strong. Down into the lungs, straight out the top of his head.

Lighting up and smoking up, free and alone on a warm summer night.

How it's meant to be.

Eli and the stars. Eli and the moon. Eli feeling better already. My head is a balloon.

What is this shit, Cyrus?

Eli can see the great big windows shining through the trees. People who made Rudy put in the new septic.

The old man's gone again in that little red car. The kid might be here, though. Kid called Willoughby, probably sleeping, the little baby boy.

How he got Honey to put her hands up his shirt like that, hands in that fairy-boy hair, the two of them out at Circle Current thinking nobody sees them, but Eli sees them.

Think they're so secret but fuck that, fuck that guy.

Look how these rich people live up here, with their big bright windows shining out for everyone to see.

Except there's no one here to see. Just some deer. A few raccoons.

And Eli. He's like one big eyeball out in the woods. I see everything, hear everything, and nobody knows it.

Hard to get a deep breath. Heart pounding like he's been running but he's not been running. Just creeping through the trees, a stealth operation.

Cyrus might be a genius, but all he's got is that stupid little Toyota. Buzzes so loud, you can hear it a mile away. Mosquito boy, the guys call him.

Eli's got his own kind of genius. Different from those people at school. Look at me now!

He sees things other people don't see. Knows things they don't know. Knows things they don't know he knows. He knows and knows.

That's like my motto now. Ha ha ha.

Jeff says these people probably have jewelry and guns, big-screen TVs. Stuff that's easy to unload. Jeff will be hitting them up in no time.

Just a little supplementary income, he says.

But Eli got here first. This one's all mine, he says. He'll fuck up the kid a little and steal whatever they've got.

What kind of guns would these people have anyway? Not hunting rifles. Not automatics. No way, no how.

Probably just jewelry. Eli will find the jewelry. But not yet. Not tonight. Tonight he's just getting the intel, smoking Cyrus's stash.

It's just the lady now, and big glass doors lit up like a TV. But more exciting 'cause it's real, even though she's not doing much.

She's just sitting there, sewing or something. Her foot tapping up and down on a pedal.

Maybe she'll get bored with all that. Maybe she'll get naked. All alone, with nobody watching, nobody but me.

Maybe she'll start playing with herself, right in front of the window! Eli's own private porno, up here in the woods.

He sits and waits. His heart pounds and pounds, his head now too.

It's like he's just a big balloon head with big alien eyes that see everything. His huge heart pounding.

This one's mine, guys. I'll take the New Yorkers and their quiet little car. Their quiet little hobbies. This one is mine.

He could just stay here in the woods all night, crouched like a ninja, until it's time to strike.

Windows lit up and she's just sitting there, working that contraption, in and out, up and down. He'll out-wait her. He'll outwit her.

But then she stands, stretches, looks straight at Eli!

But she can't see him, can she?

No way. You can't see out when it's dark like that. Can only see back in. He knows that. She's just looking at herself.

Nobody can see him, but he can see her, looking at the windows, looking at her own ugly face.

She's like a fish in a bowl. He could take an arrow and shoot. Straight through the heart.

Like with wild animals. Shoot them with the tranquilizers, and then in you go, free to roam while they sleep.

Maybe Cyrus can make some of that too. Tranquilizer juice. Ha ha ha.

Whatever this stuff is it's making his head blow up and it's pounding like a hammer. What the fuck, Cyrus?

Nobody's been out boiling sap for forever and suddenly you're cleaning the place out, making fancy cigarettes?

His head's going to float up into the windows up there. Like Oz, a big green head, and still she'll never see him.

But now the light's off. Suddenly the light's off. Where'd she go?

He should see if she left the door unlocked. He should walk right up there and see.

Not tonight, though. Not till he's made more inroads, got more intelligence on the operation. Plus, his head hurts.

There's a car creeping along Tower Road now, headlights flashing through the trees.

He'll just wait here in the dark till he's in the clear. Out of the way of the searchlights. Out of everyone's way. Alone with the pounding in his head.

What is this shit anyway, Cyrus? What are you trying to do to me?

*

Somehow he knew she didn't call McClean. Five weeks, maybe six, and she didn't buy any shingles yet either.

All summer so far she's avoided even looking at it, just looked at the ground, at the garden. It's plenty to keep her busy.

If she doesn't look too far ahead or too far behind, she can stay where she is. Day to day, doing no harm, disappointing no one.

Leonard is up there now on the roof and Nell is trying to keep busy. Trying not to hover.

How can she pay him? How much?

She almost wishes he hadn't come.

She kneels in the garden again while he works. Salvaging the last of the spinach that has bolted. Pulling the little green worms off the new kale.

The dog, Helga, lies beneath his ladder, as if Leonard does this every day—goes to a stranger's house and sets up a ladder. A roving Good Samaritan.

It's the German shepherd she saw waiting in his truck last time, unintimidating with one ear up, the other down. Like a dutiful wife.

Roofers must be fifty dollars an hour at least. Hopefully this won't take him more than an hour.

She could pay him fifty dollars, but she should offer lunch too. It's nearly noon, he must be hungry.

She was going to have tuna for dinner two nights this week. And the loaf of bread she baked Saturday, that should last till Friday too.

But it's the least she can do.

Yes, she'll give him a check for fifty dollars and offer lunch. She'll be fine with a little less next week. You can never be too thin, people used to say.

Still, why is he helping her? When she was young, men would do that all the time, look her up and down, offer their help and advice.

And she knew better than to take it, as a matter of principle. Also not to owe them anything.

But Leonard just looks at the roof. Figures he'll fix it. Seems to make no difference that she has nothing to give in return.

I just saw these shingles at the transfer station today, he said. Also saw that tarp was still flapping so figured I'd see what I could do.

Nell walks over to him now, taking off the garden gloves and stuffing them into her pockets. Helga lifts her head.

The sun is so bright she can barely see his face, he's just a silhouette when she calls up to him.

"Would you like some lunch, when you're finished with that?" she says. Her voice sounds natural enough. As if this is easy.

"Sure," he says, his mouth closed around a half dozen nails. "Lunch would be nice." He takes the nails out. "If it's not too much trouble."

"Do you mind if I watch you do that?" she says.

"Not at all," he says. "If you teach a man to fish, so they say."

He tosses some torn shingles on the ground.

"You've got a few loose patches, but this here is the worst of it," he says. "Doesn't much matter if they match in material or color exactly, just so long as they're layered right."

Nell nods, though it's hard to see what he's doing from down here.

Still, if she could learn this she could stop avoiding the roof. Without a decent roof the whole place will fall apart and her life here with it.

"You got a pretty good leak here. How is it inside?"

"A few buckets on the floor do the trick when it rains really hard," she says. "But otherwise it's fine."

"Hm," he says. "There's another section that'll need some attention. This roof is pretty old."

She watches as he goes, one shingle then another. She could manage that herself, couldn't she?

When he finally climbs down, when the patch is good enough for now, she's ready. Two glasses of water from the tap, two sandwiches on her mother's china plates.

He says thank you, but she knows it's not enough food for a man like that.

He eats fast and wipes his mouth with the back of his hand. She can see him looking around.

From where he sits he can probably see that it's a good place, even if it leaks. She painted the paneling white long ago and keeps it touched up.

The floor swept clean, the door to the back room closed so you can't see the buckets for rain. Yes, it's a good bright place.

She should be talking but she can't think where to begin. She doesn't want to ask him about money, not yet.

"This is good bread," he says finally, after washing down the last bite with a drink of water. "You make it yourself?"

"Three days ago," she says. "I'm sorry it's not fresher."

"Three days tastes pretty fresh to me. I always buy the day-old dough-nuts myself. Never understood the problem with day-old."

"It's a lot better when it's fresh, but I only make it once a week. On Saturdays," she says.

"Well, I'll come back on Saturday then. If you're not busy, I mean. If you're not busy besides the baking."

"Oh, I don't know. I might be. I might be busy," she says.

"Of course. That's okay."

Why did she say that? She won't be busy, she has no plans. But she doesn't like visitors. The waiting around, the worrying.

"I really ought to pay you," she says. "I'm sure McClean would have cost something."

"Oh, he'd charge you, all right. But I'm not McClean."

"Would fifty dollars be okay?"

"I couldn't take any money for that job. I'm no roofer," he says. "But thank you for the lunch. I appreciate it."

While he's lifting the ladder back onto the truck to go, Helga looks up at Nell, wagging her tail. Nell scratches behind Helga's soft ears and her tail wags faster.

"The Saturday after next," she says. "I won't be busy, I'm sure."

He comes around the other side to tighten a strap, then opens the door for Helga, who hops in and takes her seat at the window.

"Or really, next Saturday is fine too. I'd like to at least give you some fresh bread."

"You're busy," he says. "It's okay. Thanks for the lunch!"

And then he's gone, and Nell is alone at the end of her driveway, looking into the sun.

*

"I can't believe it's July already, and we've been up here only that once, before school even ended," Sophie says.

Honey is trailing behind her, thwacking at trees with a stick she picked up on the road.

It's summer for real now and hot enough that Sophie will most certainly swim. She'll jump right in, before she has a chance to chicken out.

She'll be first, maybe before Amber even gets there, assuming she'll be late, which she always is.

"I've been up here a bunch of times," Honey says.

"Or, a couple times anyway. With Willoughby Calper," she says. "I don't know if you remember him."

Sophie stops walking and maybe even her heart stops beating, but only for a second, because next thing she knows it's beating everywhere at once.

With Willoughby Calper, if she remembers him . . . Is that what Honey just said?

"I call him from the pay phone at the post office," Honey says. "I just leave messages on his cell. He has his own, though it doesn't work most places."

Honey has been calling him from the pay phone. While Sophie has been making up scenes in her head Honey has been calling him. She has seen him. A couple of times, she said.

"From the pay phone?" is all Sophie can manage, though at least she is walking again. Faster now.

She is walking up to the river where she hoped they'd see Will again but now, forget it, she will swim and drown her tears. What the fuck, Honey? is what she really wants to say.

Sophie is the one who has been singing for him, imagining him, "Willie o Winsbury," "Fair Margaret and Sweet William," all those ballads she learned, all for him.

So pleased with herself, too, with the new songs, not minding so much those long nights at the restaurant, waiting for him and his family to come in. She was sure she'd be the one to see him next.

But Honey's the one who actually calls him. How could Sophie not even know?

What an idiot she's been!

"I can't call him from my house because my mother is always listening. She probably has the phone bugged too. They don't trust me, after that night with the creemees."

The phone bugged. What is she talking about?

"She won't let me call Amber either," Honey says. "My mother doesn't know you were there, too, so it's okay if I call you."

Honey is just talking now, and Sophie doesn't have anything to say. The real world was turning while her own was in wait, lying still. She hasn't done anything this summer. Nothing.

"She doesn't know you were there when Amber brought the vodka.

Which made me throw up. Did that vodka make you throw up?"

Sophie shakes her head. No, it didn't. She went home to sleep and that was all. Nothing happened, nothing at all.

"I can only be gone for an hour or two when I'm by myself, or they worry, but Will meets me at Circle Current. It's the only place he knows how to find."

Honey just keeps flicking the trees with her stick, might as well be flicking Sophie across the face, the neck.

"They'll let me stay out longer if I go with you, though," she says. "They think you're okay, even though you don't go to church. Have you ever gone, even once? Will says he has never once gone to church."

Summer is like this. If you don't grab it right from the start is just floats away and nothing happens. Nothing happens and nothing happens, and yet everything happens, but to everyone else.

Even to Honey, the one who's supposed to be trapped, the one who can't do anything but work in the barn and go to prayer groups.

But things always happen for the pretty one, the princess.

She didn't need to do anything but let down her hair. And then she called him on the pay phone. What could they possibly have to talk about?

He was wearing a vintage Pogues T-shirt, which Sophie thought was a kind of sign. They liked old music, they'd understand each other, not like Honey.

Honey doesn't even listen to music! She has never even been to New York City.

It's the hair. Blond hair piled up on her head. Blond hair in braids. Blond hair like spun gold. It's hard not to stare at it sometimes, even for Sophie, who has known her all her life.

She has, as Sophie's mother says, a nice figure. Unlike Sophie, who so far has only grown tall, her hair a boring brown. Or Amber who, let's face it, will never be as pretty as her mother, not that anyone would ever say so.

"Oh, look, she's already here!" Honey says. And there is Amber, waving at them from the other side of the river. She's already swum to the other side.

Whatever, whatever, whatever. *Je suis très vexé. Je suis . . .*

And Amber's brothers too. Or cousins. Why are they here?

Sophie drops her bag, kicks off her shoes, and in she goes. Yes, she is going straight in this time.

The cold is a shock. It's freezing cold but it's wonderful, washing everything away, every thought.

She submerges, comes up for air, submerges again. She can't hear what people are saying because she doesn't care. It's best if you just go right in, right under, keep moving.

Cold cold cold, but that's all you need sometimes. She twists her hair out and lets the water run down her arms and back. She wades back to the rock.

"Wow, it's freezing!" she says. Proud, defiant.

Honey's in her bathing suit now and Amber, too, sitting in the sun. The guys have left their stuff lying around, gym shoes and T-shirts, towels.

"Sorry about them," Amber says. "I told Eli I was coming here to meet you two and suddenly the rest of them decided to come too."

They're scrambling up the rocks, taking turns jumping off. Sophie doesn't mind that they're here. They scare her a little, though.

She hardly knows them, except Eli, from when they were little, when Amber was always so mean to him.

He's not climbing up and jumping off with the others. He's so thin, hanging around like maybe he wants to be one of the girls. Sophie feels a little sorry for him.

"Get lost, Eli," Amber says when he wades over to their rock. "We're trying to have some girl time here."

Eli wanders off, downstream. He's trying to skip stones but his stones are too round and heavy, as anyone can see.

Amber has stories from the creemee stand, where she got a job, and where she seems to spend her free time too.

"I've seen everyone from school already," she says. "Everyone, even the teachers. You wouldn't believe . . ." and on and on.

Amber has a boyfriend now. A senior who works there too. "Not a boy-friend boyfriend," she says.

Nobody mentions Will and he doesn't show up. It's a secret between Sophie and Honey, but Sophie doesn't want it.

She wants to throw it into the river and drown it.

"Let's jump off the cliff," she says. "Come on, let's try it."

"Yeah, show those guys that girls can do it too. Come on," Amber says.

"No, thanks," Honey says and stretches out in the sun, smiling. So easy for her, in her nice figure, to just lie in the sun.

Sophie climbs up the rocks to the top, with Amber behind her.

She stands behind one of the guys and waits her turn.

Her knees feel soft and weak as she looks down the edge into the river. The one who just jumped waves at her from below now, coaxes her, come on, come on!

She just has to do it. She has to just jump, not think about it, just do it.

She's near the edge now. She only has to step off.

There's a cool spray off the waterfall. The rock is wet from people dripping, waiting, jumping.

"Go on," Amber says. "You can do it."

And she does. Like that, she leaps off into the air and falls till she hits the water, sinks into the water, down and down some more.

Then she's up again, on the surface, swimming with the current.

Now her arm burns where she hit the water, and her swimsuit's wrenched off to the side, but she made it, she did it!

Amber comes behind her and Honey cheers from the rock. The boys are back up again, scrambling to the top, showing off for Honey, but Sophie has had enough now.

She has jumped into the river from the high rock, and people saw her do it. Who cares that none of them were Willoughby Calper.

*

At some point Jim might do more research, interview more beekeepers, but for now this can be a one-off. For one of those farm-to-table magazines maybe.

David Mitchell didn't have much to say about Colony Collapse Disorder anyway, and that's what people want to hear about.

Jim would rather go back to the topic of water again. A fight over drinking water and who owns it, who has the rights.

Just yesterday he read a piece about Soda-Rite, how they just moved into some small town in Maine and are taking all the spring water. Bottling it up and shipping it out.

Jim can't help but get worked up about this kind of thing. Corporate pillaging of natural resources.

Hardly on the scale of the rainforests, but it's the same idea. And it's right here in the northeast! Sarah can't mind that too much.

Jim will finish up with Honey in the Rock today, then plan a trip to that town in Maine, talk to the people whose water is being bought right out from under them.

Because how can you buy or sell the land or the sky? For Jim, it always comes back to that.

If we don't own the sparkle of the water, how can we sell it?

Well, put it in a cheap plastic bottle, for starters. Soda-Rite can tell you that much.

Mitchell is right about some things, anyway, about greediness and self-ishness being our downfall.

Not that Jim would go so far as to ascribe colony collapse to sin.

He'll just finish up with the bee piece today and save the bigger story for another day. Too bad his notes are so thin.

He can't remember how it all worked. A centrifuge for extraction. Gravity-fed tanks. A hot knife to uncap the wax. What else?

Will took some pictures, which could help. Jim should've asked for them before he and Sarah left for town today.

The photos are probably still in the camera, if Jim can find it. Will isn't good about backing things up.

That time he lost all his photos from China. His grandparents paid for the trip and at least wanted some photos.

Will's not always the most reliable. He's something of a dreamer, actually, to put it kindly.

They probably let him spend too much time alone, reading Tolkien, reading *Harry Potter*. A touch of asthma and allergies making them overprotective.

It was probably the city that gave him the asthma in the first place, close as they were to the FDR and all that diesel.

He'll be better off here if he can find some work to do, stop just lounging around in the sun with his favorite books, going for walks in the woods.

Mitchell said that if people learn about hard work then they'll see the right path.

He converts people with work, he says. Addicts and the like. Then they can see God.

Hopefully Will isn't afraid of work. Hopefully all their attempts to protect him, to give him the best chance, haven't just ruined him for the basics of being a responsible adult.

Bring them to Sudan, Mitchell said, if they really need to see some hard work, to sleep well at night.

Jim has no interest in sending Will to Sudan. They'll never even know what he saw in China.

But hopefully he has some decent photos from Honey in the Rock at least. The extraction equipment. The uncapper, the conveyor, and whatever else Jim can't remember.

Will won't mind. Jim will put the camera right back on the desk where he found it.

He scrolls through photos of Will's old room in New York before they packed up to go. Close-ups of old D&D figurines before he gave them all away.

And finally here it is, Honey in the Rock. The hand-carved sign at the end of the driveway. The house with the saggy porch.

Jim hadn't noticed how green it was around the barn. In the pictures it looks so green.

Will has a pretty good eye, it seems. Maybe he has a talent for this.

Maybe this is Will's talent, finally. Not that it's a particularly useful one.

The light's dim in the barn and the pictures are rushed, but outside with the boxes and boxes of bees, it gets better.

He might even be able to use some of these for the article. They might be good enough to publish.

And here's a nice one of the girl from behind, walking toward the barn holding the bee veil. He remembers her showing them how to put on the suits while she only put on the hat and veil.

How impressed he'd been when David went without any protection at all. Jim was glad for every inch of that suit, once the bees starting pinging around.

And now more of the girl. One after the other—there must be twenty, thirty of them. Just of her. What was he doing?

Mostly they're blurry, her arm sticking out to block him. Hair swinging in front of her face. Then sticking her tongue out at him.

She's the same girl in braids from the website, but just a couple years have changed her completely.

No wonder Will's cheeks were so flushed when he caught up with him that day for the drive home.

Probably Jim shouldn't be seeing these. But if he just scrolls through quickly, he might get a better shot of the extraction equipment.

But it's just the girl, over and over. Unselfconscious and alarmingly pretty, he can see that now, even in her oversized plaid shirt, her blond hair nearly down to her waist.

Then it's back home again. Will, who used to care only to stay inside, lost in fantasy games, fantasy novels, is taking pictures of rocks and mosses.

Then there she is again. Leaning up against a rock, a green-striped T, her hair in a knot on top of her head.

Jim shuts off the camera. He'll just ask Will for a thumb drive when he gets back. He doesn't want to have seen all this, it's none of his business.

Maybe he should encourage Will to pick up the colony collapse thread himself. That's what he'll do. Do a little work on this, Will, why don't you?

Maybe the girl will help get him interested in it, set a little fire in his belly.

He can still hear Mitchell's voice, booming out all that biblical stuff about honey in the rock. *My son, eat honey, for it is good. And the drippings of the honeycomb are sweet to your taste.*

Put anything in the syntax of the Bible and it sounds like it's imparting some great meaning.

Like Chief Seattle's speech, which wasn't even by Chief Seattle.

Just like this other stuff isn't really the word of Jesus or his disciples. Just some translation of a translation.

Still, it's hard to resist the phrasing. *How can you sell the land and the sky? With honey from the rock I would feed you.*

Language like that doesn't make the message true, though it can motivate us, especially when we're young.

Motivation, that's what Will needs most in his life now. They've made it all too easy.

*

"Good afternoon, Mr. Larocque," Jeanne says.

She has the fan blowing now. It's stifling in here without it. She sorted the mail in a sweat. You can't have the fan on when you're sorting.

"Afternoon, Mrs. Hess," he says. He comes to the counter.

It's a good day when her customers bring her news of the land. *Autumn's Moon* being not much better than *Summer's Parade*, though she did finally finish it.

"Too hot for fishing, is it?" she says.

"This time of day it is. This morning, though, a decent catch by Glenbrook Bridge. Pike, mostly."

"Don's already looking forward to deer season," she says. "Too hot for fish, he says."

"Never rush the summer," Len says.

Jeanne used to agree with that way of thinking, but now July and August seem to stretch on forever. At least on days like this, long and hot and no fan until the late afternoon.

Used to be summer that she loved best, but now she likes the cool of the fall. Leaves showing off for the tourists. She's ready for cool mornings.

"Deer will be thick this year, Don says. Not that I'm looking forward to another freezer full of venison. Still haven't finished up last year's!"

"I sold mine off to Ernie," Len says. "Out-of-staters are buying it now at the general store. Local cuisine and all that. You should try it. Package it up real nice."

"You selling him your fish too?"

"Hell, no. Never enough of that to go around when you mostly do the catch and release."

"I hear Jeff LeBeau is back in town," Jeanne says. Hoping to catch something herself, maybe. "I figured he was out of here for good when he left last time."

"He's been back a while now. Shacked up in the old place with a couple other guys and a girl, too, with a baby."

"*His* baby?"

"Could be, I don't know. Went up there last week to fill the tank. They're up to no good, if you ask me."

"May be one of those meth houses," Jeanne says. "I hear they're cropping up all over the place now."

"Well, all I know's the septic hadn't been pumped in like twenty years when they showed up. They just moved in and started using it."

"Must've stank to high hell over there."

"That's what Nell Castleton said."

"What, did you go up there and check on her too? You never can resist a damsel in distress, can you, driving up there with your big truck."

"That's a good one, Jeanne," he says, and it's nice to hear him laugh. "She didn't want any, anyway. Says she's doing without."

"Without propane?"

"Yep. And without the car too. Now that she's not working the green-houses anymore, I guess."

"Must be nice, to retire early, if that's what you call it."

"We all could probably retire a bit earlier if we spent as little as she does."

"Well, good luck to her. Up there alone."

"Takes all kinds," Len says, turning to go already. "Stay cool now, Jeanne. And give my regards to your old man."

Damsels in distress—damsels on the brink of menopause more like. Though maybe that's the same thing, one way or the other.

Menopause so far less of a big deal than they make it out to be. For Jeanne, anyway. She's always been the low-maintenance type, though.

No special diets for Jeanne. No alternative therapies. No therapies at all, for that matter.

Though the doctor says she ought to watch the cholesterol. Eat less cheese, less dairy.

A creemee would be nice about now, is the thing. Even with this fan it's stinking hot. Maybe it really is just her hormones talking.

More like it's the global warming. That's what everyone says.

She stands in front of the fan and lets it dry the sweat from her fore-head. Blows the hem of her loose cotton skirt, Marilyn Monroe–style.

Then it's back to the book. Not a good series, but she likes to finish what she's started.

And it passes the time from one customer to the next. She's hardly had more than a dozen people today, buying stamps, checking their boxes. Ho hum.

Even Calper deliveries have slowed down this month. Jim was in here every other day at first, fetching new lighting fixtures and god knows what else. Sarah once in a while, too, though she hardly said a word.

If Jeanne was rich like that she'd be much more friendly. More generous. Why not? You'd have a lot to give away.

Sarah being the one from money, so she's heard. Her dad some kind of coal baron maybe. Some kind of corporate something or other.

Just the kind of people they moved up here to get away from.

Every place has its problems, though. Jeff LeBeau and the gang, stinking up the place.

Len said it smelled to high hell up there. Or, Len said that Nell said it smelled to high hell, which is a different thing altogether.

Well, he's got the time to do what he likes. On his own with no kids, a fortune socked away from his drywalling days, Don says.

Maybe after work today she and Don will head up to the falls. Like every summer, on the hottest days, they'll park alongside the road and hike into the river.

Just lying there and letting the water rush over you. Surest way to cool off. And it's free. Better than AC.

Maybe today. They can pack a little picnic. Pick up a six-pack at Ernie's.

With the fan on it's a little better in here, but they might have to spring for AC someday, if this kind of weather keeps up.

That's the other thing they came here to get away from. Rooms closed tight all summer, sucking up electricity to the point people think they need to go nuclear.

Whatever happened to nuclear energy anyway, and that plant they put in, right there on the state line?

That used to be all people talked about—meltdowns, radioactive waste, Chernobyl.

Did we just forget to be scared of it?

Maybe it's good these new people come up here with their solar and biofuel and whatnot. Someone's got to help us keep cool as the world gets hot.

*

The centerpieces will stay in the walk-in till the last possible moment. Otherwise everything's set, and the caravan will come from the church any minute now.

Tablecloths clamped to the tables but no breeze today. Leila can see the heat rising from the flagstones, huddling under the tent where the bride will cut her cake.

The sun is blazing now but in a couple hours it will dip behind the trees. It will be bearable again out there.

Leila's border beds are less lovely in the heat of July. Long gone are the peonies and sweet peas. It all depends now on the sturdy asters and the annuals, the long-suffering annuals.

Every morning she waters them—the alyssum, lobelia, petunias, arranged at the garden's edge. Needy, like thoroughbreds.

How Megan can be out for a run right now, is beyond her. Trying to stay in shape, she says. It's the only time I've got.

At least it's cool in the dining room. For now Leila can linger here, double-checking the seating chart.

In black skirt and bare legs, Sophie dresses the tables while Steve follows behind with the oil lamps, one by one.

Arguing again. Or, Steve is trying to get her to argue anyway. Teasing, she thinks you call it.

Something about music, no doubt. Sophie's been listening to his old CDs, lying in front of the stereo with headphones on.

Headphones—the death of conversation, the death of family life. First they stole her husband away, now her child.

Leila knocks on the hard plastic with a knuckle when she needs her. What's going on in there? she wants say.

She doesn't just mean the music, though that would be a start.

"You've stolen my Carter Family, I see. You've stolen my Folkways," Steve says.

When she was little, Sophie used to climb onto his lap and put her ear right next to his, trying to get in on the secret.

Now she doesn't reply, just keeps on with the tablecloths, staying one step ahead.

"Aren't you supposed to be listening to Britney Spears or whoever?"

Of course he loves that she takes his old music, the same way he always tried to get her to watch Buster Keaton instead of *The Little Mermaid*.

And he loves that Sophie is taking up the guitar for herself, something that for Steve was never anything more than a fantasy.

There was no money for lessons back when they were kids, and no time for something so impractical as that either. It was always about how you were going to make a living.

"You should steal my Joan Baez next," he says. "Though if you're enjoying the old stuff, you might actually prefer to go back even further. Blind Lemon Jefferson . . ."

Steve should have done something with music probably. Or teaching. He loves both music and telling people about it.

It's too late now, though. They could never afford to hire someone who does all that he does around here, even if he did want to try to change his life.

I wish we did something important, like Honey's dad does, Sophie said this morning, out of nowhere.

Leila was filling the watering can, feeling a kind of contentment as the cool water poured from the hose, the day not yet hot. It was going to be a good day.

And just like that her contentment dissolved. The water sloshed over the side, her pant-leg got soaked, and the moment, the day, all of it was ruined.

Of course she knew what Sophie meant. She didn't necessarily agree with her, she'd been around that question often enough in her lifetime, but to hear it aloud, to hear it from Sophie.

Megan didn't judge her like that. Megan was never cruel, like Sophie could be, even if she didn't mean to be.

I want to do something important for people in the world, Sophie said. Not put on fancy weddings, when half the people are going to get divorced anyway.

I thought you wanted to make music, Leila said. Why else are we paying for those guitar lessons?

For now. But when I'm older, when real life begins, I want to do something that matters, like Honey's dad.

Leila knows all about David Mitchell and his missionary work. The wells and roads he builds in Haiti in the off-season. His tending to one crisis after another, how important that must make him feel.

Leila just kept filling the can, and now Sophie just keeps snapping the tablecloths. As if Steve weren't talking to her, as if she didn't care about what he was saying.

At least we're making something beautiful here, she could have said. Making a place for good things to happen, memories people can store up to help deal with whatever bad things come their way, as they always do.

Steve would've just dismissed Sophie's comment altogether. Sure, he'd say, Mr. Mitchell will build you a road if you put up with all his crap about the Father, the Son, and the Holy Ghost.

And it's true, missionaries having always been a complicated business. Not that government agencies are much better. But what is there to do?

Let Sophie figure it out for herself. Maybe Sophie will do better.

As for Leila, she has her flowers, she has her menu and her maintenance. This is the kind of good she is doing and it has to be enough.

Though now she sees the rest of the night laid out before her like the rest of her life.

Jenny Rose will show up at five, the heat an excuse to open an extra button or two on her blouse. And Megan will be back from her run just in time to shower before it all begins.

Then the wedding caravan will come, and it will be one great rush until it's over. Ten o'clock tonight, or maybe later.

Leila and Steve will be out here till the bitter end. Till the beer bottles pile up in the bins, half-eaten plates of cake on the tables.

Drunk dancing on the patio, slurry speeches from the groomsmen, the old folks having long since retreated to their rooms.

The sun retreating, too, finally. Till all the lights are out in the rooms and the birds begin to rustle.

Leila senses Steve's presence behind her at the front desk, but she keeps slipping the specials into the menus. Lets him stand there, breathes him in, his good smell, his heat.

"Mmmm, Caleb's making scallops," he says. "We got a good price on them this week."

And just then she smells something else. Gin. How something so bright out of the bottle can become so sour on the tongue.

Just yesterday she begged him to wait till after dinner at least. She struggled to say it, please, can you wait till after dinner? And he said he would. He said he understood.

Can he just not help himself? Or is he making this into a struggle against *her*, a test to see what she'll do?

"Seared scallops in lemon and capers for twenty-six dollars. Do you think we're charging too much?"

She shrugs. She can feel the tears springing up in her eyes and it takes all her concentration to stop them.

She wipes around her eyes with a single finger, no time to fix her mascara, no time for tears.

Her relentless cheerfulness. Her making things nice for people. This is what it amounts to.

"Let me finish this," he says, and takes the pile of menus, taking over the easy part. "It sounds like the bridal party has just arrived."

5

Sophie is tired of the routine already. Tired of the calls, the walks. Tired of waiting around at the trailhead with Honey.

"What do you even *do*?" she says. "What do your parents think you do?"

She hates the sound of her own voice. Whiny. She has become the whiny friend.

Why does she even go along with this? It's not like Honey calls anymore just for her. She only calls so she can get out and meet Will.

She needs more than an hour or two, that's why.

"What do you *think* we do?" Honey says.

As if . . . as if what?

As if sex. As if Honey and Will are going off into the woods and having sex and Sophie is stupid not to know that. As if, duh.

Sophie has imagined it enough times. Talking to him, his face close to hers, getting to know everything about him.

But not anymore. He'll never invite her along if that's what they're doing.

Honey's snotty voice. What do you *think* we do?

Though Sophie is the one who has things to say to him, who could know him and love him as a whole person. Not just as some cute boy on his way to college.

It can't just be sex. Honey doesn't know anything about it.

Or, she doesn't know about actually doing it, only about *not* doing it. That's what she's learned.

If her mother even let her learn that.

They just keep walking to the trailhead. Will is there, and Will is adorable, and Sophie is crushed all over again.

He's the only one for her and he's with Honey. Everyone's the one for Honey with her golden hair, and Honey's job has always been just to ward them off. But Will was the only one for Sophie.

"Hey," he says, when he sees them.

"Hey," Sophie says. And she can feel her cheeks get hot. She should say something more to him. She should at least look at him.

"All right then, see you later," she says, and turns to go, as if it doesn't matter in the least.

And neither Honey nor Will seems to hear. They don't chase her, they don't call her back.

Hey, don't go. We didn't mean for you to go away. Come back—we're just going up to the falls to swim. Come back.

But no. They don't say a word, not to her. And she doesn't even turn her head to see.

So now it's just Sophie and the trees, but at least today she brought her iPod with the playlist she made for today, from some CDs Amber borrowed from Eli.

What—does he think he's some kind of battle-rapper, listening to this in his room?

She doesn't like Eli's music exactly, but she likes how it would surprise people. You're listening to *what*, borrowed from *whom*, while walking in the woods?

Dad especially, who thinks she only listens to Folkways, never "M&M's." Which he knows is wrong but thinks is funny.

If this is what a million other people are listening to she wants to know. She wants to know about the world out there.

And you don't have to like it to know that the rhymes are pretty great.

But if Eli's head is full of this. If he thinks like that. Sophie's not going to mess with him, or any of them.

It's just music, people say, just words, but it seems like more than that to Sophie.

The threats and the anger and the passion all feel real. More real than anything you can ever see.

And deeper, too, probably, than whatever Honey has going on with Will.

*

"Are you sick, kid? Never see *you* lying around till noon."

Dad's up, drinking his shit coffee. People are shouting at each other on TV, the audience is laughing. Cyrus needs to get out of here.

It probably really is noon, from the look of things, the sun coming in.

It hurts even to keep his eyes open. He's itchy all over.

Like pot, but legal, they said. Supposed to be just a little smoke, a little high, and then everything just goes back to normal.

But it wasn't good then and now it's only bad. Twelve hours later, maybe more.

His brain hurts. His throat not so great either.

Z8 times one, Z8 times two, times three. He hasn't even tested past one.

He must've been out there for hours last night, mosquitoes eating him alive. Chomping on his arms, his face too.

"You look like shit," the old man says. "Must've been a pretty good night."

Bats came out, stars came out, and it just got worse. He thought he would die. Wanted to die.

What a disaster. Eighty bucks and nothing but a headache to show for it. Plus all those hours cleaning the shack, tracking down the supplies.

He could've put in the wrong amount of any of those things. How could he know?

You can't even find the page online anymore. It's like it never existed.

If he died out there, only Eli would've found him. He's the only one goes out there. Or maybe the raccoons. The coyotes.

They'd tear me to shreds, eat my heart out.

It was nothing a halfway decent chemistry major couldn't do. Eight chemicals and some cheap tobacco.

Cyrus is more than halfway decent, isn't he?

Dad doesn't even put on a shirt. If Cyrus was skinny like that, with a gut like that, he'd put on a shirt at least.

"Where's Eli?" Cyrus says.

"Probably went back to your mother's. How should I know?"

Because he's your son, Cyrus doesn't say. Because he's probably gone over to Rudy's, gone looking for Jeff, even though I told him not to, told him to get a real job.

Then you can help me with the Z8, once I get it going, Cyrus told him. But pay your dues first.

And Eli just nodded, probably only pretending to hear.

None of the guys will do anything Jeff doesn't do first, not even Eli. He's got them all running for him now, far as Cyrus can tell.

"You got work today?" Dad says.

"No, no—I've got nothing today. Taking the day off."

Killing off his brain cells more like. One by one. Two by two. What if the next one is worse?

"Good for you, kid. Take it easy," he says. "Just don't get used to it. You'll just get old, like me."

More laughter from the TV. More shouting. Some kind of news show maybe.

"You're too smart to get old, though, right, Cy?"

Fuck you. Fuck you and your hairy belly, Cyrus could but won't say.

Dad always liked Uncle Rudy's kids better. They're more like him. Happy to take whatever's given.

But Cyrus wants so much more than that. He needs there to be more.

Maybe he'll just jump in the river today, clear it all out. Go to Circle Current and see who's hanging around, just be a normal person again.

A normal guy taking the day off, maybe seeing some girls.

And then he'll go crawling back to Shaw's, back to working full-time, 'cause someone's got to pay.

He's seen them piling up in the kitchen—electric, propane, everything on final notice.

Shaw's would take him, too. I'd hire you back in a heartbeat, Carol said. Good luck, she said, when he clocked out for the last time.

Such a show he made of putting his apron on the bonfire that night! What're you gonna do next, Cyrus? Not that anyone really cared.

Just working a few nights a week at Maplefields. Got some other things lined up, he'd said.

It's too late for the lawn crews now, though. Too late for the road crews.

He had a good idea. Such a great idea! And it was summer coming. Things were about to go his way

But you can't sell people on a burn and a headache. Or, he could sell it, once or twice, but they'd come back for him

Cyrus pours his coffee and walks out the back door, back to his sugar shack, scene of the crime. All cleaned up and no place to go.

The jobs out there are always the same. *Looking for someone to join our team!*

He should've gone to college. Those kids think they work so hard, taking the hard classes, getting the grades, but they don't know work. Not really. That's all just self-improvement.

Hosing down the walk-in, that's work. Slicing meat, zipping it up in a bag, bleaching the machinery, day after day.

Maybe if he'd gone down and lived with Mom it would be different. She would've seen to it that he got somewhere.

Honor society. Drama club. A job with D'Angelos. Amber's doing all right.

But Eli's no better off than the rest of them. Worse, maybe, and he's been with Mom his whole life.

Jenny Rose is trailer trash, his cousins say. She was using your dad for a place to sleep on her way up.

They wish. They just say that to make themselves feel better, because they know she's better than any of them.

She must've been smoking crack when she was pregnant with Eli, they say.

Jeff says it just to see Eli lose his shit and throw his skinny little body around. Throwing punches that never land.

Nobody really knows what's wrong with that kid. Maybe Mom really was drinking or something, not that he'd blame her.

Or maybe Eli's just like that. Thinks he's something special but really he's just wrong in the head.

Cyrus is at least as smart as Amber, but he didn't have anyone to pay for things. Mom pays for everything when it comes to Amber.

But what about me? What about me, Mom?

It's a nice morning today, at least. Low pressure, no sign of rain. He can be here alone for a while, where it's quiet.

Get away from Dad. Think a while.

How they made Cyrus employee of the month before he left. They put his picture on the wall, there with the manager and shift supervisor, all in their matching aprons.

At least here in the shack there's no uniform. No wall of shame. No paycheck either, though.

Jeff pays a hundred bucks a run. You just drive to Albany, meet someone in some bathroom or other, and drive back.

Jeff's making good money, the guys all say. So why's he living in that shitty house with that girl and her baby?

But even Jeff has Uncle Rudy to pay for stuff. To fix up the septic and give him the old truck.

And even Jeff has a girl. Not that Cyrus would want a girl with someone else's baby.

Maybe Cyrus should just boil some actual sugar in here. Nobody's boiled maple in forever. Not since Grandpa Rudy's time.

That'll get you about thirty bucks a gallon, after how many cords of wood, how many hours?

Jeff's the one paying good money today, paying Jason, paying Cam. But Cyrus won't do it. No, he'll be working by the hour, taking the cans to the redemption center again.

They'll hand him a slip of paper worth three dollars, maybe five. And then he'll have to stand in one more line to get the cash.

*

Nell lifts one rock, then another, from the old wall in the woods, which is hardly a wall anymore. A pile more like, as if sprung up from the ground.

She's making a border for her garden, adding a new bed for greens that don't mind a little shade.

She likes the texture of stones, their smell, and how sometimes she uncovers traces of the animals who've lived there too.

Shreddings of blue tarp. Seed fluff and snakeskins. Tiny black turds.

Laura would laugh, no wonder you've never done much with your life, content to move rocks around.

What happened to your job at the garden center? Did you quit that too?

Christine's voice in her head asking. Or Dad's voice asking. Or maybe just Nell herself, always asking.

Your series of undemanding seasonal jobs. Your series of seasonal lovers. What happened to them? You're done with even that now?

I am. I am done with all that. I have enough to get by, and whatever I don't have I can do without.

There's another voice now, though, saying, Good for you. Good for the environment.

Leonard Larocque, who has been here all this time. Fixing things because he can.

The rocks are black and damp with moss, rough with lichen. They've been here, too, for a hundred years, moved from place to place.

So different from those rocks out west. Laura's rocks, her river, her hair matted with blood.

And later her face waxy and white. At peace, said that priest who knew nothing. Everyone allowed to mourn except Nell.

She couldn't even cry. The blood on her hands, on Laura's face.

Nell is working up a sweat, working faster. When her heart beats faster than the beat of anxiety she knows she'll be all right.

You just need to keep moving. You can't go back, only forward.

I admire that, he said. Walking all that way, doing without the car.

She should not have said she might be busy. She's always busy, but also always free.

Life is longer than she thought and also shorter, each day just a series of hours to fill.

How is it that I'm still here and you're still not, Laura?

Nobody wants to hear about Laura anymore. There is no happy ending and never anything new.

But it's Nell's story and she will return to it as often as she wants, as often as she needs to.

To that night that lasted longer than any other night, longer than a week, a year, of nights.

It is hers and she remembers with absolute clarity. The quarter-moon passing over the sky so slowly. She'd never before seen how it follows an arc, from one side to the other.

How time stopped and she was trapped inside of it. Have you ever been trapped inside of time? Who can she ask who will answer?

Her heart was so tight she could barely breathe and yet somehow she did breathe. All night long, awake, alert, waiting for Laura to come back.

Calling and calling into the darkness that never answered.

She was only supposed to be gone an hour, just joining some other hikers at a campfire. Come on, they have a radio! But Nell said no, you go. And Laura did.

Finally the thick black sky lightened, and she could see again. She walked all the way back to the park entrance. My sister hasn't come back, she told the rangers.

The other hikers were gone and never found. Nobody even tried.

She died of head trauma, not drowning, the coroner said when the report came back. There'd been traces of alcohol, traces of semen, but she died from the fall.

How could they have let that be the whole story? Let it go, they said to Nell. It doesn't matter now.

But Nell knows. They sang along to the car radio all the way across the country, and they talked like sisters, and Laura said it clearly. I'm Catholic, I'm waiting for marriage.

Oh, come on. Tell me something else now, won't you? Everyone has said it. That's enough.

These things happen to people who are not used to the terrain. It's dangerous at night, a woman alone, the river so far down below. You can't change anything by finding someone to blame.

Don't you have another story?

I have so many other stories! Nells says. So many of my own adventures.

Your own careless, reckless stories of campfires, of music and drinks and of men who'd be gone by morning. Yes, I know. You've done far worse than I ever would, and yet you're still here.

You've never really gone anywhere. You never could keep up.

Nell sets down one more rock. Steadies it. It's progress, it adds order, and it will make a good bed for spinach and chard.

Maybe Leonard will admire this too.

He'll say, that's a good wall you're building. But you'll need some kind of trellis, some more mulch.

Of course, come back for some fresh bread next Saturday, she should have said.

Come back out of the woods and tell me something new. Tell me a story I haven't heard before.

*

Will describes the book he's reading—the whole intricate plot of it—but nothing about what he's doing. He seems happy, though, his skin glowing with health.

"Have you made some new friends?" Sarah asks.

She tries to sound casual. He's making sandwiches and she's stirring some of that good local honey into her tea. It's just a conversation in a kitchen.

"I guess so. Lots of people go to Circle Current to swim. Kids from town."

She wants to ask who, which ones, who are their parents? But she wouldn't know the parents' names anyway, unlike at his school in New York where she knew everyone.

She thought it would be easier here, that she'd feel safer, but instead she feels cut off, in the dark.

"Have you caught up with Amber LeBeau, the one that came looking for you that day?"

"I've seen her a couple times," he says.

"Is she on her way to college too?" she asks, though she thinks she knows the answer.

"No," he says. "She's just going to be a junior, I think."

"What about that research Dad asked you to do, about the honeybees? Have you gone back to the apiary?"

"Not yet," he says.

And that's it. His face betrays nothing. He spreads almond butter. He spreads jelly, puts the jar back in the fridge, finally without her having to remind him to.

Maybe it's Amber who makes him so happy. Maybe Amber is why he's wearing a nice shirt. If he's finally found a girlfriend, if he's happy here, she can't object, can she?

It's what she wanted all along, for him to find his way here, to be independent and happy. She just wishes he'd tell her more about it.

But he slips the food into his bag, takes the strawberries, and off he goes. His blue backpack disappearing into the trees.

Jim is gone, too, back to the city again for a few days. Hammering out the details, he said, before he starts the next book, also about water.

Water is the only thing that matters in the end, he said. You'll see.

"You'll see," Sarah says to the quiet room, the empty house.

It's never entirely quiet here, though. At first it seems like it is, but then you hear it, a chorus rising from the trees. The planes overhead, too, though not often.

And now the clacking of the shuttlecock. The whole thing almost whirs, once she finally gets going.

It took her three whole days to set up the warp. She'd forgotten about that part, remembering just the rhythm of the weave, which is the part she loves.

From where she sits she can see the three jade elephants above the fireplace. Just like in New York, marching across the mantel, though she meant to leave them behind with everything else.

Your father's colonialist knickknacks, Jim calls them. The enamel camels and porcelain incense burners. But Sarah likes them, how they were about more than just the exchange of money.

They were given to her dad at all those state dinners in China, the UAE, when his company was starting to get big.

He'd sometimes drag her mother along too. They were young and didn't know what they were doing.

Building a bridge to the future! so the corporate motto says. At one point they might really have believed it.

That was just his day job, though. What I really love, her father always said, is a weekend in the woods.

He wouldn't have loved it so much if he'd lived here, though, would he have?

No daily delivery of the *Wall Street Journal.* No television. Too much quiet.

And mother. I'm just farm girl at heart, she always said. Still says. Seven siblings and an outhouse.

To look at her you'd never know. So comfortable down there in Florida, burning a king's share of carbon for all that AC, and playing golf at the club, even now that Dad's gone.

Sarah used to be so angry with her parents for failing to stop so much of the world's suffering with their money. How they didn't even seem to care.

It's her turn now. An adult with an inheritance. And what is she doing?

Too busy making good for our kids, trying to do right by our own families, and then we're tired. Maybe once she's settled she can get more energy, find a cause.

Meanwhile she can learn to make do with less.

This yarn in her fingers, so soft, is hardly "doing with less" at twelve dollars a skein. Shorn, carded, spun. Dyed by hand, right there down the road. What could be wrong with that?

Amber LeBeau can't buy yarn at twelve dollars a skein, that's what's wrong with that. She'll buy clothes from China instead, so someone else can get rich, buy a house in the country.

How it just goes back and forth, endlessly, this exchange of money and goods and guilt. How she can never get to the bottom of it.

How when she's alone she's always just a little bit hungry. A little bit restless.

Maybe if Jim were here, she'd feel more content. If the two of them were meditating again, like they said they would. Facing inward, or facing each other.

Maybe then they could connect again, like back when he first came to be with her in the city, after that retreat up by Lake Willoughby.

They spent hours and days in her tiny apartment, talking, dreaming of all the things they would do together, barely even bothering to go out.

But he's off and running again with another project. Jim never really stops searching for a new lead.

Maybe it will just take a while longer for her to get used to having all this time and quiet all for herself.

To having a son who is strong and happy in the world, needing nothing more from her.

To finally having what she always thought she wanted.

*

David used to be able to wait till August for the harvest, but it's starting already now and what is it, the last week of July?

He just has to get the honey before the bears do. Before the ants and moths. Before the storms. He just has to collect the fruits of his labors.

The bees' labors, actually.

He switches on the uncapper, watches the conveyer roll into place, working just fine. He'll get Honey in here to feed the supers into the machine now that she's finished the labeling.

She's been doing this every August since she was six and could probably do it in her sleep.

The harvest might be early, but at least it's happening, at least there's a yield. Newsletter's reporting massive die-offs in Pennsylvania now, too close for comfort.

At least it's mostly big operations getting hit. Honey in the Rock is tiny compared to some of those places in the west or the south even.

Daisy stands now, sniffing in the direction of the woods, and Lucky follows.

Always some creature in the woods to get their tails wagging for a minute, then they're down again, lying in the shade. Spayed old girls.

Except now they're both whining at the door, and David catches a flash of something red in the trees.

"Hey!" he calls. He steps out of the barn into the light, can barely see into the woods for the angle of the sun.

"Hey!" he calls again. The dogs follow him, still wagging.

And out steps a foundling of some kind. A teenager. He knows this kid, doesn't he?

"What're you doing back here? Public entrance is around the front."

The kid looks at him, like he's just woken up. Like he's lost.

"C'mere," David says. "What's your name?"

The kid comes out into the light, pulls his hat down over his eyes as if that will make him disappear.

He's probably wasted on something or other. He would hate him if he didn't feel sorry for him.

Just David's type. Yep, this kid is just his type, not that he has time for it right now.

Still, when they show up is when they show up.

"You looking for something in particular?"

A shrug, a scowl, the usual nonsense.

"Look, why don't you come in the front door and ask for whatever it is you're looking for? Nobody likes someone creeping around in the woods."

"The dogs like me fine," he finally says, slowly, like each word is an effort.

Daisy's licking his hand now, like the kid's got treats. Lucky's just wagging and wagging.

"What are you doing here, what do you want?"

"Nothing," he says. Of course he says "nothing." They always do. So David makes quick work of it. You can't waste any time with kids like this.

"Come back tomorrow, at, say, noon, and I'll show you around. Get you hooked up with some work. Don't say no. Don't say anything. Just show up at noon. We pay a good wage here and could use some extra hands."

The kid just stares. His eyes watery and red. Has he been crying, or just smoking weed?

"You got hands, don't you?" David says. "But don't come back here unless you want to work. We can't have people hanging around in the woods. It's not good for business."

Of course it's not good for a lot of other things either, but this is what he says. Fifty-fifty chance the kid will come back at noon but better than that he won't be hanging around the woods anymore.

He knows this kid from somewhere. Maybe one of Honey's old friends, back when she used to play with boys. Maybe one of the LeBeaus.

"Noon," he says again. "And leave by the road, all right? Get out of here now, but come back tomorrow."

The dogs follow him a few yards down the drive, just as far as the edge of the day lilies, then retreat back to the safety of the barn. The kid walks away slowly, but he can see he's just playing it cool.

Why he was even here, David couldn't say. It's private property back in these woods, not far off the river trail, but it's nothing special. Just a patch of trees and rocks, like anywhere else.

David walks around back to see for himself. Some of the ferns are flattened, like a deer's been sleeping here.

A few yards back he finds a rock littered with cigarette ends, the hand-rolled kind. Enough of them he knows this isn't the first time this kid has been hanging out back here.

And he's beaten a little path all the way back to the trail.

Whatever he's been up to, it can't be any good.

Well, you have to act fast with kids like this. Act fast and don't leave any room for doubts.

Let them do the right thing like you always knew they would. Not that he even knows exactly what he'll do with him.

He certainly doesn't want him working in here with Ruth and Honey.

He can't have been back here to hang out with Honey, can he?

She wouldn't have anything to do with a kid like this. Red eyes and ugly as sin. Not with his own baby girl. David was sure she was alone out here.

But that's how it goes. You think you know something and then you don't.

In any case, it's done now. The kid will come back at noon or he won't.

*

So the old man found him out. Doesn't mean Eli can't come back. He'll come back any time he pleases.

Eli keeps a better eye on Honey than anyone. He knows when she works, knows when she plays.

Honey acts like she's hanging with Sophie Pierce all afternoon, but Eli knows what the deal is.

Today he was maybe gonna surprise them all, see what's in it for him.

Sophie's not so hot but she's something, and Amber gave her his music to listen to. More where that came from, he'd tell her.

But no sign of the girls today. Maybe Eli was late. Hard to tell when you start the day on Cyrus's stash.

He's seen her here how many times now? A thousand times over, and always the same. Always his girl.

Sticking the labels. Scratching that itch. I'll show you what kind of itch I've got to scratch.

I'll tell you what a good wage is, old man.

A hundred bucks a pop for Jeff's game. Drive to Albany, drive back.

Once I get my car. Once I get my nerve up to get the cash to get the car.

The kid goes out, the dad goes out, when's that lady gonna go out, do something besides hang around her fancy new house on the ridge?

Not that he couldn't take her. Knock her out with a rock. Smash her head in.

Easier if she just leaves the premises, though. Take the money and run. No mess, no fuss.

Get a car, get into the business.

The family business. And not whatever the fuck Cyrus is up to. Not that business.

Not the honey business either. He needs more than that, if he wants to show Honey a thing or two.

No, he sees how these bee people live. Shitty old house with a shitty old truck, praise the lord. No better than Dad's place, or not much, at least.

No, Eli knows how to pry a lock if he has to.

He's pried a few in his day. The one off Amber's bike when he needed it for cash. Or the one on his own house when Mom was so mad she kicked him out for the day.

Cheap shitty locks like Mom gets. There'll be no cheap shitty locks for those people on the ridge, though.

Probably cost a day's work just to buy one lock on that house on the ridge. A day of this kind of work anyway.

A good wage. Uh-huh. You got hands, don't you?

Shoved into his pockets. Hiding under the hat. Where's his fucking invisibility cloak now?

The guy's got Jimmy Framboise working for him. Aidan Taft. Those guys who liked to push Eli around.

Now they've got Mitchell pushing them around. What comes around goes around.

But Eli won't fall for that. He's got other plans. Making inroads, soon to be passing them by.

Sometimes you just have to use your imagination. Or kick something—whammo! Kick a stone.

Take something. Take a hit. Take a beef stick if that's all you got.

Any more of Cyrus's stash will blow his brains out. Make him miss things, wreck him for good.

Mom says get a job. Amber's got a job, she likes to remind him.

Amber has a job all right. Working all day at the Popsicle stand, cleaning up with the guys at night. Who's cleaning who, he wants to ask her.

A hundred bucks a shot, though. That's what I'm talking about! Jeff sends you down to Albany, you pick up what he wants, and you're in the money.

Soon as he gets a car.

Noon tomorrow, Mitchell said. Maybe that's his signal, maybe that's his green light. Tomorrow at noon he'll pry that lock on the Calper house.

Tomorrow at noon when the sun is up high and bright he'll bust in there and get what he needs.

Or maybe the sign is that he should come back down this road. Walk straight into that barn where Honey is.

She'd have to see him then. Have to give him something for his time.

If she's ripe enough to fall for that fairy-boy, why not a runt with a plan, someone who knows what's what around here?

Tomorrow at noon, the guy said.

You got hands, don't you?

✳

Before Nell even says hello, Helga is at her feet, tail wagging.

Leonard has a grocery bag in his hand and walks toward her in the garden, circled with stones.

The old vegetable plot is nothing more than a few straggly tomato plants that she has tied up with string. Kale picked all the way up the stem.

"How's that roof holding up?" he says.

"So far, so good," she says, and it's true. Six Saturdays gone by now, rain or shine the buckets remain empty.

"I have some bread for you," she says. "Come in and I'll get you some."

And what a relief, finally, to offer. She will do it right this time, generous, not calculating every last crumb.

"Helga—truck!" Len calls, and Helga retreats, both ears pressed down, tail between her legs.

"No, no. She can come in. I don't mind. If it's okay with you."

Where this impulse comes from. Or that one. So many at once. She thought Len would never come back.

Helga bounds in the door, sniffing around the table legs, the hearth by the woodstove, leaving a trail of caked mud on the floor.

"Sorry about that," Len says. "I can sweep that up."

"No, no," she says, and she finds she doesn't mind a little dirt today.

He leaves his own shoes outside on the mat next to hers.

"I found a couple things I thought you could use," he says. He sets the grocery bag on the table.

"These are some great tile snippers. Handy for ripping out old nails. And this here cutter works really good on shingles. Figured you probably didn't have your own," he says.

She picks up the snippers and works them a few times. They seem well-oiled. Good old tools.

"Thank you," she says. "But I couldn't take all this. I already owe you for the repair."

"Well, they're just extras I found lying around in my mom's garage. Dad's old things. She won't be needing them. And you might."

When Nell spoons the tea leaves into the blue china pot she makes sure to put in a little extra.

She slices the bread thick. "Let me get you a slice while it's still warm," she says. "Butter?"

"You'll do without propane, but you've got butter? Now that's priorities!"

"I still have a little propane," she says, but she's smiling now too.

"You ever have chickens up here?" Len says. "They're good for fertilizer. Fresh eggs. Easy to take care of too."

"No, no chickens for me," she says. She doesn't want any living creature relying on her for food or anything else.

Helga pushes up against her knees under the table, and Nell scratches her soft ears.

It's been a long time since anyone but Christine has sat at the table with her. These days even Christine prefers the phone for checking in.

Len picks up a book she's left on the table. Sibley's guide to the birds of the east. Pages through it while he eats the bread.

"I've seen a lot of these guys lately," he says. He points to the green heron. "Have you seen them, that whole family? Must be nesting under the bridge."

"I hear them but I don't see them much," she says.

"You lived right there next to that bridge way back when, didn't you? We used to pass you on the school bus, riding a bike. Always thought you were so lucky to live there, right in town."

She'd forgotten about that, riding home down Route 11 after school, the freedom of it. Not having to wait for anyone at all.

"A bunch of smarty-pants, the whole lot of you," he says. "Three girls and a boy, isn't that right?"

"Well, there used to be," Nell says. "Laura, me, Christine, then Henry, the baby."

And she feels that old surge of adrenaline. Fight or flight, they call it, when danger is near.

Nell's own face is hot now, the flush creeping up her neck like fire.

"I'm sorry," he says. "I remember when your sister died out west. That must've been tough."

"Well, that was a long time ago now. Thirty years."

"Doesn't matter how long," he says.

He sets the bread down on his plate and just sits there for a moment looking at her, as the steam rises from the pot between them.

"Do you remember that time," he says, "must've been around ninth grade, when my bag busted open on the sidewalk outside school and everything fell out—gym clothes, papers blowing across the snow. How you ran around chasing them, helped me get it all back?"

"No, actually, I don't remember that. Are you sure that was me?"

"Of course—you don't forget stuff like that."

"Or maybe you do," Nell says. She certainly doesn't remember. It's startling, really, to show up in someone else's memory. What else might she be doing in there?

"Of course I remember your older sister, too. Good at hockey. Top of the class."

"She was good at everything," Nell says. "First at everything too." She doesn't say Laura was the first to die, Mom and Dad shortly after.

Mom died of a broken heart, Christine always says, as if just by living Nell had no real claim on grief.

Her hands are shaking a little now, holding the teacup, which is hot like her face is hot.

"She was the first at our school to wear bell-bottoms," Leonard says. "I remember that. A real trendsetter!"

"You're right," Nell says, remembering now. "I forgot about that too."

And she can see Laura now, hand on hip, standing in front of the house on her way to school. She could get away with anything, even in Glenville.

"Did you ever wear jeans like that?" Nell asks, though she can't imagine he did. A tech-school kid, living in the mountains. Going nowhere, is what she would've thought back then, and in a way she would have been right.

"Oh, god no. All that hippie stuff pretty much passed me by," he says. "We were just glad when the war ended. Not before it got my brother, though."

"I'm sorry, I didn't know that," Nell says. How could she not know that, when he knows about Laura?

He empties the cup in one swallow, as if about to go. Nell refills it before he has a chance to say he's had enough.

"The seventies," he says, picking up the cup again. "Not as much fun as everyone thinks." Nell just nods. Wills him to say more.

"Eighties weren't much better, come to think of it," he says with a smile now. "Reaganomics. Remember that?"

But Nell would rather not move on to the eighties. Back home with Mom and Dad. One getting ill, then the other, as Christine and Henry moved on with their lives.

No, she wants him to talk more about the time before. Back when she was just the girl on the bike with long hair, her sister walking along in bell-bottoms and beads.

Before she became so difficult, unable to stay on a single path in school or work or love even, unable to fulfill any promise.

You're too sensitive, you care too much, Christine would say. Then the problem was that she cared too little. Nell could never get it right.

But Nell can't think of a way to bring it back to before, and he's quiet too.

"I'm sorry I don't have any milk for the tea," she says finally. "Milk always spoils faster than I can drink it. But I do have honey."

"No, I don't need anything. And don't worry, I won't suggest you get your own cow," he says. "Though it is the best way to keep the milk fresh, of course. Most environmental."

The conversation doesn't circle back again to that life before, but at least she was here for a second, the young Helen Castleton, that girl who would go somewhere.

Her sister, too, alive in that house by the river, but in someone else's memory now.

"Thank you for the tools," she says when he gets back into the truck.

Helga's already in the seat beside him and a loaf of bread on the dashboard.

"I hope you can use them," he says. "There will be lots of rain come the end of the summer and you'll want that roof sealed up tight."

*

They walk through the trees, farther upriver than before, where there is no trail. No sign of human life at all.

It's so unreal up here—all the rocks and the thick green moss. The way the water sounds.

Will could get lost up here. He'd never find his way back, if he didn't have her as a guide.

Honey who knows the way. Honey who is going to save him today.

He stands by the river now and begins to unbutton his shirt, a dress shirt because she told him to wear something nice.

"No. As you are," she says.

She pulls off her sneakers and steps into the river. He's never seen her in a dress before. He's not sure if he likes her better this way.

"Jesus could save you, too," she said last Sunday. That's exactly what she said, and he could see from her face she wasn't joking.

"In my religion it's the priesthood of the believer and I'm a believer," she said. "So I can be a priest."

"If you choose grace over sin, you could be saved," she said.

And he said, "I'd choose anything for you."

Or something like that. It sounded like the kind of lies people say in movies, but it was true.

So they got dressed and made a plan. The plan they're doing now. "We'll go upriver to a place where the water is smooth and deep but nobody ever goes."

She pulls the rubber band out of her hair now and shakes it out from the braid, signaling something, though he has no idea what.

All that hair. Nobody else has hair like that, in ripples down to her waist.

The sun is bright, but the river is still freezing cold. You can't believe how cold until you dip your feet in.

"This seems like a good place for it," he says, stopping, and hoping she'll stop too. The water has reached the edge of his pants to where he's rolled them.

"No, deeper," she says. "You have to go in all the way."

She pulls him by the hand till he's in up to the waist and her dress is floating around her.

This girl is going to save me! This girl in a dress.

"Not now. Later," she says, when he moves in to kiss her face.

She glides through the water away from him, and back, and through her dress he can see the thick bra she always wears. The granny bra, he calls it when she takes it off.

He wants her to take it off now. To see her breasts through her flowered dress, to touch them in the freezing-cold water.

"Now," she says, standing still again. "Listen to me."

And she says some kind of prayer. She calls on Jesus and they both look up to the blue sky peeking through the treetops, white clouds rushing past.

"Do you accept Jesus as your savior?"

"I do," he says, and she grabs him around the waist and tips him back.

She presses his shoulder and his feet come out from under him. He nearly pulls her under too. It isn't funny, to have your feet go out from under you in a river like this.

"Just let go, I have you," she says. And like a baby he floats in her arms.

Her strong freckled arms. He can feel the current pulling at him, but she holds him steady, weightless.

"You have to put your head in," she says. "Let me do this."

He looks into her face, her mouth, which soon enough he'll be kissing, and says, "I trust you."

She pushes him down then, forcing his head all the way into the cold water.

Water pours up his nose and he's coughing, struggling, like his head might burst.

"There's nobody between you and God now," she says. "You are saved." And she smiles and he smiles back.

Are they serious, or are they kids playing games? I'm the boy and you're the girl and this is what we'll do.

There's always food after a baptism, she told him. People come out starving. "Are you starving?" she says now.

She brought a bottle of sparkling blood-orange soda to share. "It's more ritualistic, with the blood-orange than regular," she says.

He brought sandwiches and strawberries, "which are an aphrodisiac," he says, even though she doesn't know what that means. Even though they won't need it.

Their wet feet pick up pine needles and they're shivering in search of a warm rock where they'll eat, which is also part of the plan.

Has something really happened? Is he really saved? He doesn't believe in that, but he might believe in something. He believes in all the religions. He told her so.

Buddhism, Taoism, Judaism, they all have something for us. Jesus, too, he told her. He did some good in the world. I like Jesus.

She just said, okay. As long as you let Jesus into your heart, you can be baptized.

He has no problem letting Jesus into his heart. His heart is full to bursting already with Honey and with the summer and all of it. Why not?

And the baptism was okay. That was good. But it's very cold. His jeans are heavy, his shirt sticking to him.

"Can I take off my shirt now?" he says. "It's just making me colder."

She's cold, too, he can tell, her lips bluish. Even Honey, who's always warm, is covered in goosebumps.

"Of course," she says, and she lifts her dress from the skirt and up over her head. She stands there in wet panties and that thick bra.

He goes to brush the pine needles off her wet skin but they stick.

"This is wet, too," he says, and unfastens the bra from behind. When it falls into the pine needles she laughs.

"Stupid ugly thing," she says.

She takes his hand and places it on her breast, which is warm. The only warm place between them.

Then they are kissing, like they always do, and peeling their wet clothes off, every last bit.

This is not pretending, this isn't kids playing. This is more real than real. The most real thing he has ever felt.

It is happening now. She's not stopping and he's not stopping and he pushes her panties aside, pushes everything aside.

She says "stay," or he thinks she says "stay," and he does, and it happens, much too fast it happens.

He's sure now that something has changed.

A cloud moves away and the sun shoots through the trees and onto their bare skin.

"It's a sign," Honey says. She pulls closer to him, pulls the blanket of her damp hair over their shoulders.

And maybe it is. Maybe this is what it is to be saved. To have direct access to your god.

This is what it is to believe in heaven and hell and everything in between. He has never felt so much peace.

6

Jeanne will never get used to it. That the end of summer doesn't mean the beginning of school, the beginning of anything anymore.

Just a feeling of autumn in the air, and soon the yellow buses will be going by.

All it does is rain these days. Soon there will be mushrooms sprouting in the garage again. Mold on the bathroom ceiling. All while she stands here watching the time pass.

Jim Calper's got a book tucked under his arm as he flips through his mail now, coming her way.

"No packages for you today, sir," Jeanne says. "Can I maybe get you some stamps?" She's always supposed to offer stamps. Part of the USPS upsell.

She reaches under the counter for the new ones, National Parks. He might like those. Better than the boring old flags.

"Not today, thanks. But I'm sure I'll have something to mail out soon. Will's heading to school next week, and his mother thinks he's going to the moon."

"But I do have something for *you*," he says.

"For me?" And he hands her the book. His name's on the cover, and the photo on the back is the author, serious, arms folded across the chest. She looks from the photo back to Jim. "Is that you?"

"It is. Or, it was, anyway. That was a few years ago now."

"You look younger now, if you ask me," she says. "Without the glasses."

"I always see you reading in here, so I figured I'd give you a copy. I hope you'll like it. Or find it interesting maybe."

"*Growing Gold: The Rise of Biofuels*," she says.

"Yep. And I've got a new book on the way. Just finishing up the proof-reading now, actually."

"Really? Wow, another book already. Is that one more . . . uplifting?"

"*Rising Tides: The Fate of Island Communities as the World Warms.* I'm still not sure about the title. Do you like it?"

"Catchy," she says and flips through the pages. There are some color pictures in the middle at least. Fields of yellow flowers.

She wonders if she'd ever finish a book like this. Maybe if she stopped reading this other crap she would.

"Here, I'll trade you," she says and reaches under the counter.

"*Winter's Glory*. Wow. That does look more interesting than my book," he says.

He hands it back. "But I better not take it. That's quite a pretty lady there on the cover—my wife would be jealous."

"Ach, your wife's a pretty lady, too," Jeanne says, though she's never really thought so. "She's got nothing to worry about."

"Speaking of winter's glory, do you think we'll get much snow this year?"

"It's hard to say about snow except I hope so. The ski areas will go belly-up otherwise. Probably the inn too."

"Colorado's got the same problem, with not enough snow. I grew up out there."

"Then you're spoiled for snow."

"Sun and snow together, yes. But I've been on the east coast long enough to know what I'm in for."

"We'll have a couple weeks of color early October, but then it's just stick season till the snow comes. *If* the snow comes."

"Stick season, that's good," he says.

"Hunting season, too," she says. "You ever hunt?"

"No, I never have. Sarah's father was wild about it, but I wouldn't know what to do with a rifle if you put one to my head!"

"I could hook you up. Turkey's first. My husband always says it's a good excuse to hang out in the woods. A nature lover like you might like that."

"I don't think so. Not this year anyway," he says and turns to go. "But I hope you like the book!"

"It really would help if you took this one," she says, trying again. "Not so tempting to read about fuel oil when you've got this hanging around."

"Oh, my book's a real page-turner, you'll be surprised. Once you get started."

She'll finish *Winter's Glory* first. Third of the series. Then she'll get going on Jim's book.

She'll try, anyway. But Jeanne has never gone in for doom and gloom, which is what this is, you can tell. It's what the environmentalists are all about these days.

It's trying to fool you with the fields of flowers, but everyone knows you can't grow gold. Not even with all this rain.

*

Eli waited a few weeks to take him up on the offer, but Mitchell didn't mind. Sure, I can find some work for you, he said.

But it's Eli's third day in a row and he hasn't seen her. Just him and one of the little cousins, working the damn machine.

Probably be done in about three hours today, Mitchell said. It's only been one but feels like forever.

There's a whole truckload of this they've got to get through. Frame after frame.

And here he is wearing a fucking shower cap and gloves. Like what Cyrus wears at Shaw's when they go in there and make fun of him by the deli slicer.

Maybe Eli will just shave his head so he doesn't have to wear this thing and look like an idiot.

At least what Honey was doing with all the labels and jars this summer was clean. This is a mess, his shoes sticking to the floor every time he tries to move.

He pulls the nasty frames out of the box one at a time, sets them on the conveyer, and all the wax gets sliced off the top, then into the extractor it goes.

It's nothing like what you see in those plastic bears with their little red caps, all clear and gold. This stuff is thick and full of junk—wax pieces, bee pieces.

Mitchell explained all the rest of it, how they get the wax out, showed him some cute little candles shaped like Christmas trees, but Eli's just here for the job.

Just show me the money, man. Show me the fringe benefits.

Where is she, anyway? His third day and he's only seen her like once.

Apparently she's got a different job in the operation.

There's the old lady in the front office keeping track of things. Boss man walking around. But hardly any sign of Honey.

The little kid's job is to pop the sticky thing off the conveyer and put it in the spinning machine.

You put them on, he takes them off. Don't worry about the rest, Mitchell said. Roll it in, roll it out.

The cousin's got headphones on under that bonnet, MP3 player in his pocket. It'll take Eli, what, forty hours working here to have enough for one of those?

And there's no sign of Aidan and Jimmy. Maybe they're out in the trucks or something.

He liked it much better when it was just him outside and Honey inside all alone. So damn busy now with all the honey coming and going, trucks and people and bees all over the place. They even got a forklift down there.

They could at least let Eli drive the forklift, but instead he's nearly falling asleep on his feet up here with all the machines rattling and the little kid kind of singing to himself.

Ah, but then here he comes up the stairs, the boss man himself! And why does he have that shithead, Willoughby Calper, with him?

And Honey, too, finally. Finally he sees her, wearing braids like some innocent little country girl. Can't fool me!

Boss man is lecturing again, and the kid is taking notes. Yeah, yeah, he's heard this before, the magic, the miracle, of honey.

Mitchell hands Will a piece of honeycomb on a paper plate and says what he always says. "You know this was one of the first foods they gave to Jesus when he rose from the tomb?"

And he gives him a little plastic spoon to dig into the drippy mess, just like he did with Eli the other day. "Here, have a taste," he says.

Same old routine. But Will hands the spoon to Honey when he's done, and she takes a little bite, too, looking at him the whole time like he's God's gift.

How can Mitchell not notice that? They're using the same damn spoon!

The cousin doesn't take off the headphones but looks at Eli. Smiles. Probably he likes seeing Honey too. Who doesn't?

College boy's got his own lecture to give now, though. Starts talking ancient this and ancient that, and Honey listens, hangs on his every word.

"Aristotle said honey was like dew, distilled from the stars and the rainbow," he says, looking right at her.

This is just too much. Is that how he got her scratching his itch? Stars and rainbows?

"Well, the ancients also thought bees came from the belly of a dead ox," Mitchell adds to his sermon.

Like—take that, motherfucker.

But Will just keeps going, like it really matters, like he cares about this stuff. Greek gods ate honey, Norse gods ate honey, blah blah blah.

"Yes, it's always been considered a delicacy," Mitchell says. "As it should be!"

But probably he doesn't like hearing about other gods. Only one God for that dude. Probably doesn't like the kid being all smart like that either.

But they go on, the three of them just standing there, puffed-up and yammering while Eli works, eavesdropping as best he can with the rattle of the machines.

Then Will says how bees are better than people actually. They build better societies. They'll probably still be here after we wreck the planet.

Good one, Will! That's a way to charm the ladies.

"If we don't kill them all off first somehow. With colony collapse," he says.

And yet he's the one who's got Honey licking the comb for him, a nice house up on the ridge.

Why are these supposedly smart people always talking about end-times when they've got everything they need in the here and now?

Mitchell's comeback is pretty lame too. Something about it all being up to the will of God, which is what these people always say.

And now he finally sees Eli, working there this whole time.

"You know this young man here?" he says. "Eli LeBeau. Just started on the job this week."

They nod at each other, keeping it cool. Yeah, I know this jerk, Eli wants to say. Though he doesn't know me.

At least they don't expect him to shake hands, what with the gloves and everything.

Eli grabs another tray, lays it down on the conveyer and in it goes, *clunkety-clunk*.

And off they go, back downstairs. Honey following behind with just a glance in Eli's direction. A tiny little nod.

He knows she knows him better than that. She was best friends with his sister, and they played all that hide-and-seek as kids! And yet that's all he gets, not even a word.

Maybe she's seen him spying. If she has, she likes it, 'cause she's never said anything to make him stop.

But what was that nod, the eyebrow raise? That was nothing.

"I hate that kid," Eli says to the cousin, though of course the cousin doesn't hear. Nobody hears Eli. He's just got to be louder maybe.

"I fucking hate that kid!" he shouts.

Cousin takes off the headphones. "What?"

"Nothing. What are you listening to in there?"

"VeggieTales, *Where Art Thou?*" he says.

For fuck's sake. What is he, like six years old?

Why did they have to stick Eli up here in the barn with the four-footers, when all the good stuff is happening somewhere else?

*

The pack is full and heavy, but Nell has grown stronger this summer.

She's sweating from the walk along Route 11, the walk through town, but the air is always cooler by the river.

She stops to rest just far enough past the bridge that nobody will see her.

Not that anyone cares. It's just she can feel their eyes on her as she walks through town, judging.

She feels eyes in the woods sometimes, too, though, even when there's nobody around. Or is there?

She came down a day early because she feels darkness coming. Dreams she's grateful to wake from but that linger on, even in the bright sun.

She knows it's coming when the shimmers appear. Rifts in the air, like a mirage.

She sets the pack down on a rock. She's just a bit bleary, is the thing. From the heat maybe, and the headache coming on.

Summer without the car was fine, but winter's on the way, the days getting shorter already.

In summer she could count on some greens from the garden. Plenty of peas, though not much for tomatoes.

Until Leonard showed up with a whole box of them. You've got time, maybe you can do something with these, he said. Otherwise they'll just go to waste.

He shows up sometimes like that, her place in the woods like a stop along his way. But on his way to what?

She should have canned those tomatoes, should have learned how by now, but instead she made a sauce and put it in the freezer, which is on the fritz.

Yes, the fridge will go next.

She still hasn't even fixed the roof. The tools are still there on the porch where she left them. He didn't say anything, but she knows he saw them.

Why doesn't she get up there and fix it? It's as if she's willing it all to come crashing down.

She probably needs to go back to work. Then she could get a new roof, a little more food for the winter.

Or you could just get some chickens, Leonard said. In the spring you keep the chicks here in your living room till it's warm enough to put them out in a coop.

And when they stop laying after a couple years, let them free range a bit. Make a nice lunch for a fisher cat. Or a fox.

No, she's not ready for chickens. Not in the house and not out with the foxes either. Though it would be nice not to have to carry the eggs all this way.

Maybe she just needs a little more income. One part-time job.

But then she'd need a car, which means working twice as much so she can pay to keep it going.

And she has not missed that feeling every time you turn the ignition. The fumes, the smoke, going up into the air, coating the leaves of the trees.

It's just wrong to burn in five minutes what took forever to make underground, is what she'd say if anyone would ask. Just so that you can drive into town and earn a little money to buy some eggs.

And it is wrong to take those medications that stay forever in the water. Medications that make it possible to go to work every day.

But maybe it is just wrong to live, to be human, taking more than your share.

She doesn't have to live at all, really. She could just walk into this river. Finally see what it's like. It would take her quickly, her body crashing over the rocks.

She might have to walk farther upstream, where the rocks are rougher, the pitch steeper, but she could do it easily enough.

She looks at the river. The rocks. Inviting her in. Laughing at her a bit. Why not? The ultimate "doing without."

But something keeps her rooted here. Fear maybe. And Christine would be upset, though of course she'd recover and could finally stop worrying.

Nell can see it, the current pulling her under, tossing her downstream, but she won't do it. Not today.

She feels the cool of the sweat drying on her face, the warm sun on her back, and she stays where she is just a little while longer.

*

Leila is counting down. Five more weddings till they get a break, but first they have to get through fall—the busiest time of all.

Megan's back in Boston, Sophie starts up in a week, and still she hasn't really talked to Steve about the drinking. Or about Jenny Rose.

That time she came into the kitchen and the two of them were standing so close. They seemed startled to see her.

Maybe she's imagining things about them. If she is, let him tell her so.

She just has to find the courage to say it. Maybe after this weekend she will talk to him.

This weekend should be easy enough. Just fifty-seven guests and an older bride who, as she says, doesn't need a tiara. Let's keep it simple.

Steve, it has to stop, Leila will say. It's every day now, and starts earlier too. Can't you at least wait till the weekend's over, or till the kitchen closes for the night?

She's said it already. In so many ways. For your health, Steve. For me. For the girls, what kind of example is this setting for the girls?

Meanwhile they just fight about other things. The other night it was a comment about Amber's friendship with Sophie that set it off.

You're just a snob, he said. You say that *she* is, too busy hanging out with the popular kids, but really it's you.

Because Leila had said what careless thing this time? Something about being glad Amber'd been too busy to hang out with Sophie all summer. That she'd rather Sophie hang out with someone better.

Someone *better*? That's what Steve fixated on. What do you mean, better?

All she meant, but didn't say, was that she didn't trust Amber's mother. Her whole family, for that matter.

Eli walking around town in his hoodie, doesn't even say hello when you see him anymore. Doesn't even look up. Didn't she used to feed that kid cookies?

The other brother, Cyrus, still living up there with their father on Tower Road. Graduated from high school a few years ago now, and doing what? You never hear Jenny Rose bragging about him.

Amber has the lead in the play, Amber's in the honor society, Amber's practically manager at the creemee stand, and only sixteen!

Amber's a great kid, Steve said. I like her gumption. And she's been a good friend. Just because she doesn't come from money and culture, just because her name is LeBeau.

Leila had just handed that one to him, handed him the righteous card. It's not what she meant. Amber is fine. She likes Amber well enough.

It's Steve she's worried about, it's Jenny Rose, and of course, by extension, herself.

She doesn't say anything, but she sees every day how he gently touches her on the back when he wants her to move out the way. How he laughs at her jokes, *their* jokes.

Leila's the one who takes his gin glass, rinses it out, and says "enough" every night. So Jenny Rose gets the charm. The old Steve.

The look he gives her, too, when Leila takes the glass off the arm of the easy chair. It's not a look of love, that's for sure. He might grab her arm and pull her down onto his lap, touch her breasts, but it's not for love.

He's barely even there. She doesn't see him in that face.

But it is him. This is him too. His inner jerk, his inner asshole. We all have one inside us—the selfish, the mean, the crude. He needs to rise above.

To Jenny Rose it's all a good time, finding the rocks glass on the shelf at the hostess station. Calling his name, laughing, Oh, Steve, did you forget something?

When the break comes she'll tell him: You have to stop. Now. Or else. Or else what?

It's not like she could leave. Or kick him out either. This place wouldn't exist without the two of them. There'd be no Birches Inn without Steve and Leila both.

Though Jenny Rose might like to think so. She might like to take my place. She might think she can just push me out and pick up where I left off.

It doesn't help that summer is ending. Leila hasn't seen the sun for days, but it feels like weeks.

And she doesn't have a Jenny Rose to flirt with. She doesn't want one. She wants just to be alone. No customers calling night and day, no brides, even the ones without the tiara.

A little apartment with a view of the river. One room for her, and one for the girls. She doesn't care how small, how simple. She could just sit and stare at the river. Get a job somewhere to pay the rent.

Yes, that's what she wants. A little place of her own. Some peace.

Love is not always patient and kind. Sometimes it devours you. Sometimes it's mean and selfish. But that's love, too, isn't it?

Through sickness and health. For richer or poorer. They don't say for soberer or drunker, but they mean that too.

Just five more to go this year. Five more cakes, five more catering contracts, five more floral deliveries.

And tonight is just a nice party for fifty-seven. We don't need all the frills, the bride said. Just a handicap-accessible room for my father and a peanut-free cake for my niece.

Oh, and if you could make sure my mother doesn't drink too much, she said.

She laughed a little then, but Leila heard only resignation.

*

The thick calluses on Sophie's fingertips are not what she wanted from the summer, but she'll take them. She's proud of them.

She picks at them now, though, as she walks up to the trailhead where they meet every Sunday.

Except this is the last Sunday before he leaves, the last before school starts, and Honey has refused to come.

Tell him I'm sorry, she said. Or I don't feel well. Tell him I have to work.

Which means now Sophie will see Will alone. It would have meant so much to her back in June, but Sophie doesn't care about him anymore, doesn't even think of him.

She has blocked him out entirely, except on these Sundays.

If anything, she might be feeling a little nostalgic about it now, knowing this is the last time and summer is ending.

Dorothy, your friend is here! Her mother calling from the upstairs window, and Dorothy, so-called, running out to meet her.

Then they'd link arms and sing all the way down Honey's driveway to the road, in step.

We're off to see the wizard, the wonderful Willoughby of Oz. *Because of the wonderful things he does!* Sophie would sing. What a joke it had all become.

Yes, it was all just a joke to her. A song and dance with a friend she's not even sure is a friend anymore.

And when they'd get there, to the trailhead where the path opens up into the woods, Will would say hello, and Honey would say goodbye, and off Sophie would go to her own business.

Alone with her knapsack, her notebook, and whatever new music she loaded onto her iPod.

She's listened to a whole year's worth of music this summer and played a lot of it too. Her teacher says she has a good ear, and good taste.

But it's simpler than that. Sophie likes what she likes. Who cares if nobody else listens to the music she knows best, if it isn't even from this century?

Nobody cares, is the thing.

It's not what she wanted but it was what she got.

Today will be different, without Honey here. It's nothing to be anxious about but she's anxious.

All she has to do is say hello, tell him Honey is sick, and head back home.

And being home will be fine, because she can finally play and sing at the same time, the song that she's been chasing for weeks now, every day, every hour when she's not working at the restaurant.

Honey may have got Will, but Sophie got "Pink Moon."

Eli can have his rappers. Other people can have their autotune. She knows enough to know it's not for her.

They can have it, because Sophie's got Nick Drake, who is hers alone.

She should have brought her iPod, should've brought her earbuds. If she'd known she'd be walking alone she would have.

And when she got there she'd take one earbud out and without a word put it into Will's ear and say to him, shhhhh, just listen.

Then he'd finally know something about her too. Know what he was missing, all those days with Honey and leaving Sophie behind.

But she doesn't have her iPod. She only has the music in her head and she's breathless walking alone, even though she's in fine shape and the slight upward climb is nothing to her.

Willie o Winsbury. Sweet William. Her songs of love are not for him, at least not anymore.

As she gets closer she can see him through the trees, hands in the pockets of a rain jacket. His blondish hair sticking up the way it always does.

She sees him before he sees her.

Now it's not just her heart and her breath losing ground, but her mouth is dry, she has to lick her teeth to keep them from sticking to her lips.

It's her own mouth, her own heart, her own body—why won't it do what she wants?

She waves when he looks up, and he waves back, and there's a look of surprise on his face. Not the smile she's used to.

As if to say, Why just you, where's my Honey, my beloved, my very own delight?

Would he even use a word like "delight"? Sophie will never know.

"Honey's sorry," she says, before she even catches her breath, before there can be any silence between them. "She doesn't feel good. She said she has to work."

"On a Sunday?" he says.

"I don't know. It's a big harvest, I guess. They have a lot of honey."

"Did she say anything else?"

"She said she was sorry."

He just looks at her, but that's all she has to say. It's all she can think of, with him standing there, looking at her finally.

"Well, I better be going," she says. And it's Sophie who turns away first. Sophie who leaves him standing there alone.

And as she makes her way downward, her heart racing even faster now, her mouth dry as if she's guilty of some crime, she can't find the tune in her head.

"Pink Moon" has left her. *It's a pink, pink, pink* . . . no, that's not right. She can't sing like Nick Drake.

She hurries now, nearly tripping her way down the trail, while he stands there, watching her retreat. Or did he turn to go too?

If only she'd had her iPod she would've said to Will, listen to this.

And given him an earbud, and he would've heard it too and not felt so disappointed, left standing there without his girl.

Maybe he's still there. There might still be time to redo the whole thing.

But of course he's gone. Or maybe she just can't see him now through the trees. She's too far down, and he's too far up.

She'll stand still for another moment, in case there's some trick of the light, some movement of the trees that will change things.

Does she see his rain jacket, his backpack, a bit of blue?

No. It's just the rocks and trees and the sky so gray.

*

Will can't stand it in the house, can't stand his mother, who keeps nagging him to talk to her. What's the matter, is something wrong?

He even slammed the door on his way out. Let her worry. Soon enough I'll be gone.

He could just go all the way down from here on this trail. Three miles, that's not so much, that's not so bad, even in the dark.

Why has he never come down in the night, come down the trail to see her? Why have they been so ready to play by the rules?

Not anymore. He can't wait any longer. He'll just see for himself. If they're really so busy working they'll be up late, they'll be in the barn.

Lights will be on in the barn, and he'll see for himself how hard they're working.

One foot then the other, over rocks, over roots, slippery from the day's rain.

That's all there is—the roots, the rocks, the light bouncing over them from his flashlight.

Sweating now where the trail flattens out, he can see the light of houses through the trees, can see Honey's house.

There's a kind of trail here, less traveled than the other path through the woods to her land.

As if someone else has already walked this way tonight. As if someone walks this way often.

He passes the goats in their shed sleeping. He hears them snore. Passes the chickens in their coop, no sound at all.

He can see the house now, just a single light on, downstairs.

Lights in the barn too. It's Mr. Mitchell alone, working the machinery, working into the night but she's not there.

He'll go to the house then. She must be in the house. He's come this far now, he just has to go up to the door.

His heart thumping and the dogs barking now, racing up to meet him. On goes the porch light.

He's only been on this property twice before, and just in the field, in the barn. He's never been this close to her house.

Mrs. Mitchell opens the door as if she's been standing there, waiting for him.

They've never met but he knows all about her. Knows her ways. My dragon lady mother, Honey calls her.

"Can I help you?" she says.

And he has to say something. Has to speak.

"I'm Willoughby Calper. My dad is the journalist?" He reaches out a hand.

She doesn't reach back. "I know who you are."

But she can't know him. Unless Honey told her about him, about them, but she wouldn't tell, would she?

"Is Honey at home?"

"Yes, she's home, of course. But she's sleeping. It's late."

"I'm sorry. Could you tell her I stopped by?"

"You're wasting your time. You boys who come sniffing around. You're wasting your time with her. She has work to do. She doesn't have time for boyfriends."

She doesn't have time for boyfriends. As if there are many. Sniffing around.

But Honey loves only him—there's barely time even for him!

It doesn't make sense. None of it. Why she didn't come out today, their last Sunday, and why her mother knows him.

Why he's here now and Honey is home, upstairs hiding.

Mrs. Mitchell says good night and turns back into the house. He can hear her turn the deadbolt, against him. She turns out the light.

He can see a light on upstairs now, but he doesn't know which room is hers. He knows so little, really, about her.

He heads back now, to the pathway, worn down in the woods. Sniffing around.

Maybe she doesn't love me.

The words come suddenly and ring like the truth. Of course, he should have known.

This sneaking around, the meetings at the trailhead, only at a given time, only when she said so. Maybe it's not her parents at all. Maybe it's her.

Too beautiful for him to have all to himself. She belongs to this place, to these people, not to him.

He knew something was wrong when he came that day to take notes.

She seemed surprised to see him, but not in a good way.

Maybe he crossed some kind of line. He thought she'd be happy to see him, and he wanted to get Mom to stop asking about the damn bee article.

Will really doesn't know anything about these people. Religious, country people, with dogs and goats and chickens.

If she really loved him, she'd have found a way out. She would have known he had come.

He catches his breath in the woods, back in darkness. A stick snaps nearby. What was that?

Is someone else here too? He holds his breath. Someone is here. Sniffing around, you boys who come sniffing around.

Probably just an animal. A raccoon or something.

He shouldn't be terrified of a raccoon or a possum, but he is now.

Terrified. Turned away and rejected. He'd do anything not to be here on this trail. To never have come to Vermont. To be in the city with the lights and the noise. People out in the light not hiding.

This place is too strange. The baptism in the river, the sneaking around in the woods. He does not recognize himself.

He turns on his flashlight now and shines it around. Sees something, someone, ducking down in the ferns. "Hey," he calls.

His light flashes over the ground, over the black trees, and there's someone there, or maybe not—oh, yes there is.

"Who the fuck are you!" The voice yells, it shrieks, not a man, not a woman either. "She's mine, you get the fuck away from here, you fucking fuckhead!"

It's a guy, a small guy, but it doesn't matter, large or small, if you have a gun. If you have a knife.

And it doesn't matter because Will's running now, running as fast as he can away from here.

Racing up the path, stumbling, tripping, as he goes, out of breath. Falling on his knees, falling over a root, a rock.

He cuts out of the woods toward a clearing where there's a road, some light.

He runs without turning, up the mountain road till his legs and lungs are burning.

Someone was there. A boy like him. Another man.

7

The colors seem to be arranging themselves, unfolding with each turn on the trail, just for her.

Sarah stops on the logging road up to Mount Jerryfield, her eye caught by the greens so bright and clean, the gold coming in on the trees.

A yellow monarch has been following her along the open trail. It's here now, hovering above her shoulder.

This will be her new project. To attempt to weave something out of this place—the dark gray rocks piled into a wall, backdrop to dark mossy green, a fringe of pale lavender.

Now that Will's finally at college, she can get focused. She's spent the summer getting her rhythm back with the loom, and now she has to make something of substance.

It's why she's here, it's what she's been waiting for—the practice of weaving like the practice of meditation, only in the end you have something to show for it, to give away or to sell.

It will take longer than a few days to break the habit of always thinking about Will, though—that constant awareness of when he'll be back, whether has he eaten.

What train, what streets, what playground—all of that was only replaced by trails, roads, and swimming holes when they got here. If anything it made her more vigilant.

Now it's time to focus back on herself, and on Jim. She'd given up on this over the years, worrying about how long he'd be gone, or whether he missed her as much as she missed him.

Will filled the void while Jim got deeper into his research, and now Sarah has to find meaning in her own work too. It has to be more than just re-learning the loom.

She doesn't even know what it would be like if Jim were to come back to her the way he used to be. Attentive, amorous, attuned to her every thought.

He couldn't understand why she was so distant from him when Will was young, so dull when he got home from his trips.

Is there somebody else? he'd always ask. But no, there never was. It was just that she was exhausted. No time for herself, much less each other.

He doesn't worry about that anymore, though, and never should have. She's always been faithful to their best selves.

At least Will let them drive him up to Strattenburg last week. He was insisting he'd take a bus, go it alone, a gesture toward independence. Egalitarianism maybe.

Until he discovered it would take three buses and twelve hours to do what would take four hours in the car.

I knew he'd come around, Jim said. You just have to let him make his own decisions, which won't always be the ones we'd make for him.

His choice of Strattenburg, that soulless public university, that was his own decision, and one she still hasn't made peace with.

He'd listened to them all too well over the years, it turned out. Their anti-elitism, their sworn allegiance to public education, which for high school in Manhattan had been no sacrifice at all.

It's possible to get a good education anywhere, Jim said, once the decision was made, though he too would have been happier to see Will at his own alma mater.

Will's roommate didn't help matters. A cloddish kid from New Hampshire who'd tacked his Bobcat paraphernalia all over their tiny cinderblock room before Will even arrived.

She can't help but see it as an opportunity already lost.

Sarah stops where the logging trail ends, giving way to a steep switchback through a thick stand of pine.

The three of them hiked here together just before Will left, though it wasn't the family outing she was hoping for. Will barely spoke, and Jim couldn't coax him out of it.

It was a disappointing end to the summer, in which he had blossomed so beautifully, so completely, so she thought.

She'll always remember that time he came in from an evening walk in the woods, flushed and exuberant. Mom, I saw a fox. Right up close! It looked at me!

This triumph that felt so short-lived.

It may have been coincidental, but as soon as they got the internet going his mood deteriorated quickly.

They were doing just fine without it. Sarah didn't mind just checking email once a week in town, and Will seemed more relaxed, happier than he'd ever been.

He was probably just worried about going to college when the summer started winding down. Of course that's all it was.

Sarah will build her own life again now. Fill it up through a series of real choices, knowing Will will make his own, too, just as Jim has all along.

When she gets back from her hike she'll drive up to the fiber shop in Kingsbury. She'll see if they have any workshops, maybe sign up to do some teaching like she used to at the craft guild.

And she'll make something significant of her own. A new kind of weaving, picking up where she left off eighteen years ago but with the accumulated wisdom, desire, vision—

Another turn and suddenly she's reached the summit. A great flat rock opens onto a view of the valley, which gives way to more peaks, more valleys. The treetops both ragged and jewel-like with the sun shining through green and gold.

And this is it. It is enough. The present, vibrating and electrified.

She just has to absorb this, hold it still for a moment, so she can attempt to capture it in silk and wool later.

If she can get her hands and feet and eyes working together in a rhythm, the threads sliding together according to plan, she may finally be able to transform that beauty into something she can hold on to.

*

It's nearly dark though it's only 5:00 p.m. and the rain keeps lashing the windshield of the truck. Lashing everything.

All day they've been driving from one beeyard to the next. Laying stone and brick on the hives, giving them ballast, tying them down.

Normally David waits till the harvest is done to bother with all this, but now and then a storm comes. Now and then it's worth the trouble.

It's good he has the whole team today. Aidan, Luke, and Josh. Even Eli showed up this morning, said he was ready to work. And Honey of course.

They stood there in the drizzle while David gave the orders. Divide and conquer, men, he said to them. And woman.

He has to remember that Honey's not one of the guys anymore. Ruth says she sees her flirting, rearranging her hair around her face, whenever Aidan comes around.

Told him that she found a book under Honey's pillow. *The Lord of the Rings*, with the name Willoughby Calper written inside of it.

Something's not right, Ruth said. She wants David to keep a closer eye. She hopes it's not too late.

Too late for what? David looks at Honey now, all soaked through, even in a jacket and boots.

She's always been a beauty, he knows that, but she's as strong as any boy and she has worked hard today.

He doesn't see the harm if she flirts a little. She's sixteen years old.

And she's a good kid, racing out into the rain, hardly needing to be told what to do.

With weather like this you can just forget about everything but the matter at hand. Past and future don't matter, it's just you and the hives and the need to secure them as quickly as possible.

David takes Route 11 as fast as he can, the wipers on full speed, as they head to Misty Hill Orchard, where the hives are most exposed to the elements.

He turns the heat on full blast, but it fogs up the windows. He changes it to AC and Honey wipes it with her hand, smearing it worse than before.

It feels like God is sending a Great Flood on them again, but he knows it's just another storm.

Nothing like they see in Haiti every year. Storms they never even hear of up here, storms that have no names, blow whole villages to bits.

The bees hate it. Trapped in their hives all day when there's not much time left in the season.

It used to be once every couple years, but now it's nearly every summer he has to call all the farmers with hives on their land, ask them to take the bricks and stones he's left nearby, lay them on top.

Those who can't or won't help will get covered by his team. The hives too far out are left to chance. Or to God's will. Though it's hard to believe God would micromanage to that degree.

"How many more, Dad?" Honey shouts. The rain's so loud they can barely hear each other speak.

"Just a dozen at the orchard here, but then we've got a long drive up to the field out by the airport. The guys have got the rest."

She pulls the jacket closer, and he wishes he could turn the heat all the way up without blinding them. She's shivering now and there's nothing to be done.

"Mom will have the woodstove going when get back. We can dry our things."

She nods and wipes her face with the back of her hand.

God's just keeping it real, as Aidan always says when some challenge comes up. He's come such a long way.

He'd never do Honey any harm, would he? And is it really so bad for her to be borrowing books from a boy on his way to college?

The others should be done by now. He asked them to check in at the barn, when they finished, report any problems in the log.

If he's planned it right he'll be the last to turn in. He and Honey. He and Dorothy. A good kid by any name.

*

Jim watches the swirling patterns of color on the screen. It's the prime of hurricane season, and this one's tracking up the east coast, Hurricane Isis, they're calling it.

Sarah's in the other room, laying out her colors. Content, finally, and oblivious to the storms outside.

Jim doesn't mind being stuck at home for once, and he can admit it, he's glad he doesn't need to go to the town library for internet anymore.

Of course you won't go back there, Sarah said. Even the chairs in there have bad breath!

Sarah was right, but to Jim it seemed virtuous somehow, to sit in the library sharing the internet with the old folks and their notepads. The young folks hiding under their caps.

He thought he might be able to change his habits for good, waiting to get the internet up here.

But no, he can't help it now, it's so much nicer at home. And he has a job to do. He can't do his job without information.

He can't track the hurricanes the way he likes to either when he doesn't have Wi-Fi at home.

A Friday night, and he and Will would sit there in their little kitchen in New York watching the storms. Eating popcorn.

Maybe Will's in his dorm room now doing the same, watching Isis swirl up the east coast, getting closer, with tropical storm Jasper right behind.

This storm has already strayed from the usual course of things. From the usual trek through Haiti and the DR, tearing everything to shreds.

Normally it might track up to Florida, maybe crash into Kitty Hawk, but this one's still going strong.

No, Isis has something else in mind. He's tempted to show it to Sarah. She'd want to know how it's already knocked out power in New Jersey.

You could feel the wind up here in the mountains yesterday. A kind of balmy wind after a week of autumn cool and drizzle.

It's what brought that spectacular sunset last night. So warm and wild, out there on the deck, the trees flipping their leaves upside down. Sarah's face glowing in that light.

If only that happened more often. Sarah straddling him on the deck chair, her heavy thighs on his.

Maybe having Will gone at college won't be so bad.

Those last couple days were hard. Will's moody outbursts, and his sudden indifference to anything outside his room, all of which she blamed on the internet.

Now that he's gone Sarah's finally able to focus on something. She's taken to that weaving project now in a way she hasn't done anything for years.

It's her way of meditating, she says. And she wants Jim to find that kind of focus of too. As if mindfulness might somehow save them.

But he doesn't have time for that anymore. He can't sit still when so much is happening, so fast, one human-made crisis after another.

Even hurricane season isn't just a predictable series of disasters anymore.

You follow hurricanes on the storm tracker like other people follow sports on TV, Sarah says, and it's probably true.

He watches the screen for the play-by-play. He follows the stats.

This one's a class four now. Wind speeds at 150 miles per hour. The largest hurricane to hit as far north as Jersey since 1972.

If they were still in New York, they'd be on the other side of it by now. They'd be worried about all those beaches washed up with debris and torn-up jetties. There'd be trash in the streets.

The rain's been falling fast now since this morning. The trees out the windows are bending and whipping their branches.

The rivers are all so narrow—what will happen to all that water?

They're calling for rain through the night and into the morning. Could be ten inches in twenty-four hours.

The colorful swirls of the storm tracker bounce up the coast then start over. Green and yellow spirals move inland and westward, the red center now heading this way.

Would the red ever land in these woods? It's never happened before, but things are different now. Regular weather patterns don't hold.

In some places this is just what happens, these hurricanes. He's seen the pictures often enough. Palm trees bending to the ground, cars up to their roofs in floodwater.

People somehow get used to that. They put up with it, year after year.

But not here. Here it's just snow and cold. Enormous plows and Quonset huts full of road salt.

The river, when he passed it in town an hour or so ago, was already high and muddy. He asked Jeanne at the post office, What do you think? Have you ever seen anything like it?

Sure, she said. We get gully washers like this at least once a year. But we don't get hurricanes. Or tornadoes or earthquakes either. One of the good things about living here.

But the water looked awfully close to the bridge when he drove back this afternoon.

Even just in the past hour he can hear how the rain has picked up. Sheets of rain slap against the windows.

And Sarah just sits there under the lamp as if nothing's happening.

Maybe he'll take her to Tuvalu next time he goes. Take her up to Alaska. Before, she didn't want to leave Will so far behind. It would take too long to get home in an emergency, she'd say.

If she comes along it'll be easier for her to understand why it matters so much to him, and why it should matter to everyone else too.

The storm tracker's been repeating the same pattern, over and back and over and back up the coast. So gradual he didn't notice exactly when the red swirl bit into Massachusetts.

"The red's in Massachusetts now!" he calls out loud. "Look," he says. He brings the laptop over for Sarah to see.

Of course he doesn't want the storm to come and pull the trees from their roots, wreak havoc on the mountainside or down in the valley.

But he can't help feeling a bit excited about the possibility.

*

Eli's first week on the job was boring enough, but yesterday, what was that? Driving around in the rain with Aidan Taft?

Now that her college boy's gone, Mitchell probably wants to marry Honey off to Aidan. Kiss-assy know-it-all's what he is.

Rain just ran right off him while Eli soaked it up like a sponge. Soaked his sneakers and sweatshirt. How was he supposed to know it was gonna rain all day?

Aidan in a slicker with a hood and Eli didn't even have a hat. Did anyone offer him a hat? Nobody gave him anything. No gloves. Nothing.

Honey didn't even say "hey," didn't so much as look at him. Just got in the other truck and waited, while Mitchell bossed them around. And make it fast, the rain's coming hard.

Mile after mile all around the county, one field after another, hives and hives. He never wants to see another one of those things again.

Go over there. Do that one. I'll do these. Hurry up now. Lording it over him like he's the big boss.

Wouldn't even turn on the heat. Probably liked seeing Eli sitting there all wet and cold. Probably wanted to see him suffer.

His teeth chattering and his hands numb. Christ on a cracker.

All he wanted was a nice hot shower, but no. He can't even have that.

Just forgot to pay the propane, Dad says like it's some kind of joke. I'll pay up next week. Ha ha ha.

Eli should've moved back in with Mom by now. It would be worth the harassment to have a little heat.

He just wanted to get away from her and Amber and all the shit they give him, but he'll probably die of pneumonia up here. He hasn't been so cold since hunting with Uncle Rudy.

Should've learned from that never to wear sneakers in the woods. But what was he supposed to do? It's not like he has a pair of hikers. Not like he has anything better than gym socks.

Dad's out there, watching TV. Cyrus coming and going, not even checking to see if he's alive.

Probably he's crying over the Z8 again. His product turned to shit, turned to mouse droppings, and working back at Shaw's again.

The other guys are making five hundred bucks on a bad day now, selling product. Just don't use it, Jeff says. Or not too much.

Not me, though. I had to go out in the rain and freeze my ass off for nine bucks an hour. No chance with Honey when Aidan's around.

One hour of my time not even worth one jar of honey. Ten bucks a pop with a ribbon on top. Fuck that.

He should've just hit up the place in the woods. Pried a lock, taken the money and run.

He would just stay here under the covers forever if he wasn't so hungry, but you always have to get hungry. Always you have to get up.

Dad's probably got some cans of soup at least. Some bread.

He'll put on some clothes and go out there for something to eat. But once he's out of here it'll just be more of the same.

Unless he can get a car, get his cousins to help him out. Get into it together like family should.

Like lords of the land and I don't mean the beehives.

*

There's nothing but pain. Pain is all Nell has now, and all she wants is for it to end.

One leg's going numb now, twisted beneath her, while the other one throbs. Maybe if she holds still enough it will stop altogether.

But then the pain radiates through her again, from so many directions at once, like a flash of red and black, like screaming.

She must have shouted when she fell. She must have cried out when the ladder slipped away, with nobody to hear.

Nobody but the birds, who are still singing, and the sky, which is still blue, the day after rain. You'd never know that just last night the world was ending.

All night long, the pounding and crashing on the roof, just feet above her bed where she did not sleep.

The rocks in the river were grinding and moaning, as if a flood was coming and by morning the whole world would be washed away.

But with the morning light everything was the same. A small puddle on the floor, and some trees down, but the world was still here.

And she had the idea that she'd fix the roof finally. It would be easy enough. She'd seal up the weak areas, keep the buckets from filling up again.

Now all she has is this. Pain that keeps her from getting up. Pain that stops and starts again, a throbbing.

The cold ground seeps in, deeper and deeper. As she makes her breath shallower and shallower it hurts less.

She'll be like a lizard in winter, breathing slow until the world is safer for its thin skin, so slow that the pain will stop, is already stopping.

It must have stopped like this for Laura too. Slowing, stopping, then finally painless. Nell could just let it take her, too, the end, here it is.

But no, she can't do it. She shakes herself awake, shakes off the numbness. She still wants this, all of it, what little she has. She doesn't ask for much.

If only she could be inside and warm. It's all she wants, to be warm again. If only she could be inside, if only someone.

She tries pulling herself by the arm that hurts less. It can take the pressure, but she's not strong enough.

She can bend one leg but when she tries the other her vision blurs. Seeing stars. Then shades of black.

She could drag herself but it's too far. She is so heavy and the ground is so wet. Then there's the pain again, shocking in its intensity, its insistence, this too is life, you want this too.

The phone inside is ringing now. Five times. Ten. Someone is calling. Someone is thinking of her.

Then silence again, just the sound of her breathing and the woods around her. The dripping with every breeze.

Oh please, someone come, just this once. Please, someone, just this once, and I'll never ask for anything again.

She never knew she could want anything this badly, all of it, the pain even. The blurred vision.

And there's the ringing again. Ringing and ringing because she has no machine, never paid for voicemail.

It rings in rhythm now with the sounds of the birds, the woods, the dripping from the roof. Or has it stopped?

The cardboard is split, the shingles scattered on the ground. The tile clipper on the ground, too, out of reach. Her hand that she can see but barely feel

And then the sound of tires on gravel. Oh, blessed sound!

Has he come, has Leonard come? If only he'd come when she was still up on the ladder. How impressed he would have been!

How impressed she was with herself, climbing up there finally. Saying yes to the job that would make it possible for her to stay. She should've known better, the morning after so much rain.

The sound of car doors. Voices.

But it's not Leonard. It's Christine and Edward. Christine's voice now, her warm hand on Nell's forehead. How did she know to come?

8

They'd only finished the first full week of school when Honey called her. I haven't seen you in forever. I have news. Bring Amber.

And now Amber just talks and talks while Sophie says nothing.

All the way down the road to Honey's house, blah blah blah.

"What do you think she wants? I don't know why she can't just tell us, like a normal person. Though since when is Honey a normal person, right?"

Sophie kicks a stone and Amber kicks it, too, taking turns till the stone lands in a puddle and they find another one.

"You don't think she's pregnant, do you?" Amber says.

"No," Sophie says. "Of course not."

Though it's exactly what she's been thinking since Honey called after school today, maybe since even before that.

Maybe she knew way back when Honey refused to come out that last Sunday with Will. Maybe she thought of it even then but forgot.

Why should she worry about Honey when Honey never worries about her?

Bring Amber, Honey whispered into the phone. I want to tell you together.

At the bottom of the driveway Daisy and Lucky come trotting out, and Honey, too, wearing a jacket, her hair tied up in a bun.

"So," Amber says, "what's the big idea?"

Honey links Sophie's arm, then Amber's. "I never get to see you anymore. You've been so busy!"

"I know, right?" Amber says, and gets talking again.

Junior year and the fall musical and weekends at the creemee stand till October. How they'll probably make her manager next year. How she finally got her license.

None of which matters, of course, if Honey is pregnant.

Tell him I'm sorry, she said that day. She didn't feel well. What else could it be? Why didn't Sophie even ask?

"That would be great," Honey says, "to be manager. Wouldn't that be great, Sophie? And Amber can drive!"

And they walk, like normal but faster, because the sun's going down. And because they're anxious to get there, to get the news.

Will Sophie be disappointed if she's wrong, if it's just that Honey is coming back to school, or that she's learning to drive too?

The river is still high and muddy since the storm. The sky is blue through the trees but not for long. Fall comes on so quickly once September begins.

"So here's the thing," Honey says, sitting down, taking one of each of their hands.

And she tells them everything, and it's true, she's pregnant, six weeks, she's certain of it. At first she thought it was bad news, she says, but now she sees it for what it is.

Wonderful, terrifying, good news. Not like it's the end of her life, which it is.

Which it has to be. Boys like Will finish college, go to grad school, move on. And girls like Honey, they just become teen pregnancies.

"I knew it!" Amber says. "Didn't I say so, Sophie? On the way over?"

"But I need your help," Honey says. "Both of you."

And they both start talking at once, trying to be helpful, they'll do anything for her, anything at all.

Because even if they don't see each other much anymore, they're still the best they've got. They're best friends in a crisis, which is what friends are supposed to be.

Amber could drive her to the clinic. There's a clinic in Kingsbury. Amber can borrow the car.

"Absolutely not," Honey says. "No clinic. God gave us this baby and we're going to love it, no matter what anyone says."

How can she think of God in a situation like this, as if God has anything to do with it? But that doesn't matter now. No, they just need to take care of her.

"My mom keeps looking at me funny. She stares at me and asks if something's going on with Aidan, but she has no idea."

Maybe Honey could stay in Megan's room for a while. Sophie's parents will understand, or at least they'll be nice to her.

"Yes, come stay with me when your parents find out."

But Honey will not tell them, not ever. They'll never understand, and they will kill her for not waiting till marriage.

They'll make her give the baby up for adoption. They'll hide her away somewhere till it comes.

No, she's not telling them, at least not until after she sees Will and he comes back to be with her.

If only she can see him, she says, everything will be fine, she's sure of that now.

"Let's go to Strattenburg then," Amber says.

"Oh, could we? Could you take me?" Honey says. "I knew you would help. Both of you."

Amber will borrow her mother's car. They'll tell her they're visiting Will, which will make her happy. A real college boy.

Sophie wants to go too but there's a wedding tomorrow and next weekend too. She'll ask her parents, though, she promises. They'll let her, won't they, for a friend in need?

But first there are more questions. How do you know for sure? How does it feel? Why don't you just call him?

"If I can tell him in person, it'll work out," Honey says. "We have to be together. He has to see my face to know that it will all be okay."

And for the rest of the afternoon Sophie almost believes her.

*

Eli can't wait anymore. It has to be today or someone else will get there first. Jeff, or one of the others.

They've been talking. It may be just talk but they think they can do anything now. They'll take everything and Eli will get nothing.

Eli will show them who can get the job done. And he'll show that kid too. Honey was Eli's girl, not his.

Eli will make him see that you can't just come in here, take the best of everything, and leave.

He'll grab the wallet, grab anything worth taking, then tear up whatever shit the kid has left behind.

Take the Xbox. Probably he's got the latest model everything. Eli wouldn't mind the latest for once.

Eli just has to get inside. Just focus now on getting past the gatekeeper. Once he's in that's the easy part.

Let me in, ma'am. I'm hurt.

Help, I just need a little help, he'll say. She'll feel sorry for him. She'll see a scrawny little redneck hick and she'll feel sorry.

Jeff can have the rest of the town, but Eli's getting this one. This one's his.

They'll be drinking out of his hand. How'd you do it, cuz? We didn't know you had it in you.

That's right. He's got this one, just you wait. Jewelry and what-else. Tear the shit up.

He's got to walk steady, the rifle over his shoulder, the orange cap cocked.

Ma'am, I was just out huntin' squirrel and got a gash here, fell on a rock. She'll see his leg.

The ketchup packets Dad's too cheap to throw out. Well, Eli's got some use for them now.

Eli's got a use for everything. Uncle Rudy's old rifle, shoved into the closet with the hockey stuff.

Crouching ninja-like now, he can see straight in. And she's there all right, working the yarn, like always, making whatever she's making.

Okay, Eli, be cool now. Be cool, Eli, 'cause finally here's your chance.

Check your wounds, check your nerves, get to the door.

He goes around and knocks on the kitchen door. Waits. Works up a face of pain. His heart pounding so fast he might have a stroke.

He bangs on the door. Solid. He tries the handle. Locked.

And there's her pointy little face. She pushes aside the curtain and there she is, finally, up close. Looks nothing like her kid, that proud little fucker.

"Help me, ma'am, I need some help." Can she hear through the door? Can she hear him?

She doesn't move. "My leg," he says, louder. "I hurt my leg." He lifts up his knee so she can see the mess and the rifle slips off his shoulder. He shoves it back up.

"Look," he says, "I hurt it real bad. I just need a bandage or something. Got to stop the bleeding."

And she stands there, like she's thinking about it before she's gonna open the door.

He puts his heart into it now. "Please, help me, ma'am. I just need a bandage. Stop the bleeding, I'm bleeding out here."

Then she motions something. Motions like a phone to her ear like she's going to call someone and lets the curtain fall. Disappears.

Where'd she go? She won't open up! She won't open the fucking door!

He tries the handle again. It's locked tight.

He has to get in, he just has to. It has to be now, today, it has to be now.

He climbs up on the deck and bangs on the big glass door with his fist.

Where is she? She's not coming around. She's hiding back there.

He hits it with the butt of the rifle. Hits it hard now, has to break it, has to get in before she calls the EMTs. Or the staties!

This glass must be bulletproof or something. It won't break. He hits it hard, harder, and then alarms start squealing like crazy.

It's like he's surrounded, like some helicopter or something might just drop out of the sky. Maybe she's got her own security SWAT team or whatever.

No, no, he just has to get out of here. Get away from the racket. He holds his ears and runs while the alarms squeal.

His lungs burn from running so fast, and soon the staties will be here. But he's off her property now. He didn't do anything!

He knocked on the glass, that's all. Nothing wrong with that. He knocked on the glass and ran. Nothing broken. Just a kid out hunting squirrel and rabbit.

So what. So fucking what. Only, he dropped the rifle. He dropped the damn rifle!

He has to go back for it. When the noise stops. He'll wait in the woods and hide.

But what if the staties have dogs, and they sniff around and find him? Yes, that's him! She'll point.

He needs to get out of here, get back to Dad's. But they'll find him at Dad's. They'll find Uncle Rudy's old gun.

No, Eli needs to go to Mom's. If they come knocking at Mom's he'll just say, Who, me? Not my rifle. Just me and Mom and Amber here.

Sirens still going. Lights flashing back in the trees. Or maybe it's in his head.

He just needs to go back to Mom's and calm down.

Calm down, start over, 'cause he can do this. Even if they find him, all Eli did was knock on the door. Knocked hard on the glass.

But they won't bother. They got meth labs and poachers and shit. They won't bother with a kid knocking on the glass, asking for help.

He'll figure it better next time. Let the alarms do their thing. He won't be scared of them next time.

*

Cyrus slices a box elder into two-foot logs, leaves them where they fall. It's a small chain saw but it does the job fast.

So many branches came down in that summer storm. A few trees too. Dry enough now to cut.

It feels good, clearing out the dead stuff, piling it into the truck, with the sun out finally.

He's got the younger guys helping, Eli and Jason and Cam. They pick it all up, one load after the other. Even Dad was here for a while, till he just walked away.

Something's wrong with Dad. He never used to let anyone else use the chain saw. Have at it, boys, he said.

He didn't even care that Eli dropped Uncle Rudy's gun up on the ridge. Tried to laugh it off when Rudy called, saying the staties traced it back to him.

What were you doing up there anyway, trying to stage a heist?

He acts like it's funny, but it's probably true. Eli's stupid enough he probably really was trying to rob them.

Lucky they just let it go at that. No harm, no foul, the cops said. Just leave those people alone, would you?

It'll be a good bonfire this year, though, with all this dry wood. Maybe Amber will bring some girls from school.

Jeff's always bugging her to bring her friends to their parties, though her friends really aren't the type Jeff has in mind.

They're the type that goes to college, gets out of town. The girls Amber hangs out with think they're too good for any of us LeBeau boys, and probably they are.

What Cyrus really wants is to ask the new girl Emily to come. She always talks to him in the break room like she might like him. She's stuck at Shaw's too for now, but she has a plan.

You could take classes, too, she said. At the community college. Business management, maybe communications. You have to start with tech literacy, though.

Nobody's ever suggested he could take classes. Maybe Emily sees what other people don't see. That Cyrus is smart. He's more than halfway decent. He could really do something with himself.

He'll ask Emily to come up for the fire, and she can tell him about it while they stand around keeping each other warm. A nip of whisky under the stars. That's what he needs.

Jason's in a good mood today, too, practically jogging between the truck and the heaps of branches Cyrus has been piling up so quickly.

Jason bought his own truck last weekend and brought Eli up here in it. Just three months working for Jeff and Jason's already got his own truck.

Cyrus can see Eli looking down on him, rubbing his nose in it. Like he's saying, look what Jason got and all you have is that shitty Toyota.

They're getting Z8 from New York now, Jason says, in shiny little packets that make it look like incense. The feds aren't onto it yet, he says.

It's nasty shit, though, no matter where it comes from. And costs way more to make than it sells for.

Cyrus sold his whole lot off to Jeff for eighty bucks, a good deal for both of them. He's washed his hands of the whole thing now and the money's back in his pocket.

Not that eighty bucks will be enough to pay for school, even part-time at the community college.

Cyrus cuts the branches off a fallen pine, slices the trunk into logs.

The bonfire used to be such a big thing for Uncle Rudy. Early November after youth deer-hunting weekend.

Cyrus hasn't hunted in years now. He should do it again. Could use a day in the woods, just tracking something. All day long till your face freezes, and your hands.

Rudy'd give them each a shot of something strong afterward, standing around the bonfire, stomping their feet and making up stories about the deer they got, or the ones that got away.

Neighbors would come, and Aunt Stacy brought out bowls of snacks for everyone. Caramel popcorn. She doesn't come anymore either.

It'll be a good party this year, though, if it doesn't rain. Someone will bring music, someone will get a keg.

He'll put his arm around Emily, there at the fire. Talk to her about all the things he wants to do with his life. Ask her about her own.

He doesn't even know where she lives yet, or how old she is. She could have a kid for all he knows.

But at least he's got something to look forward to. Emily in the break room. Maybe tech literacy this spring. Why didn't he think of this before?

Plus nothing beats a chain saw on a bright October day. Getting things ready for a party.

Someday he'll have his own land like this, not here next to Dad and Uncle Rudy, but with the same birch trees, and the same bright sky.

*

Christine's house is clean, pleasant, stifling. Nell's only been here a few weeks but it's an eternity. A purgatory.

The crutches she can handle but the cast is too much. She just has to breathe through it—the itching! It's nothing, just skin, just breathe, it'll pass.

And it does pass.

Soon she can take it off, they say, this bright blue monstrosity that probably cost as much as a new roof.

Winter's almost here and Nell needs to get ready, but all she can do is wake up, move from the bed to the window, see the big white sky crossed with wires. And not scratch.

She hobbles around, eats their food, even takes the pills that cost she can't think what. She has asked, but Christine is too kind to tell her. Don't worry, we'll sort it out, she says.

She says that now, but they both know Nell won't be able to pay her back. Not for the cast or the crutches. Not for the ambulance, all the way down into town.

She tries to read, offers to bake bread, can't knead, can barely even walk to the end of the block and back. But she does it, slowly and in pain.

Lonely is the problem. "I'm lonely," she says, to the bedroom and its clean yellow walls. She was never lonely at home.

Paige is away at college. Take her room for as long as you like, Christine said.

Nell had no other answer, and so here she is, with the jewelry box on the dresser, a closet full of shoes.

She doesn't belong in this house with its carpet, the heat humming in the walls. With its little sounds and the smells of last night's dinner.

The garage door bangs up and down as Christine and Edward come and go from work. This is their life and it's good for them.

What you need is a little place by the lake, they say. A condo, where people take care of things for you. Where you don't have to work so hard.

As if she's still that woman in her twenties, needing her family to protect her, wallowing in guilt and grief, while Christine's off starting a family of her own.

There are a lot of things Nell doesn't have—things Christine has, that Laura would probably have too if she were here. Successful things.

But she likes her chipped blue plates and her whitewashed paneling. She liked waking up there every single day this summer. And walking home from town with her heavy pack, even in the rain.

She can handle the headaches too. They always go away eventually, and then everything is clearer than it was before.

She just should not have let herself fall. It was a stupid mistake and one she won't make again. She can't let any ambulance come and take her away again either.

You're so lucky, the doctor said. That fall could have been much worse. You're lucky your sister came when she did!

Every time she sees him he puts on another pair of latex gloves, and she can only wonder where they go when he takes them off.

At least now it doesn't hurt so much to take a deep breath, not like before.

I couldn't bear to lose another sister, Christine said, and keeps saying, as if Nell would've died there on the ground if Christine hadn't saved her.

Which maybe she did. Maybe Nell would've died. She certainly deserved to.

Somehow I knew, I just knew, Christine said.

It was cold and she couldn't move, but Nell might have found the strength eventually, to pull herself back to the house.

Her urge to live is relentless, it turns out. Much stronger than she knew. What she would've given for just another slice of bread, another cup of tea.

Why, though? Why does she do it? And now, again, with the hideous cast, there's this urge to go on, to get out of here.

All she wanted was to get off the ground, for the pain to stop. But she wanted it with every cell in her body.

Now she wants more, a little more each day.

And what about Leonard. Has he come by and wondered where she is? He would've seen the mess. The ladder on the ground.

Leonard doesn't have any of the things people like Christine have either. No career to speak of. No kids of his own. He was never first in the class, first at anything.

If only Leonard had come and found her on the ground instead of her sister.

But why should he have? She's never been anything more than a stop along the way, never offered much more than a cup of tea.

*

The smoke, so thick above the flames, is just a wisp once it reaches the sky and joins the clouds that move against the moon, bright then dark.

It's in Sophie's hair now, her sweatshirt, too, and she doesn't mind.

She hadn't expected it to be so easy. To be out like this, at a keg party, with strangers in the woods.

They found their way to the party though they didn't make it to Strattenburg.

Sophie knew it wouldn't work, the plan to take Honey up to see Will, to tell him before her parents found out.

Amber tried to get the car every weekend for the three weeks in a row, tried again today, but it was the same problem every time.

Her mom had an appointment. Her mom changed her mind. One thing after another until Honey gave up, or maybe her parents just caught on.

Sophie wouldn't have been able to go with them anyway. You're not driving up to a university, just a couple of girls. No way, her dad said.

A bonfire party in Upper Glenville was a small thing to ask compared to that. Dad probably knew there'd be drinking, but at least she'd be home by midnight.

Erin and Amber have wandered off, but the fire is Sophie's company now and it's just how she likes it. Nobody talking to her, nothing she has to do or say.

Parties like this once seemed so out of reach, something other, more daring people did, but now, who cares? She's not pregnant.

Sophie's parents were too busy being mad at each other to worry about what Sophie might be doing tonight anyway. Sure, a bonfire sounds nice, sweetie, Dad said.

She hates it when they fight. Mom rolls her eyes and Dad says, I know, I'm a terrible person, as if begging her to disagree.

My mom thinks your dad is so cute! The way they look at each other, they should just get a room and get it over with, Amber said. Then we'd be stepsisters!

But it's too sickening to think about. Sophie wants her parents to stay the way they are.

Let's go to the party, Amber said. Somebody might as well have some fun around here. You know Honey can't.

So Sophie's here, her carefully chosen outfit covered in a sweatshirt, her clean hair smelling like smoke.

She doesn't even know who else is around. Some of Amber's cousins and who knows who else. It doesn't matter.

All she needs to do is stand here and watch the flames, a silhouette among a handful of silhouettes. It's not like an indoor party, where everyone's watching everyone else.

Amber and Erin have gone out to the sugar shack with some guys. Someone said that was where the real party was happening.

Another peal of laughter breaks out of the woods now, maybe Erin, maybe Amber, and then there's applause in the distance.

They said they were going to try smoking Z8 tonight. It's totally legal, you should try it, too, Sophie!

But Sophie said no. No way. She has a hard enough time getting her voice to work right as it is.

And LeBeaus are bad news, everyone knows it. Amber used to be different but now she's trying to be just like the rest of them.

Sex all summer long at the creemee stand with some senior who's long gone now. Smoking whatever comes her way.

At least Amber wasn't stupid enough to get pregnant. And she somehow still managed to get the lead in the play!

Yes, Amber has things figured out, she'll be fine. It's just not the way Sophie wants to do it.

Sparks explode and the smoke spirals upward, then a breeze takes it off in another direction, white against the black sky.

Whenever Sophie comes outside after dark like this, looks up at the stars, and feels the cool air on her face, she wonders why she doesn't go outside and look at the sky every night.

Why does she stay inside when this is here—it's always out here?

She could just stand and watch the flames for hours, like people used to do, gathering by the fire and making up ballads, telling stories of love and death down by the river.

The fire crackles and a guy in a camo hat pokes at a log, sends more sparks flying. Stands back again. His face is lit up for a second but then it's back in the shadows.

Amber's brother Cyrus. He's the only one of the guys who's going anywhere, Amber always says. He's the smart one, you'll see.

But there he is, twenty years old and still hanging out at a bonfire with a bunch of high school kids, a bunch of stoners. Maybe some people just get stuck somehow.

Honey will be stuck here too. With a baby. She might think she got what she wanted, with Will, but Honey's never going to be able to go out on a night like this, she'll never be so free.

She won't be able to be alone, like Sophie, or go and do whatever fucked-up things Erin and Amber are doing in the woods.

They can have it, the "real party," the stories to tell in the cafeteria on Monday. Sophie doesn't need them.

If they get wasted, if they don't come back from the woods, Sophie will just have to go looking for them. Save them from themselves.

Or she'll just walk all the way home by herself.

She could do that. Yes, that's what she'll do if it comes to that.

Sophie doesn't need any of them. She hasn't even met the people who will matter in her real life.

She wants something completely different now, and she's only just starting to figure out what that is.

*

David will start by checking on the hives farthest north and make his way back on 33. He'll take a good look at every last one of them, like he hasn't done in years.

Anything to get away from Ruth and Honey right now. To get away from the house and the fact of it—of Honey's pregnancy.

His first thought was to kill the man, whoever he was. I swear to God, he said. An urge deep in his gut. I'll kill him.

Now he's on to second thoughts, more complicated thoughts, but he still has no idea what to do with them. Or with this rage, which has no place here but nowhere else to go.

I love him, I love him. He still hears Honey's voice yesterday afternoon. *But I love him!*

He doesn't know what to do with that either. It can't possibly be real, can it?

Teenagers don't know anything about love. He sure didn't. It was just animal instinct back then, following the ancient code to go forth and multiply!

They've known for less than twenty-four hours, and yet yesterday morning seems so long ago now. Since yesterday everything has changed.

He should turn off here, Old Farm Road, but he drives right past. It's not important and he doesn't want to. He wants to keep driving.

By now he should be getting ready for the missions, leaving this all behind. His hives did well in the storm, they're ready for winter, and he should be going.

But he won't join the trip to Haiti this year. His plans, and what he needs, are not what matter right now. God has bigger plans, apparently.

I suspected something, Ruth said, as if it was David's fault for not listening to her. I knew something was wrong. But pregnant? How can it be?

Ruth kept saying it, over and over. However did this happen, how can this be?

Until finally David said, I'm sure it wasn't the immaculate conception, if that's what you mean.

He shouldn't have said that to Ruth, but he was out of patience. And if he keeps talking, he'll just upset her more when they need to be a team.

David skips the next turn too. The hives at the solar array can wait. He'll just go straight to 33 and head north. Nobody will know the difference. He needs this time alone to figure things out.

The highway is empty enough this time of day. He can just go and go, get away, at least for now.

He could drive all the way to Canada, and still not know, but at least he'll get away from what he might say next.

Maybe it will take care of itself, Ruth said. It's early. In the young and the old, sometimes it just takes care of itself. It will all just have been a lesson of some kind.

A lesson for Honey, certainly, refusing to come out of her room today, and at first even refusing to tell them who the father is.

They were yelling at her, finally. Right to her poor childish face. Just tell us who it is!

A boy they hardly know. The kid from New York. How's that even possible?

The Calper boy? Ruth was nearly shrieking then. That kid's probably some kind of atheist for all we know, or maybe Jewish. We know nothing about these people!

And Honey shouted back. You're right. You don't know anything. But Will's been saved, she said. Baptized. He's one of us.

David doesn't believe it. The journalist's son off at college, a Christian, a Baptist? No, he doesn't think so.

Honey tried to run to him, the son, all the way up to Strattenburg. Waiting on the porch, agitated like bees with a wasp. They didn't know what she was waiting for.

Then Amber finally called the house, called it off. Honey just stood there with the phone in her hand. Blank-faced, till they begged her. What is it?

Figures it was Amber LeBeau, the same one who got her drunk this summer.

At least it wasn't one of the disciples who got her pregnant, wasn't

Amber's brother Eli, creeping around the way he did. Or Aidan, whom he trusts.

David watches the speedometer go up over 60, the old truck rattling as he goes, then up to 70, which feels even better.

Sounds like the paneling might shear off but let it. He'd rather deal with that than this.

Pregnant. It just can't be. Not Honey. She's always been so smart, so good.

Should he have known about Willoughby Calper? How could he? He was only here twice all summer, and always with his camera and notebook, helping his dad.

And Honey was always at home, except when she was out with Sophie those Sunday afternoons. Going swimming, going for a hike.

He takes it up to 75 and gets passed by a motorcycle on the left. The truck won't go any faster, though. It's old. Like him. Too old for running away.

But he has to understand. Has to figure out how in God's name . . .

It must have something to do with Sophie. Was she in on a lie? Taking Honey away from them and hiding her secrets? Ruth always said her family was too lax, too liberal.

All those weddings at the inn and not a priest or a minister in sight, she said.

He wanted to trust Sophie, she seemed like a nice kid, but now he knows. Sophie is to blame.

But no, he can't try to pass it off on her. It was Honey, his daughter, she's the one who knew better. She brought this on herself.

And David should have been paying better mind, not assuming all was fine like he so often does.

You see the way she plays with that hair, Ruth said. You see the way the men look at her.

Yet he refused to see. He only saw his sweet little girl growing up so strong, so like him in many ways. He was too proud.

He can't keep going like this, though. Wasting gas, wasting time. He has to go home and face them even if he has no idea now what to do.

In days, in weeks, they'll know better. It may take care of itself, Ruth said. Not all pregnancies come to term, especially in the very young.

Yes, that would be hard lesson, but that's what he wants.

David's not saying he knows better. The Lord has plans for you, sure, he knows that.

He's not wishing the baby's life away. He's just praying.

Please, God, we don't want to kill this baby. We just want it to come back later.

He puts on the signal before he even sees the exit. The clicking will remind him to get off and turn around.

You will suffer a little while over this, but it will make you strong, firm, and steadfast.

So says Peter, and so he has to believe it.

*

"Why couldn't they just tell us what they want? It's outrageous, keeping people guessing like this," Sarah says. And Jim stands there, staring at her, like he already knows.

Of course Sarah knows too but she can't, no, she won't allow it.

Ruth Mitchell calling on the phone, saying, We have to see your son in person. As soon as he gets home for Thanksgiving break.

Sarah has never spoken to her before. Didn't even know her name. And now she has to go down there with Will, the moment he gets home, and talk to her?

It's ridiculous. To withhold like that. It's a family matter, she said. You and your husband should come too.

Of course, there's only one thing it could be.

Jim says it first, but Sarah won't believe it.

"Was he even seeing her this summer, their daughter? Do they even know each other?"

"I don't know. There were photos of her," Jim says.

"What, from that time he went down for research? Is this all because you sent him down there? Why doesn't anyone tell me anything?"

Sarah was always there for Will. She was asking, ready to be told, and yet he told her nothing.

She won't believe it. Will, getting a girl pregnant. No.

"I hope to god he stole something," she says. "Broke something. But not this."

"We should call him," Jim says. "I'll call him right now."

"Yes, and ask him what the hell he was doing all summer when we thought he was out walking in the woods."

She didn't make much fuss about that LeBeau kid at the door, setting off all the alarms. Police told her it was just a prank and let the kid off with a reprimand.

Don't worry, ma'am, he won't be back, they said. We know Eli LeBeau.

She was trying to get along, not to cause any trouble for people who have enough troubles of their own. But now there's this strange family down the mountain, making claims on Will.

This place has always promised some kind of magic to her, a place apart, but maybe she's just been lured into a trap.

If it's true that the girl is pregnant, it's probably been at least three months. Sarah doesn't know the laws here, but there's no time to waste.

*

They act like it's the end of the world, but for Will it is really more like a beginning.

It is the end of college, of Strattenburg, for now, and the end of the endless possibilities people have always been talking about for a guy like him.

But it's the beginning of one thing certain. It's a confirmation of something he one time knew for sure but that he made himself forget.

Day after day telling himself it's not real, and she's not real—there must be other guys, not me—and now this.

It took weeks to talk himself out of her, shutting down every thought she showed up in, but only one phone call to bring him back in.

Not the call from his father, with Mom fuming in the background. But the call from Honey herself.

Why didn't you call me sooner? I would have come right away, he said.

He's supposed to go home in ten days for Thanksgiving, but he won't wait. There's no way. He'll take that bus. He'll hitch home from the station.

This can't be an argument between the parents about right and wrong. It's not their life, not their decision.

It has to be only about him and Honey. Only they get to decide. And if she's sure he's the one—

I'm sure, she said. There's nobody else, there's never been anybody else.

But why didn't you come out that night? If only you would've come out I never would have left!

I would have come in a second, if I'd known you were there, if my mother had told me.

Of course I'll come back, Honey. We'll do this together. Whatever it might be.

You and me and this baby, she said.

Yes, he said. And it was like his whole body lit up with certainty, defiance. With love for her and pride too.

He'll stay with her and take care of this baby. His parents complain that he has no drive, no direction—well, here's a direction.

They talk about the future and how the world is ending faster than we can imagine. Dad and his books, it's all death, all the time. Even when he talks about bees.

His parents didn't do anything about it, so how dare they tell him what to do with his future?

And it's the right thing to do. You can't make a girl like Honey get an abortion. He knows her enough to know that much.

Her parents say adoption, but Honey wants the baby. My baby, Will says to himself. Our baby.

And he knows what they had—what they have—is real. It was not just a summer fling but a revelation. Maybe they're too young, but this is bigger than both of them together.

This is life, and he's part of it now.

Later that night, lying in his narrow bed, the bus ticket printed out and in his backpack, he can't sleep. Joy and terror both. What they add up to.

A baby? He never wanted a baby, doesn't even know how to imagine it.

9

It's Thanksgiving today, but Nell has nowhere to go, nowhere she has to be.

The snow is falling lightly, and the woodstove is burning hot.

Two weeks she's been back but still every day it feels new again.

She can walk now, and breathe, and her head is clear.

She has so much.

Groceries to last the week and bare trees creaking in the wind.

Eddy could come get you, Christine said this morning. Just for the day. You can see all the nieces and nephews.

Nell could hear them in the background over the phone. A burst of laughter.

She's glad they are together but more glad to be here alone.

When she opened the door for the first time since she fell, it smelled clean and good. As if the wind and trees had been living here while she was gone.

No more water in the buckets. No mice, not that she could tell.

Everything as she left it. Tea leaves dried in the bottom of a cup in the sink.

That morning after the storm Nell had just one cup of tea. If she'd eaten breakfast she might not have fallen.

She just has to be more careful. And she is being careful, avoiding the ladder to the loft for now, sleeping on the couch and eating when she's hungry.

Christine didn't want her going home until she had recovered completely. I just won't be able to stop worrying about you up there alone. And without a car?

Really, Nell, it's not fair to me. You're my sister. I need to know at least somebody's looking in on you. Don't you know any of the neighbors?

Nell finally found the phone book in Christine's kitchen. There was a whole column of Larocques.

She couldn't do it. She couldn't call. But then she did, getting her nerve up over and over until he finally answered.

Jeanne told me you took a spill, were staying with your sister in Kingsbury, he said. Said he checked on the place a couple times. Finished the job she started on the roof.

To him her leaving was nothing more than the natural cycle of things, then, of people coming and going, like deer coming up to the pond for a drink, then going back into the woods.

He said he'd be glad to stop by once in a while. If it will help ease your sister's mind. I go over the gap all the time anyway, it's no trouble.

You want the fuel delivery guy dropping in on you? Christine said, raising an eyebrow.

But the next Saturday she drove Nell back home. A relief to everyone involved.

Nell has a pie now cooling on the table, and already it's nearly dark. All day yesterday cooking pumpkin into mash.

There's a lot of meat on a pumpkin, but not as much as on a deer. You have to kill some of the deer, or they starve, Leonard said. After they strip all the cedar trees there's nothing left to eat.

Leonard will be here soon with the venison stew. And more for your freezer, he said.

Her whole place is so warm now that she takes off the second sweater, takes off her hat.

No need to go outside anymore today. Just waiting now for the pie to cool. For the sound of tires on gravel. Helga on the porch.

She has folded the blankets neatly on top of her pillow and hidden the sheets underneath.

She folds and refolds the old crocheted afghan, blue and white squares for the college she dropped out of.

It's probably the last thing her grandmother made for her, and she barely even sees it anymore. Maybe she could learn to repair it before it unravels completely.

She has so much to do now that she is home.

The woodstove is going strong, and Leonard is bringing his venison stew. Thanksgiving, and Nell is thankful.

It tastes like how the woods would taste, he said. Acorns and ferns and river water. He can't believe she's never had venison.

Her leg's still weak from the cast, and she still has some pain where the ribs were broken.

And yet she can feel the bones healing, knitting back together all on their own. The torn skin on her arm now just a faint trace of pink scar.

Staying in town would be easier. No wood to carry, no leaky roof and ice on the doorstep.

But life's not painless and it's not supposed to be. She just wants to be ready for the pain, for death even, when it comes. She wants to be able to bear it. But first to try the venison stew.

*

Sarah hears the shots explode in the woods outside. One last week of deer season, then it's on to grouse.

She wears the ugly orange hat when she goes walking and makes Jim wear one too.

The hats sit on a bench by the door now, above their muddy boots. They're real Vermonters now. Just like their son will be.

Get used to it, Will says. Life goes on. There are worse things than to get married too young.

He has no idea what he's getting into, none at all.

Did they teach that girl nothing in homeschool? And what part of basic sex ed did Will not understand?

She can't speak for the girl, but Will was educated well. He was taught to respect women and himself. He took AP biology, for god's sake. They handed out condoms in health class!

It's impossible to concentrate on her work. She has to get up, shake it off, before she settles in to try again.

It was humming along so beautifully, the pattern of shifting greens working exactly as she planned across the gold warp, but now she keeps messing up. Her head is too much in it.

All those conversations with Will over break. Then yelling at him on the phone, regretting it, trying to make up for it, and then doing it all over again.

She can't help herself. She loves him so much. And she set aside so many of her own days and dreams to give them all to Will.

It was your idea to come here, Mom. And now I'm going to stay so you should be happy.

Isn't he the least bit worried? Is he keeping that a secret too? If she were him she'd be out of her head with regret and grief.

Jim tried over and over to talk to him on the drive back to Strattenburg, but there was no moving him.

They've said all there is to say. He's eighteen, he gets to decide.

As soon as Sarah achieves a rhythm, sliding the shuttle back and forth with the treadle and beater moving in time, there's another round of shots.

They're really out there today. Men in the woods shooting animals just like her father used to.

She never meant for Will to make a home here, not for real.

You need to take advantage of your advantages, Will. *That's* the right thing to do! She said that too. She said so many things.

The love you have is a delirium. It wears off. She won't always be so pretty. What will you do then?

At least they were able to convince him to finish off the semester. And he says he's applying himself to his work. Doing exactly what you said, Mom. Finishing up.

And next he'll get a job, anywhere, who cares where, he says.

But what kind of job will he even find around here? He's never worked a day in his life. Not really.

She should not have shouted at him. She should not have raised her voice.

It's my decision. I made a mistake, I know, but I really think it was meant to be.

Meant to be! Such a weak-minded, patently useless way of looking at things. Didn't they teach him better than that?

Jim has already told his mother. Susan will tell the family, will spread the word, and make it all real and irreversible.

If they'd just keep it to themselves a while longer it could continue to be not quite true. There'd be room for Will to change his mind. For Honey to change her mind.

Sarah won't tell her mother until she absolutely has to. At least she'll never have to tell her father.

Sarah goes to the great big window, looks out over the bare trees. Everything's brown and gray now. The gold and green have gone.

She can see the tops of strange little buildings. Sugar shacks, burned-out sheds covered in leaves. Of no use to anybody, just left to the elements.

She can see the cars pass on Tower Road below. One every few minutes. Who are those people who come and go?

When Will comes back for Christmas, when the baby is born this spring, will he become one of these people, who work five jobs just to be able to pay the heating bill?

His savings will only go so far. Of course, when his grandmother dies, which one day she might, she'll leave everything for Will. But that's no way to live.

He'll need to go back and finish a degree. Find his real calling. And the girl, Honey, will need to at least finish high school.

Adoption is the only other choice, Ruth said that day they finally met, that terrible day in that terrible little room in their terrible little house.

But Honey said no, over and over, no, hanging on to Will like he was her savior. This girl Sarah had never met before, hanging on to him as if he were her own.

And Will himself seemed so steady, so certain. Sitting upright and proud, saying, We've decided. We're getting married.

They offered all the arguments, the facts and reasoning, so many times, that awful Thanksgiving break. Nearly a week of it, and Will just wanting to run down the mountain and see her.

You can't stop me, is what he said. Is what he keeps saying. You can't stop me from doing the right thing.

*

Once even the late-season dahlias and mums have withered there's really no choice but to dress the place up for Christmas.

White lights on the trees out front, white lights in the lobby, and evergreen boughs to hide the dead garden.

Still, Leila is saving the all-out red-and-green for another week or two, at least in the dining room. Christmas decorations are depressing when the ground is still bare and brown.

The dried heads of coneflower, and dried hydrangea blossoms that she snipped this morning from the backyard, will do for now.

She tucks them alongside the evergreens on the mantel. Just different shades of brown, but it's the texture that surprises.

She stands back to admire it, nearly steps on Steve. "I didn't see you there," she says.

"Sorry. It looks nice," he says. "Not as nice as you, though. Is that a new dress?"

Steve's mood these last few days is already changed. He must notice it, too, how much better everything looks when he's not drinking.

What a relief that he listened this time! Weekends only, he promised, which around here means Monday and Tuesday.

Weekends will be reasonable. They can go back to drinking like reasonable people, a glass of wine with dinner.

She didn't bring up Jenny Rose yet, but maybe she won't have to.

"Not new, I just haven't worn it for a while," she says. "A few years, in fact."

It's a younger woman's dress, with its long zipper and pink silk lining, and she was surprised to find this morning that it still fits.

He wraps his arms around her from behind, and she pretends to be interested, still, in the decorations. It's good just to stand here a while.

"The birds are mad at me for taking away their seedpods. But they look good, don't you think?"

"Sure, they do," he says. He kisses her neck.

He seems to like her again. And he's less angry at everything, everyone.

Leila, too, now that she can stop repeating and refining in her head what she needs to say to him, now that she has finally said it, is not angry anymore either.

Just wine, and just weekends. None of the hard stuff. This is how it's going to be from now on, and such a relief.

Without the drinking, Jenny Rose will stop being a problem too. It will all vanish without her even needing to bring it up.

Well, the problems will vanish for them anyway. She nearly forgot about poor Honey.

And Willoughby, too, and his parents. Certainly this isn't what they were hoping for when they moved up here.

"Do we have anything on for December twenty-ninth?" Steve says.

"Why? Are they asking to have the wedding here?"

"No, no. Just thought it might be nice to offer the place for a reception, if they want it."

Honey's in the office with Sophie and Amber. Sophie asked this morning, could we use the internet for a while, to look at wedding stuff? And of course Leila said yes.

It's good seeing the old trio again. She wishes they'd do something other than occupy her office searching the internet, but obviously they're not little kids anymore. She can't expect them to play dress-up.

"I doubt they'll take us up on it, but should we go ask her now?"

The three girls are huddled around the computer, scrolling through wedding dresses. When they turn around they look stupefied.

"It's just an offer, and only if it's useful to you," Steve says. "We're pretty good at weddings around here."

Amber comes out of the daze first. "That would be great, you should do it, Honey! Isn't that great?"

Leila is startled to see Honey's face looking so vulnerable and pale without the hair. She chopped it off herself, Sophie said. Trying to prove something.

"Thank you, Mr. Pierce," Honey says. "We're probably doing everything at the church, though." Always polite that Honey, with the Mister and Missus.

Leila's never been able to read what's behind that politeness. Either she's just a simple, sweet girl, not particularly bright, or she's very good at maintaining a surface.

Given the situation, probably the latter.

"Of course, of course," Steve says. "We just meant afterwards, if you're looking for a place for your family and friends to get together."

"Thanks, Dad," Sophie says. She closes the window so all they see on the screen now is the logo for Birches Inn. In other words, You can go now, Dad.

Steve shrugs. "Well, let us know. Happy to help."

And it's true, they're happy to help. And very happy it's not their own daughter pregnant. Such a relief when the bad thing that happens doesn't happen to you.

Leila and Steve leave the door open to the office and hover nearby. The hostess stand is close enough for them to listen while pretending not to.

Amber and Sophie are arguing, but Honey's either not talking or her voice is too soft to hear over the others.

Probably she just doesn't care. How could she think about a dress when there's a baby on the way? Babies take over everything.

"Here's a whole pregnant bride collection!" Amber's voice this time. No wonder she's so good in theater—such a voice!

Steve smirks at Leila. They're conspirators now, in eavesdropping.

Leila loves to be in on something with Steve. You and me, Babe, so much better together than apart.

"What about this one? You might as well show off a little," Amber says. "Your tits have gotten so huge!"

Leila rolls her eyes and Steve laughs.

"Should I tell her that the proper word here is *décolletage*?" Leila says.

He looks alarmed, as if she might actually march in there and correct her.

"We should probably close the office door now," Steve says. "Give them a little space."

"You're right. It's not like the old days, when they'd be expecting a plate of cookies."

"And how much trouble can they possibly get into when they're only ten feet away?"

*

Cyrus goes on autopilot at the deli counter. It's all he can do to get through the day. One pound of this, half pound of that, it's all the same to him. All the same slimy bullshit.

Why they have to have nine kinds of turkey and eleven kinds of ham and like a hundred kinds of cheese. One of this, one of that, make it thinner, no, thicker.

No wonder Emily wouldn't do it. She looks at him in the apron, in the hairnet, no way, she says. She laughs a little, too, which is nice.

A dollar more an hour adds up, he says. And she says, Not fast enough.

She's a couple years older than him and she has a kid. Two years old. A bit of extra pay should matter, shouldn't it? $9.85 is that much better than $8.50.

Plus, I'm manager there, Cyrus wanted to say. Wanted that to matter.

At the Ski Bowl, even the subs make eleven an hour, maybe more. He shouldn't have signed up as a sub when he has this other gig and paid time off. And he shouldn't have had to beg for it either, but he did.

Waiting for a cold snap, and one big storm to lay down a base coat.

He'll probably have to call in sick at the deli, but he'll do it.

When Cyrus is not slicing he's wiping. When he's not wiping he's stocking. When he's not stocking he's listening to people bitch in the break room.

Cashiers have no idea how easy they have it, it's just, Please enter your rewards number, thank you and have a nice day.

A dollar an hour makes a difference, though. And another couple bucks if you close. Carol puts him on to close as often as he likes.

You show up, Cyrus, she says. As if that's some big compliment. As if he should feel proud.

Emily doesn't always show up. It's hard to show up when you've got a two-year-old. You have no idea, she says.

He doesn't judge. He's on her side. Mostly he just hates it when she's not there.

If you don't think about what you're doing too much, you can get through. If you don't ask why it matters how thick the slices are, which kind of ham you get.

How's that? A little thinner? Oh, that's too thin now? Okay, no problem.

Just ask, nod, adjust the slicer one more time until it's time to close down.

Never mind the hairnet. He forgets he has it on sometimes. Talking to people at the counter all day long.

Jared's mom. Kylie's mom. How do they even remember him? Jared and Kylie went off to college or something. He doesn't ask.

Mom thought Eli'd be going to college. Probably doesn't think that anymore, though.

He's just lucky that lady didn't press charges. Attempted robbery, attempted assault even. Not that anything would've come of it.

Everybody's buying the Nature's Bounty today. No additives! It's on sale but still $1.10 more a pound than the cheapest stuff. They don't buy it other days. What, does nature only matter when it's on sale?

Not that he blames them. Turns out it's hard to resist a special if you make the signs big enough.

Cyrus could go into advertising after this. He's getting to know how people work. Watching their stupid patterns and how to break them. Maybe he'll do marketing after tech literacy.

He'd drop it all in a second if it snowed, though. There's supposed to be a big snow next week. Maybe he could even learn to drive the groomer.

What, are you a ski bum or something? Emily said when he told her how much he wished it would snow.

Right, he said, I wish. He barely even knows how to ski, but he can't wait to get out there. All night long, the lights of the snowcats bouncing up and down the trails.

No hairnet. No yes, ma'am—thinner, thicker? What's on sale today? Today's special. What difference does it make?

He's working with one of the grandpas today, the slowpoke who takes five minutes just to slice the wrapper off a new hunk of ham. The customers start looking around, they get fidgety.

Cyrus better not be here when he's old like that. He'd rather die first.

He'll cut off his finger first, though, if he's not paying attention. He really can't afford to lose any fingers if he's doing that computer class in the spring.

*

Nell hangs the towel back on the hook and slips into her blue shirt, still buttoned. Washed so many times now it's nearly white.

Her bones and muscles are warm from the bath, no longer aching from the day's long walk in the cold.

A gift of propane to last the winter. That's what he said, and this is how she's spent it. This bath an indulgence, a one-time thing she can't afford to repeat.

Not for herself and not for the trees either, poisoning the air with her old propane furnace.

She sits on the edge of the toilet, and the cool feels good on her bare thighs.

Nell told Christine today that she managed the walk to town, that she's able to carry a pack now.

What does Leonard think of that, of your walking all that way? she asked.

Christine likes having a man around for an opinion, as if the opinion of someone she barely knows would be more reliable than Nell's own.

But Leonard just laughs it off. You walk as long and far as you want to, he says. That's what I think. One less car on the road for me to get stuck behind.

And just yesterday he asked, How's your sister? Has she recovered from your fall yet?

Nell wipes the steam from the fogged-up mirror and looks at her face. There's color in her cheeks from the bath. She's not so bad looking when there's color in her cheeks.

Her skin is crepe-thin where the cast was. The cloth on her underwear is so worn it's nearly transparent.

She has strong legs, though. They've always served her well.

And her breasts are still small and firm, the nipples soft in the warmth of the steam but taut the moment she touches them.

It's okay to want things, as long as it doesn't cost too much for others.

The girl from Honey in the Rock must've wanted things, and look what suffering that cost her, and everyone around her too.

That must have been her last summer, the blond-haired girl Nell saw sunning near the summit, a half-naked boy lying face down on the rock beside her.

Their story belongs to everyone now, that timeless old story of young love—mutual, natural, and unstoppable.

That was never Nell's story, though. After Laura all she wanted was to make a wreck of herself. To be taken and discarded.

Everyone tried to get her to go back to college and make something of herself. You'd be a wonderful nurse, Dad said, not noticing that she could barely care for herself.

She's never asked much of others. She doesn't ask Leonard either, but he gives her things anyway.

Here are these tomatoes, can you do something with them? Here are these old tools. Take them off my hands.

And he thinks in a way that makes sense to her.

Pay your sister what you would've paid for the fuel. Little by little and you won't have to owe her anything.

She agreed to that, she thanked him, and he brought her the forms she needed.

Advance Directive they call it. Refusal of Medical Assistance. She has it all in writing now.

No more doctor bills for Christine to pay, no more hospitals and their toxic waste, latex gloves tossed in the trash.

Why so many promises, when you have no idea what's next? he said. Makes it hard when you change your mind.

Which is the point, of course. Now she can't change her mind when something like pain comes.

My dad wanted it simple, too, Leonard said. When he was strong he said he'd just crawl off into the woods like an animal when it was time to die.

But in the end he died in the hospital, dementia, five years of forgetting, and then was buried with everyone else.

A funeral and the whole bit. Cost a fortune, Len said.

He'd come by to give her the forms but stayed an hour, then longer. Nell cut open a loaf of bread, and when the sun went down she lit the woodstove.

Once you get old enough, he said, you don't remember what you wanted before. Human instinct kicks in, and you just want to live. And everyone else wants you to live too. No matter what.

That's just how people are, he said. And he ate the bread she put in front of him.

Not me, Nell said. I like the thought of leaving no trace, just a bucketful of ash tossed to the wind. But how do you go from this, to that?

So much has to happen between being alive and being dead and nobody really knows how to go from one to the other. And yet we all have to do it.

You're right about that, he said. And I can't say that I know any better how it's done.

She slips on the old gray sweatpants now. Places a glass of water next to the couch where she'll sleep off the rest of the day's exhaustion.

It's your life, he said, when she signed the forms, refusing treatment or transport. Refusing everything.

*

Jeanne better hurry to make out the package slips this morning. A big stack of boxes came in today, and by lunch hour it'll be nonstop in here.

She's not used to that kind of traffic anymore, but at least it passes the time. Time flies when you're having fun!

Drop it on the scale, rattle off the questions about hazardous materials, and show them their choices. Maybe switch them to the flat-rate envelope.

That's fun all right.

Everyone complaining about the prices. They never mail anything anymore, no wonder they're surprised they actually have to pay.

Paid more for the postage than for the gifts, they say.

What do you think, that you'll get that box for the grandkids all the way to Chicago on a dime? Think of all the trucks and planes!

Not to mention people like me. I'm not just going to stand here all day, at your service, for nothing.

Jeanne turns on the station that plays Christmas music. Maybe it'll get her in the mood for all this bounty.

A handful of boxes from L.L.Bean for the Calpers. Some squished paper packages for D'Angelos, with tape every which way. Must be the annual haul from Grandma.

Yep, here it is, the holiday fruitcake, all the way from Englewood, New Jersey! *Perishable* written in old-lady cursive on every side of the box.

Big Catholic families like that get a lot of cards too. The thin ones from UNICEF or whatever, and some of the thick gilded ones, too, from the rich cousins, or the truly devout.

Jesus, Mary, and Joseph—how many different versions of "Jingle Bells" are they going to play? Or worse, "Jingle Bell Rock." Jeanne's getting sick of it already.

And the commercials! Excitable men shouting over and over about some deal on snow tires.

You've got to tune out the commercials, focus on the festive stuff, like you tune out the complaining. There's a line of two or three in here and people get huffy.

Younger folks don't even bother coming in. They just have their presents shipped directly, with one of those little printed cards stuffed in the box.

Like this one here. Big square box, probably a fake wreath, lovingly made, packaged, and shipped by robots in China.

Merry Christmas, Mom!

They never even touch the gifts they buy, just *click click click* and it's done.

Jeanne's lucky she can deliver her own gifts. Christmas Day with the boys and their wives, all together in the old house. And once they have babies it'll be like real Christmas again.

She thought Kingsbury was too far but now she sees. Other people's kids gone to Ohio, Virginia, Delaware.

You can't babysit the grandkids if they all settle in Virginia.

Luckily Ruth Mitchell will be able to babysit her own grandbaby. Maybe she'll even let Honey go back to school after this.

Keeping her home sure didn't help. Good Christian people protecting their kids from the heathens. Good luck with that!

She was just too pretty. All that blond hair, those big doe eyes—what good did it do her?

And now she's gone and cut off all that beautiful hair, probably her best quality.

Jeanne hasn't seen anything come through for the happy couple yet, come to think of it. Maybe after the wedding they'll get their own P.O. box. Mister and Missus.

But first they'll have their Christmas wedding in the big white church. Honey and Willoughby Calper, like homecoming queen and king.

All down the tubes after that, though. Get a few good pictures and then deal with what you've done.

Up all night with a screaming baby. And forget about sleep, forget about school!

The Calpers might have money, but all the money in the world can't get a baby to sleep at night.

No, money can't protect you from the chaos of a new baby, but a condom sure would have!

Stupid kids.

Jeanne hasn't seen Sarah in here mailing things to Will at college, not like Leila. No care packages for that kid.

Maybe she's just too angry with him. Or maybe she's too ashamed to face the public, face Jeanne, after what her son has done. Ashamed that he's just one of us now.

Thankfully Jeanne's sons weren't stupid enough to get any girl pregnant at that age. She wishes they would now, though.

It's time now, boys and girls! Nature only gives you so many years, she wants to say.

She never did finish that book Jim gave her. Don read it. Did you know you can run a diesel engine on old fry oil? he said. And he just might try.

Don's always been smart about things like that—save the earth and save money at the same time.

People think he's just the guy you call when your wash machine breaks, but he's always got something checked out from the library.

That's not why she married him, though. More to do with what drives the young people.

Maybe if it was actually snowing they'd sell some of those damn tires and shut up about it.

Maybe she should just turn the radio off already. Put the slips in the mailboxes in peace, Christmas spirit be damned.

What she really needs for Christmas is grandbabies. And snow. A little snow always helps.

It used to snow before Christmas. Now it seems like it waits till after New Year's and then before you know it it's time for the January thaw.

Jim Calper said it's not just global warming they have to worry about. It's big storms of every kind. The rainstorm this summer was just the beginning.

You can't count on things like the hundred-year flood anymore either, he said. That's all changing. Droughts and floods all around—not just down south, he said.

Yes, and you have a good day, too! Jeanne said.

At least she got him to smile.

*

Now that the date is set, December 29, now that it seems almost inevitable, Sarah has to try to believe it.

If they're really going to do this, a church wedding with all the family assembled, she at least wants to host a small reception.

She's come here today to talk to Ruth about it face-to-face. On the phone she's so curt, so definitive. And she's used to having her own way seen as the right way.

It's just the two of them in the kitchen, in the silence, while Ruth pours coffee that tastes like it might have been sitting in that pot all day.

Then out of nowhere there she is. Honey herself, the cause of all their troubles.

Just a girl in a T-shirt and jeans but her presence takes over the room somehow. So feral, so unselfconscious.

She's wearing a wool cap on her head and Sarah recognizes the shirt as one of Will's own, the band logo stretched across her chest.

"Hello, Mrs. Calper," she says. "It's nice to see you." And when she reaches for a cookie Ruth pushes her hand away.

"Stop it, that's not good for you," she says. "You have to mind yourself. And please put on a sweater."

Honey takes the cookie anyway and turns to go. "I'll be upstairs if you need me for anything," she says.

Sarah is glad she didn't have a daughter. People always say that teenage girls are cruel. Teenage girls and their sexuality, which they have no idea how to handle.

Though of course not having a girl hasn't protected her from them.

If Honey's parents can't handle her, how is her sweet and totally inexperienced Will going to manage?

"I know the kids have agreed to have the wedding in your church," Sarah begins, there's no point in waiting, "but Jim and I think it would be nice to have a reception at our house—at Will's house."

Jim doesn't actually have an opinion about it, but Sarah knows that Christian people respect male authority. Maybe if she brings Jim into the conversation it will go better.

She's still clinging to the hope that the whole thing will be canceled for some reason, any reason, but for now she just wants to salvage at least some part of it.

"There's a large kitchen in the church basement, if that's what you're worried about," Ruth says. "The church is old, but the kitchen is new."

"We don't need a big kitchen. I'll just get a caterer. It would be nice, our families could all come together . . ."

"Which they will do, at the church."

She hoped to get Ruth with the word "family," but she has an answer for everything.

Sarah could have taken no over the phone, without the bad coffee. She takes another sip, trying to be polite.

"Our family would like to have a part in this too. This is not just about your daughter, but it's about our son, our family, too."

"Tradition dictates that the bride's family arranges the wedding," Ruth says, "and the groom follows suit."

"I know, but the groom's family arranges the rehearsal dinner," Sarah says, knowing before Ruth even responds that this is a dead end.

"We don't need a rehearsal for this. It's not a show."

"Well, in place of that, our family would like to have everyone to our house for a simple meal and a cake."

"We always have cake right after the service. It's an important part of the covenant, the sharing of the covenant, and joy."

Since when is joy some kind of obligatory sacrament? This woman is impossible, but Sarah can be determined too.

"What about the children," she says. "Maybe we should see what they want to do."

"Children?"

"Will and Honey. They're still our children, no matter what they've gotten themselves into."

"I think they've already had plenty of say in the matter. I can't deny I'm disappointed in my daughter. I don't know how . . ."

Ruth looks away, looks down at her hands. Finally, a crack in her facade.

"We've always been so careful," she says. "We've done the best we could for her. Your son, I don't know what . . ."

"We have, too," Sarah says. She has to control herself now. Does Ruth really think she's the only one with a moral claim here, the only one with a child whose life is about to end?

"We've done the best for Will, too," Sarah says. "We taught him respect for women. Not to mention the basics of human reproduction."

Ruth doesn't respond to what Sarah meant as a direct hit. She just nods.

Maybe Ruth knows it, that she failed in this regard. That quite possibly Honey did this on purpose to tie herself to Will, to find a way out of her life here.

Will would never see himself as attractive in that way, or in any way really, but to Sarah it's the only thing that makes sense.

They're quiet a moment, gathering themselves. Sarah's anger already cooling back into despair.

They don't want to cry, not now, not together.

"Still, we could ask Honey," Sarah says as patiently, as kindly, as possible. "She might like to invite your family, your parish, to our house afterwards. Everyone could stay as long as they want, get to know each other, it's all so new . . ."

"Dorothy clearly can't be counted on to do what's right on her own, and neither can your son."

"But surely . . ."

"It's been very hard on her. On all of us. She's not feeling well. I hope you understand."

Sarah should not have come alone. She should have let Jim take care of this. He and the girl's father get on fine.

But Jim doesn't care about the ceremony or the reception. He cares about Will, certainly, but the wedding is just something to get through until the real marriage, the real challenge, begins.

"I'd at least like to order the cake," Sarah says.

Ruth's face softens a little, into the first faint smile of the day.

"Yes, okay. You can order the cake."

*

If Sophie were vacuuming she could listen to music in headphones, but cleaning the bathroom—forget it. The cord keeps getting caught, the iPod comes unhooked, tangled around her arm.

She tears the headphones off and dumps them on the floor. Not broken at least. She hasn't broken anything.

Why today, though? She doesn't have time for this. She needs to find a song. She has only a few more weeks.

That's plenty, Mom says. The world doesn't stop turning so you can listen to every love song in the book. You have to learn to multitask like the rest of us.

Which is what she was trying to do. Listen and clean at the same time. Five weeks—but that's with school and Christmas and everything else.

She just has to clean faster. She's done with the toilet, the sink, now it's just the tub.

Sophie sprays the tile, watches the bubbles slide down. She sprinkles baking soda on the faucets, the rough bottom of the tub.

How can she think of a song worthy of Honey's wedding when she's here doing chores?

Rubber gloves and brushes. *Tra la la la la.*

She envies Honey. Her certainty. Her worthiness—for him to sacrifice everything, to see her like that.

And she's horrified. Giving up your body, having a baby, when you haven't even figured out yourself alone.

Will's real life was just beginning, and now he's coming back here for what? To set up house?

Nobody else can understand, but that's okay, Honey says. You'll see. As if she knows something Sophie will only one day learn.

What it really means is that she'll be cleaning bathrooms and kitchens and diapers for the rest of her life. Forever.

Cleaning, scrubbing, a housewife, a mother—no way.

But the way they stood up to everyone, how they're doing what they want when everyone thinks they're wrong.

Sophie could not have done that. She always follows the rules. Do well in school, go to college, make your escape. That's what smart people do, ambitious people.

What is wrong with them, that they're throwing that all away?

The grime is stubborn. The floor of the tub never comes clean. This is reality. This is what they'll be facing. The time for playing around in the river is over.

She's seen her own parents. What happened to their true love? Or was it never true, like Honey and Will's?

Maybe they just work too hard. The restaurant, the inn, they never get to leave. They never even get a weekend at the lake.

And they make Sophie work too. Every weekend, clean the bathroom, sweep the porch. Nights after school: Bus the tables. And people think they're rich because they have the inn!

Will's parents already found a little house, where Honey and Will can live together, every day like a holiday, in love with their little baby.

What song can she possibly sing for them?

It's impossible but Honey insisted, Honey chose her. She said, no, not Amber. She doesn't understand. I want you, Sophie.

You'll figure it out. My mother has to approve the music, she said, but I'm sure you'll find something perfect.

Perfect would be epic, apocalyptic, something with worlds ending, oceans roiling, but love in the middle of it all. A love like that. Defiant. Certain. Dangerous but true.

Like in the old ballads, with all that darkness, because Sophie feels that, too, the darkness surrounding them as much as the light.

But no, in those songs the lovers die, the mothers curse, the fathers threaten—everyone keeping them separate.

Only sometimes they escape on a milk-white steed—it's nearly always white—leaving everyone else behind. And that feels like Honey and Will too.

Sophie leans into the brush, sweating now, the grime running off the tiles in a rush of foam and water.

An old tub like this is never really clean yet it's only in cleaning that you notice how dirty it is. Better not to look.

But what if the wedding song has to have Jesus in it? Jesus smiling down on them all, because of the church. Because of Honey's parents, who will have their say, they always do.

It's an impossible task. She should not have said yes.

But Honey insisted. Sophie was flattered. She said yes, and so she has to do it. She wants to do it.

Dad will help her find something. He said, you're becoming a real musician, Sophie. He said it when she didn't know he was listening to her play.

She sprays it all down, the water swirling and bubbling down the drain, finished. But she still has the faucets, the mirror.

A real musician, he said. So she'll figure it out. Not the sad music she loves—but something happy on the outside.

Maybe something from when they were kids, something they used to love. Like *Camelot*?

But Guinevere falls in love with the wrong guy.

Besides, Sophie hates musicals now, as much as she hates the crooners.

Love and marriage, horse and carriage—what bullshit!

She closes the shower curtain with a snap, the rings sliding and clinking.

She takes a dry cloth and wipes down the faucets till they shine.

She steps back. Satisfied, but only for a second.

The mirror is last. It's the easy part.

When she wipes off the last smudge with a paper towel she sees her own face. Is that the girl who will be singing in the church?

She'll have to close her eyes. She closes them now. The right song will come to her soon. It just has to.

Love and marriage . . .

No, I'll never, never leave thee . . .

Open the door, Maid Margaret, open and let me in.

*

What a relief to finally be leaving town, making their way down to New Jersey. With a little more peace at home David can get away for a few days, be of use somewhere.

The church van is loaded with tools and snacks, and a half dozen boys are settled in the back with their gadgets. Their first trip to the Jersey shore since Hurricane Isis blew through last summer.

David can handle them for a week, just a bunch of kids from the home-schooling group that he can take off their parents' hands for a while. Make good use of all that energy.

He's shown them the pictures. Mud in people's basements. The board walk torn to shreds. Still so much work to be done after the storm.

And there's something about a roller coaster crushed in the sand that intrigues them. More exciting than a soggy carpet in a church basement, though that's what they'll be dealing with when they get there.

When he called up their sister church in Jersey they said yes, we could make use of some strong Vermont boys. And so these boys will have to do.

He glances into the rearview mirror. They're finally sitting still. They're probably glad to get away for a while too.

It's hard to believe these kids are so close to Honey in age. Their pimply faces and all that fidgeting.

Maybe girls just grow up faster. They take better care of their skin.

As soon as the billboards start popping up, you know you're in New York. *Don't let addiction sideline your dreams! Marines fight to win!*

Jesus is talking, they say. But who do they think He's talking to out here?

He passes prison fences and worn-out little towns. Weeds in the parking lot of the McDonald's.

It's why you've got to make an impression on them now, show them all the good they can do, before they get caught up in other things.

David can't save them all, though. Eli, for one. Showed up a few times but hasn't been back. Not since that same storm that tore up the Jersey shore, matter of fact.

Unless he's sneaking around again. Though at least David knows he's not bothering Honey. Or—what does he know? He's been wrong enough times before.

Hopefully they won't hit any traffic on the thruway. They got a late start when one of the boys lost his game charger and they all had to wait around till he found it.

As if they needed it for the trip! From the look of things in the rearview, though, he can admit it's come in useful. Every boy to his toy.

These kids don't know about Honey yet, but they will soon enough.

Reverend Peters will be doing the ceremony, so of course he knows. They've told a few of their closer friends, like these boys' parents.

It will be good to get this wedding over with. To have everyone at the church know, to come out with their blessings.

Also to have them get it out of their systems, whatever judgments they want to make.

It'll probably take longer for Ruth to get it out of her system.

Tearing up those wedding magazines right in front of Honey. Who do you think you are? Where did you even get these?

They're from my friends. For me! Honey yelled back at her, just as righteous, just as loud.

She could've let her look at the pictures at least. Just a bunch of cakes and flowers. She'd get tired of them soon enough.

At least when he pulled out of the drive this morning the two of them stood together, waving. He knows they're at least trying to get along.

Ruth's bringing the bassinette down from the attic was a step.

She also brought out her mother's wedding dress. I didn't have a gown of my own, but my mother did, she said. Want to try it on?

Honey threw her arms around her, and thanked her over and over, as if all was forgiven. She knocked the dress right off the hanger onto the floor.

She's too impulsive, is the thing. A little too much like David probably, when he was that age.

And passionate too. It was okay for a boy to be that way. Girls just pushed him away. That's the way it was back then, that was the girl's job.

But what if the girl is impulsive too?

He can't help but wonder what the reverend will say at the service when he's never married a couple of sinning teenagers before.

Something about God's love, of course, and its many ways of showing up here on earth. The power of it, forceful in its mystery but with a purpose we may never understand. That's how David would put it.

How it's a trial, too, a trial He has brought upon these kids, or that they have brought upon themselves, but it's a trial that can be faced with love. The love between the two of them, and Jesus Christ.

Something like that. Hopefully he'll say something to encourage them and encourage the parish to support them, even if they aren't exactly a beacon of righteousness right now.

It's definitely good to be getting out of town. Good to get some perspective on the whole thing, see the world out there, even if it is only New Jersey.

Maybe once he sees the wreckage in the flood zone, whole neighborhoods destroyed by the ocean, all those families living in shelters, the situation at home will feel less tragic.

And it'll give these boys something to do besides play with their gadgets, blowing things up on their little screens.

Nothing like a flood to show us the power of God, then our own power to recover, working hard, working together.

There are far bigger troubles than a teenage pregnancy. He knows that. Of course, he does. And yet it's just so hard sometimes to see past what's right in front of you.

*

It's only four o'clock but it's already dark, and Steve already has the headphones on. The wailing of the opera singers is so loud Leila can hear them pouring out of there, even from across the room.

A glass of bourbon too. Just one more, he says. Why not? It's Monday. Our weekend!

Leila will make dinner, but she just doesn't care about food. How can you care about food, every single damn day she has to care about food.

And Steve can just sit there. He needs a day off, he says. Thank god it's Monday. Well, Leila needs a day off too.

It's supposed to be reasonable. Wine with dinner. That lasted a few weeks, if that. Now she can see the level in the bottle going down, day after day.

Reasonable, he says, you mean like your way? It has to be your way, is that what you're saying?

Sophie will come in and he'll be all laughter, all fun.

How was your lesson, Pumpkin? And she'll want to show him what she learned, finally coming out of her shell a little.

He'll help her find a song to play for that wedding. He'll ask Jenny Rose her opinion, humming a little love tune—how about this, what do you think?

He doesn't ask Leila. He doesn't suggest the songs they played at their own wedding, which they picked out together, before they had any idea what they were getting into.

Leila bangs the pots and pans not because she's trying to but because she's not trying not to. They make noise, so what.

If they had snow everyone would be happier. The few hours of daylight would be twice as bright, reflecting off the white ground, and they'd be busy. They'd be taking reservations, making money.

Not enough for college, never enough for college, but something.

And Steve's there pissing it away, and his health along with it. What will they do when Sophie goes to college and it's just the two of them again?

It's only Monday. He can drink on Monday and Tuesday and that's it. She can take it for two days a week, she just needs to let it go, stop making it out to be a big deal.

She's heard from Jeanne that even people around here are getting hooked on pain pills, stuff they take for backaches and football injuries, just regular things like that.

It's not just the meth heads anymore, she says. Not just the LeBeaus. Just regular people and suddenly they're hooked.

Yes, it could be a lot worse. Steve works hard, he deserves to relax. They're keeping Sophie safe, giving her a good life. Leila needs to lighten up.

She just needs to think about dinner and how good it will smell when she adds the coconut milk. How Sophie loves Thai food, something they can never have at the inn.

And she'll have a glass of wine. She can certainly do that. Wine will help change the weather, take the edge off.

Steve needs everything louder, more intoxicating. Not just some nice music in the background, but opera music in headphones, to block everything out.

To block out Leila, who doesn't get it. Who never responds to music the way he and Sophie do.

Tears streaming down his face. Fuck me, this is just so beautiful, he says when he finally takes them off.

Unless he falls asleep in the chair, in which case, Leila will wake him. Come to bed. Come on, Steve.

She'll still recognize him in there, in the eyes, and he'll say, I'm sorry, I'm sorry, Leila.

But first the laughter, too loud. Not eating the dinner she made. Not hungry, why do you bother? Don't make dinner if you don't want to, he says.

But Leila knows Sophie loves Thai food. And if they don't sit together in the kitchen and eat it Sophie will know something is wrong.

If it would just snow then they'd be too busy for this. Or if Honey was having her wedding here, they could be busy with that.

But nobody wants to come to Vermont when it's dull and dark at 4:00 p.m., no light till late the next morning.

No wonder people are getting into pills. Or drinking. It's the weather. Russians have their vodka, and Americans have their pharmacies. Their doctors and their refills.

One more week and then it will turn around again. Reverse course. Sunset will be one minute later, then two.

She sets the candelabra on the kitchen table, a wedding gift from old friends, and lights the three candles.

What's the occasion? Sophie will ask.

Darkness, she'll say. Darkness is the occasion.

10

Every time someone opens the door they bring a draft with them, making the silver and gold garlands flutter above the Priority Mail display.

"Big snow coming Wednesday," Leonard says when he comes up to the counter with his slip.

All day they've been doing it. They come up to the counter, lay their package slip down, and say it: big snow coming.

And Jeanne says, "I'll believe it when I see it."

She lost interest after the fourth or fifth time, but it's better than just "I'll take this, give me that."

She hands Leonard his box. Sierra Trading Post, the package says in about a hundred different ways. "What, the old Rack & Reel not good enough for you anymore?"

"Rack & Reel's fine, but this place has better prices, better stuff."

"Hmph. Well. I hope you got me something good," she says. "Or is that something for your girlfriend? I see she's up and walking again. Walked past here just yesterday."

"If I had a girlfriend, I'd be sure to get her something good, but probably not one of these," he says.

"Why, what is it, some kind of new fly rod?"

"How'd you guess?"

"Oh, just my women's intuition," she says, though by now Jeanne knows her package shapes.

"I suppose you've heard all about the latest from the LeBeaus," she says. "Old hay shed burned down overnight, straight to the ground."

"Oh, I heard about that. Probably just trying to warm the place up with a little campfire. They're not too smart, you know. Or maybe it was part of the plan to scare the neighbors."

"Police log didn't give any reason."

"Police log never does," he says.

He takes the box under his arm, makes ready to go. "But don't you go worrying about LeBeaus. They'll always be up to no good, and nothing's going to change them. Just enjoy your snow day when it finally comes. It's going to be a big one!"

"Oh, you know the feds don't close for anything."

"What the feds don't know can't hurt them," he says. "Take a day off. Take your old man out skiing, he'd like that."

"You have a good day, too, Len."

She let him off too easy about Nell Castleton. So many other things she could have pulled out of him, if she'd been quick enough.

Don's filled her in some already, about how Len's been helping Nell out with the house since her fall. Reason enough to keep his beard trimmed, it seems.

If he wants a woman there are plenty of better ones Jeanne could recommend, women with more get-up-and-go.

Of course a guy like Len's probably had his share of lady friends. Charming guy like that, steady income. Why not Jenny Rose? She's still single, and still looking.

Then again, Len's probably no peach. Don says he cleans up the kitchen about once a month, if that. You just walk into the place and you know no woman would ever live there.

Still, he's a decent guy. Some people are just not the domestic type, meant to be bachelors.

Jeanne shouldn't judge Nell any different. It's fine if a guy like Len lives alone, doesn't help out at the town-wide tag-sale, but for a woman it just seems weird. And selfish.

That's double standards, though, isn't it?

Jeanne's always been a feminist, since day one, but maybe Danny's right.

You're out of touch, Mom, he's always saying. Though it usually has more to do with computers. All anyone really cares about these days is getting on the computer.

Online they have better prices, better stuff. Even Len said so. So where does that leave the old Rack & Reel?

Well, it's good for the old P.O. at least. And what's good for the P.O. is good for Jeanne.

*

They've finally come into the barn where it's a little warmer than outside, though they can still see their breath.

"We've talked more today than we did all summer," Honey says, and it's true. Over the summer they were too busy with other things. They never had enough time.

"We're doing everything backwards, I guess," Will says. He finally got back from school yesterday and last night had dinner with her parents, everyone on their best behavior.

Her dad drove him home afterward, after Will gave Honey a good-night kiss at the door. It was like a first date, quick and chaste.

But the dreams he had afterward keep coming back to him today, that feeling of frustration and shame, of kissing her in rooms he's never seen, getting caught, but doing it again over and over.

He feels like they were together all night, that she was there with him, guilty and desperate but together. It's confusing now, how separate she is from him.

"I wouldn't change anything about last summer," she says. "Backwards or not." She moves some crates of jars off a long wooden bench next to the honey vats.

"Here, have a seat," she says. "Welcome to my elf kingdom!"

She's been making fun of him ever since he told her the story of Arwen from *Lord of the Rings*. How when he first saw her out at the river, he thought of the elf princess who gives up eternal life to be with her love.

Which is me, he said. And she agreed, with complete seriousness. I didn't doubt it for a minute, she said.

She's reading other books now, too, hiding them in a dresser drawer during the day. He can't believe she's never read Tolkien.

He puts an arm around her and pulls her close. It's good to sit finally, and to feel her body next to his, even if they are both wrapped in winter coats.

They've been on their feet since morning, first with Honey showing him around the property, then walking along Chubb Road so they could pass by the house they'll be moving into in January.

"I can't wait to show you New York," he says. He'd like to touch her like in his dream, make sure it's all still real, but he also wants to prove that he can wait. He'll wait as long as she wants to.

"Maybe this summer I can show you where I used to live," he says. "And we'll go to Central Park, maybe the Cloisters, I think you'll really like it up there."

"I wish I had somewhere new to show you, but you've seen all my best places already," Honey says.

"That's all right. You showed me some really great things. Like Circle Current. Which is better than New York any day!"

"Hmm," she says. "I doubt it."

"And those goats," he says. "You can't beat a yard full of goats!"

"Shut up," she says and hits him with her mittened hand.

"No, really. It's great how when you go in there they all line up, pushing to get up close to you. They're all so in love with you!"

"Yeah, well the goats are just as bad as my dad's helpers. I'm pretty tired of them."

"That's what happens, I guess, when you're the most beautiful girl any of us has ever seen."

"Not anymore," she says. "Now I look just like you!"

She pulls Will's hat off and messes up his hair, then her own. "See?"

With her hair all spikey like that she's even more perfect. To Will she is. But he knows she's had enough of that subject.

"Did you know that Strattenburg has family dorms, for students who have kids?" he says.

"So maybe we could go to college together sometime? Once I pass high school?"

"Of course—why not? We can do anything we want."

What a relief it is to finally have things settled, to be able to think for themselves. This fall every conversation was about what their parents wanted, what they didn't want.

And what a torture it was. At Thanksgiving, everyone trying to get them to change their minds—give the baby up for adoption, finish college, and on and on. Then he had to go back and finish the semester without her.

They may be young, which nobody will let them forget for even five minutes, but the two of them have been through so much together already.

He knows he has to get a job, but that won't be so bad. With a job you get off at five and then you're done, unlike school, where there's always some lab or a test to study for.

"The sun's going to set pretty soon and you're going to have to go home," Honey says. "Should we go watch?"

"Sure, okay," Will says. "It's not much colder out there than it is in here."

"Plus, it's romantic," she says. She pulls him by the hand, but he can't tell now if she's happy or sad.

Her face has so many different expressions, and he doesn't know what they all mean yet.

They cross the road to the cornfield, all cut down to stubble. Just beyond is a clear, wide view of the sky.

"Do you still have my grandmother's necklace?" she asks. "Are you wearing it?"

She'd given it to him at Thanksgiving. My most precious possession, she said, when she handed it to him, though it was just a little gold cross on a chain.

"Of course," he says. "I never take it off." And he pulls it out of his collar to show her.

"Good," she says.

"Even though the chain's always getting stuck in my chest hairs," he says, hoping she will laugh.

But she doesn't. She just says, "Then you'll think of me every time you feel a little tiny pain near your heart."

She takes his hand then and kisses him on the mouth. The first real kiss since he got back.

"I missed you so much," she says, taking a quick breath, her face cold against his.

"Me too," he says. And it's true. He's never missed anything before. Not New York, not home, not anything.

When they turn back to the sky, it's pink around the edges, even though it's only four in the afternoon. Soon he'll have to be home for dinner.

What will it be like to be with someone who's never seen a Harry Potter movie and never been to New York but who goes out in the cold for things like sunsets?

It's like they have two whole separate worlds between them. That's what he tells her. And when they put them both together it's going to be amazing. You'll see.

*

"Can't you stay a little while longer?" Sarah says. It's his third day back and she feels like she's hardly seen Will at all.

He's trying to strap his sleeping bag to his knapsack, which he's packed with a few things for overnight. He still hasn't learned to drive. Still a typical city kid that way, at least.

"Do you want to maybe try on your suit before you go?"

But he didn't want to do that either. I'll have time later, he said.

He slept till nearly ten, it's not even noon, but he's already anxious to get back down there and see her. Sarah barely saw him at all yesterday either.

Though at least he came home for dinner. It was such a relief to be together again, the three of them just talking and laughing, like they hadn't for so long.

Maybe they really have forgiven each other. Maybe the ugly words are over now.

All the things she'd said since he told them. Did you just do it in the barn, like animals, is that what happened?

She'd said other things, too, ugly and unkind. She was just trying to understand how, when, where did this happen. It was not like Will.

She'd begun to fear what else she didn't know.

I'm just trying to finish up the semester, he'd say when she called. Like you keep telling me to.

Let's try to keep it in perspective. That was Jim's favorite line. If he really loves this girl like he says he does, it will all work out. Did he really believe that?

Will stands up now and the sleeping bag wobbles off the bottom of the pack. He takes it off to start over, unwinding the bungee cords, reconfiguring.

"Well, I don't see why you have to go so soon. I could drive you, save you some time. Don't you have some planning you need to do, some job research? You'll be there all night tonight, and . . ."

"You're just trying to find a way to waylay me," he says. He's smiling, though. He knows she loves him.

Ever since he's come home, he's been exuberant, affectionate, like a little boy. It's just a little bit contagious, the way he's been singing in the shower like she's never heard him do before.

He even said I love you before he went to bed last night.

Now that she can see how happy he is, she is trying to let go a little. Like Jim says, we just have to support him now in whatever way we can.

Willoughby stands up again, and the sleeping bag stays in place. "Better," he says.

"Why do you even need that? Are you planning to sleep on the floor?"

"I'll be sleeping on the couch, actually." He smiles, maybe even blushes. "Don't say anything. They're just really old-fashioned."

"Well, I don't blame them," she says. "If she were my daughter, I wouldn't let you anywhere near her."

"A little late for that now," he says, and now he really is blushing.

Last night at dinner they talked about what next, about the little house near town that Jim found for them to rent, and finally she could see into the future a little.

Jim even suggested that maybe Will could help him out this spring, take some photos of the water-bottling plant up in Maine, before the baby comes.

As long as I can fit it in with whatever real job I get, Will said.

Sarah suggested maybe he take some courses online this spring. Why not? College is proving pretty hard for her to let go of.

Maybe we can just think of this as a gap year, he said. Lots of people take gap years.

And all three of them laughed. Not because it was funny, but because what else could they do? At least they're in it together now.

He's sliding into his jacket. "Make sure you wear your boots," she says. "It's supposed to snow tomorrow."

"Good idea," he says—another thing she hasn't heard him say to her in a very long time.

Supporting him in whatever way they can, not judging anyone, not even themselves. That's what they're doing now. If he's happy today, then today is a happy day.

If tomorrow he regrets it, they'll see him through that too.

The wedding is in ten days. Sarah has a shawl to finish. Her first attempt at something like lace.

She had to force herself do it at first. But it calmed her a little, to make this thing for Honey.

And when she showed it to Will she could tell he was happy with it too. He didn't care about the soft silk, but he could see it for what it was   a move toward acceptance, and welcome even.

Sarah kisses his soft cheek. She hands him a pair of ski gloves and watches him go down the drive.

Now that he's gone there's no reason she can't work on it all day. Maybe she will finish it in time for the wedding.

*

Nell thought she'd have at least one more day to fill the woodshed.

But the air is heavy with snow today. Imminent, and all the birds seem to know it.

Loading the woodshed by herself is tedious but she can do it. Two logs at a time, from the pile to the shed near her door.

Her hips still ache from the walk, which seems longer now than before. She had to hurry to get back before dark.

Had to bake the bread a day late. One chore at a time.

No, no, I'm all set, she said, when Leonard asked if he could help.

All day Sunday just talking, and then talking and eating the burnt bread.

What—you don't use a timer? he said when he noticed the smoke from the oven.

Nell hasn't needed a timer in years. She always just knows, or she used to.

Speaking of cremation, he said.

Speaking of dementia, she said.

And they laughed. And talked. And eventually ate the bread anyway.

Steamy and white inside. Delicious, he said, tearing off a piece. And it was true.

It was getting colder outside, and dark, and she figured the wood could wait till the morning.

It's not so bad if she moves just a couple logs at a time. Don't try to carry too many, or you just drop them, and then you have to pick them up twice.

Always the temptation to carry more—and always she drops one.

How did they sit there so long? The afternoon into evening with just bread to eat, and pickles from Leonard's sister.

She makes the best kind, he said. Three days and three nights in the sun, is how she does it. And a whole head of garlic.

Len has been here all this time, in Upper Glenville, in the valley below, and she'd barely noticed him.

His family too. So many of them, with so many years and all the things they know.

Like how it takes a bear a long time to bleed out if you don't shoot it right. The heart rate is so slow, he said. They cry too. Like humans.

You never seen a deer swim either? Leonard said. Their hollow hairs help them float. A whole family of them living on that little island near the swimming gorge. You haven't seen them?

But they're wrecking the cedars. Too many of them, hungry, with nothing else to eat.

They make good eats themselves, though. You've got to aim for the heart and lungs, he said. Shoot them right in the boiler room.

Leonard doesn't seem to mind putting things bluntly. Or asking what he wants to know.

Like, have you ever been married yourself? Marriage didn't work for me, he said.

And, what happened to your sister anyway?

An accident, she told him. But maybe not.

Permission to say the worst out loud.

About the autopsy. The other hikers, young men all gone by morning, and nobody even bothered trying to find them.

She wanted to say more, until finally she did. How she'd said no, you go, and let her sister go out alone. How it was all her fault.

And he didn't deny it. Just let the words sit there, heavy, above the kitchen table.

No wonder you never took up with a man, he said. I don't blame you. But there's more than one kind of man, you know.

And they ate the bread. The room was getting hot from the stove. Her face was growing redder, and still she wanted him to stay.

Leonard had chores to do, though. Busy day tomorrow, he said, finally getting up to go.

And all that while her woodshed stayed empty.

Not for long now, though. One small load after another and the job will be done.

She's sweating under her coat now. Old leather mittens shaggy with scraps of bark and wood splinters.

They say it heats you twice over, but it's really more than that. Chop it, stack it, move it, burn it. And then you move out the ashes.

All winter long it keeps you warm.

And in a few days the world will tilt back toward the sun, and spring will come again. The darkest day is nearly here, though winter, it seems, has barely begun.

*

There's a pot roast in the oven, with carrots and potatoes, Honey said. Mom's making her best dish just for you!

It's so stuffy in here with the cats and the fire, he can't smell a thing. But no matter, he's hungry after today in the woods, out there in the cold and the trees.

He can hear water running in the sink, the clank of pots and pans from the kitchen.

His mother would kill him for just sitting on the couch while they work, but they insisted. No, no. Relax, son, her dad said. Just a couple more loads of wood. You can help another time.

Will tries to relax. He picks up the Bible from the coffee table. A fancy one, with gold-edged pages.

Love covers a multitude of sins, Honey's father said Sunday after dinner, when the four of them sat in this room, so serious, so polite.

Peter, he said. He was quoting from the Bible, as if that would make it true.

What else is in that Bible? Peter, Paul, Luke. Honey's dad seems to know them all.

The paper is thin and sticks together. Has she really read all this?

Will has never actually considered reading the Bible. It has always seemed more like a decoration.

He'd like to know, though, if that baptism last summer was real.

They'll probably have to sort that out soon. Maybe even before the wedding. There's so much he doesn't know.

At least now they found a place to live. After Christmas he'll find a job, and they'll move into that little cottage on Chubb Road.

Shopping for their own sheets and towels. Stocking the kitchen cupboards.

He doesn't even know what she likes to eat!

But to sleep and then to wake again with her there, that's what matters.

And never to have to return to the dorms. His roommate so impressed when he told him why he wasn't coming back.

My girlfriend is pregnant and we're having a baby, he told him. Trying out the words.

Today in the woods we made love, Will says to himself now. Repeats it, while he waits, paging through the Bible.

Just to say it makes him want to do it all over again. Make love to her, his almost-wife.

She's so young but she has always seemed older to Will, much older than he is.

Her body is not young. Her body knows things he'll never know. Her breasts so tender now. Be careful, she said.

He can't think of it, not now in this room full of knickknacks and granny afghans, the cats coming and going.

In this room with her mother so near. Her father in and out of the door with wood for the stove.

But he can't think of anything else! The two of them outside in the pine needles, naked under old blankets from the barn.

Honey comes out of the kitchen to put some plates on the dining room table. She looks at him, then turns and goes.

All she has to do is look at him and his face burns. Knowing what they did today.

And she showed him her belly, how it's getting puffy, put his hand right there where she swears she's felt it kick.

His eyes already burn from dander and woodsmoke, this tiny, cluttered house. Earlier she laughed and handed him a box of tissues.

But she won't come to him on the couch tonight, she'd said earlier. Not with the way this house creaks, and with her mother still angry.

So let's do it now, right here under the trees, she said.

He thought she might be waiting till after the wedding, trying in some way to set things straight. He would've waited if that's what she wanted.

But he was even more glad not to.

While he's lying on the couch here later, he'll be thinking of her up in her room, naked under a nightgown. An old-fashioned one, probably, with lace and ribbons.

But tonight is for family. For being good, she says. Having dinner. Then breakfast in the morning. Eggs and toast.

"Last load," Mitchell says now, shutting the door tight behind him. He hangs his coat on a hook by the door. Drops his gloves on the hearth.

"Wood box is good and full now," he says.

He settles onto a rocker, puts a foot up on the dusty bricks around the stove. Honey's father, with eyes like hers. Something in the face, too, Will can see now.

"We'll all be warm when the snow flies tomorrow," he says.

And maybe he does know what they were up to today, this preacher man with his multitude of sins.

*

The skiers came a few days early. A young couple from Boston. They pulled into the lot with a Thule rack on the car, came up to the desk all flushed and happy.

I hope it's okay, the man said. We tried to call from the road but there was no service.

Of course, it's okay, Leila told them. She was glad to see them. Like a good omen before Christmas.

And an older couple from Connecticut too. Wanted to get here before the snow tomorrow, they said.

Leila and Steve now bustling to get the rooms ready. They won't have their full staff until Friday, but that's okay. Snow changes everything.

Steve's consulting with the cook. Thaw a little more of that salmon. No time to get anything fresh right now. And they'll need breakfast for these people.

The phone's been ringing all day. People booking for the weekend before the holidays. They've gone from two rooms to nearly full!

Leila is glad their "weekend" is over a little early. Everything's better when they're busy.

There's a clogged sink in the suite, which Steve will sort out while Leila freshens the rooms. Places a small vase of holly on each dresser.

She is calm with work. Untroubled when she has a plan, a Swiffer in her hand, a skirt hanging in the office for later.

And when Sophie gets home from school, she can pitch in if they need her. She won't want to, but she'll do it.

She'll bring her homework and sit at the front desk. That's her life. Part of the family business, it could be worse.

It could be milking cows, 4:00 a.m., day after day, and delivering calves. Families do that too. Kids Sophie knows at school.

How do these people from the city change their work schedules around a forecast for snow? They were going to come for the weekend, and now here they are on a Tuesday night.

Just like that. Such freedom. Even before Birches, Leila never had such freedom. Though she's never had cows either.

She feeds off their energy, a little. The excitement over the weather. Their bright faces as they sit in the bar waiting.

These people want to be where she lives. They've come a long way just to be where Leila wakes up every day.

She needs to keep that in mind. She is lucky. When she's busy, she and Steve each doing their part, it's easy to see that.

*

"What's this?" Sarah says. Jim hands her a bottle of the local wine she likes, but she doesn't light up the way he hoped.

He only meant to stop in and chat with Ernie, but when he saw the wine there he had to buy it.

"How can you not love a general store that stocks bait, Campbell's soup, and a twenty-dollar bottle of wine? To go with dinner," he says. "Calm you down."

"I am calm," she says, but she keeps opening the lid on the rice.

"He's out who knows where every night while he's at college," he says, "then he comes home and you worry."

"It's different when he's home," she says.

"It's different when he's with a girl," Jim says. "Even if she is his *betrothed*."

She turns off the rice. Stirs a pot of greens on the stove. "I know. But he just got home, I didn't want him to leave again already."

Jim puts his arms around her. He wishes she would relax. Ever since the pregnancy she's been agitated like this.

She works on that loom, which is usually so meditative, but he can see she gets frustrated whenever she makes a little mistake.

He burrows his nose in her hair, which smells like woodsmoke, and her ears smell like the winter cold, but Sarah just turns back to the stove.

If they could just take their clothes off and dispense with all this stirring of pots, things would turn around quicker, they always do.

At first when Will left they had sex almost every day, but for the past few days it's as if she leaves the room every time Will does. She's not really here.

And she has dinner going. They have to eat it. And then after dinner they'll be tired, especially if they drink this wine.

Which is the not effect wine used to have, not the effect he's going for, but he still tries.

Then he remembers the gift he bought for Will and Honey in Maine. He was going to save it for Christmas, but why wait?

"Hang on a second," he says. "I want to show you something."

He goes to the bedroom and comes back with the heavy box he's been hiding under the bed.

"I got them a kind of housewarming gift."

She opens the box, lifts out the wall-mount weather station. Thermometer, hygrometer, barometer, all in a row. An antique, handsomely made.

"It's their very own weather station," he says. "I found it in a general store up in Maine, just hanging on the wall. For sale—can you believe it?"

"Is this for them or for you?" she says, but at least she's laughing, like he hoped she would.

"See here. The barometer is between 'change' and 'stormy,' on account of the snow coming. It works!"

"I wouldn't mind 'very fair' at this point," she says. "But it's a nice present. Very grown up. I still think of them as kids sneaking out of their rooms at night."

"Believe me, I do too, but we can try to treat them like adults, anyway."

He wraps it back up. He really would like to get something like it for himself, but he wanted a special gift for Will and Honey, something you couldn't get just anywhere.

Maybe he's also trying to introduce some basic science into their life from the get-go. Take a preemptive stand against whatever crucifixes and things the girl is likely to bring with her.

"It will be beautiful with the snow," Sarah says. "Finally brighten things up around here."

"In time for Christmas, too," he says. "And the wedding."

"As long as it clears in time for our parents to fly in here."

"It'll probably be cleared the same day. They know how to deal with snow here, it's not like the city."

Jim sets two plates on the table, some silverware, and sips the wine. All wine is pretty much the same to him, but it's nice there's a local wine that pleases her.

They still haven't covered the big glass doors, and he can see large flakes falling in the light that spills out onto the deck. It's starting early.

Sarah comes to the door, and they stand and watch together.

Her hand is warm when she slides it under his sweater and holds him by the waist. He remembers when they first got together, how much fun it was just to be in the same room.

How when they first saw each other across the meditation hall something sparked. Visions of the two of them taking it further than anyone else in the whole place, as far as India, together.

Will and Honey are in that phase now. A kind of giddiness, with no basis in reality.

Jim only hopes they still like each other after they grow up.

There's no way his own son will get caught up in the family's religion. Leaving everything up to God's will instead of trying to do something about whatever crisis is on the horizon.

But what will they have to talk about?

Jim looks back at the stove. The burners are off. The roasted chicken is cooling on a rack.

He reaches for Sarah's face and kisses her. She responds softly. Then harder. He thinks he tastes blood, but it is probably just that good local wine.

11

It's dim, and still early morning, but Nell can tell by the silence that it has snowed.

It may even have snowed a lot already, though it wasn't supposed to start until later today.

She's not sure till she climbs down the ladder. One foot then two, one rung at a time. Just how it fell, one flake at a time, then faster.

She looks out the window, and there it is—the first snow, so much of it, and so beautiful!

When she opens the door she sees it's still falling gently, and the ground is completely covered. A foot already. Maybe more.

She slips rain pants over flannel pajamas. A parka over her morning sweater. Boots over the wool socks she slept in.

Just for a few minutes then she'll come in for tea and toast. Then she'll shovel a path, soon, but not yet.

Even without tea, and just minutes from sleep, she's wide awake this morning. Because the world is new today, because of the snow!

A thrill in her whole body, stepping out into the bright white world. The first snow can be magic like this, if you let it.

Like when they were kids and they'd stay outside all day, plunging into it, digging and building, or sledding out by the frozen river.

She's sure Leonard must be out in it now, too, just like he would have been then, sledding with his brothers, his father, too, before his father forgot who he was.

So many first snows have come and gone since then. So many times Nell has felt that magic edge in but then shut it out.

She'd clear the car, get to work. Snow was just trouble. But not today. Today she can feel it, her heart opening up.

It really feels that way—like an opening, with light pouring in.

The snow is piled high over the garden, smoothing everything into soft mounds—the stone wall, the car, the trellis, all like perfect little igloos.

Like that snow fort they built one winter when Laura was back from college. She brought peppermint schnapps and the two of them sat in there, warm and protected and laughing.

Nell had forgotten, but the snow remembers, the smell of it, the piles inviting her to play, to fall into their feather pillows.

To fall into joy, however it comes, and to stay with it—she can do that too. Today. She can stay here with it.

There's Laura in a stocking cap. Her face bright with cold, handing Nell the minty green bottle.

There's Mom at the door, calling them in for hot chocolate, everyone in town in their hats and mittens, the children up in the mountains, too, everyone caught in that thrill of the first big snow.

Nell's heart is bursting wide now as the snow falls like down from the comforter of the sky.

Or maybe it's not her heart so much as it is her lungs, opening wider, letting in more air, filling her with oxygen and light.

She holds out a hand and catches the flakes as they fall. She lifts her face and feels the tiny snowflakes dot her skin.

When it stops, when the sun comes out, everything will sparkle.

Len will drive up with his plow in polarized sunglasses, bringing who knows what this time. Snowshoes maybe.

There will be skiers in the woods, making their thin, elegant tracks, and a bus will make its way up Mountain Road, taking kids to the Bowl.

But not yet.

For now the animals are still hiding. Squirrels in their nests, snakes buried deep in the ground, waiting for warmth, their hearts slowed to nearly nothing.

And for now Nell can plunge forward alone in pajamas and boots. She is that girl with mittens covered in balls of ice. She is with her sister in the fort, sipping schnapps.

And she can have this now, too, this perfect first day of snow.

She breathes it in and presses forward through the drifts, her footsteps hardly making a mark.

*

For the third time in the last hour or so, Jeanne sees the staties with their lights flashing, pausing at the stoplight, going through.

Maybe they're onto Jeff LeBeau finally. Comes back here with his druggie friends, thinks nobody will notice he's got money but no job.

But why would they come out just after a snow like this? The roads are barely cleared, and more is supposed to come down tonight.

It makes her anxious, seeing the lights flashing like that. The third time today already.

Maybe she should've stayed home. Taken a snow day, like the schools did. Gone out for a ski with Don.

But she's always so duty-bound. Just like her old Subaru, no matter the weather she starts up and off she goes.

A couple kids come in and drip all over the floor. Cheeks ruddy from playing. You're the only place open on the block!

Their moms probably at home saying, I don't know, just go out there and do something. Go to the post office, for Pete's sake! Pick up the mail.

If any adults come in she can ask what's up with the staties. Though more likely they'll be asking her.

Leonard might know. He gets his coffee at Ernie's after lunch. Fills his thermos before coming to check his mail.

Jeanne empties the recycling, sweeps the floor. She can't just stand around with all those troopers passing by.

The broom slips right over all the little sticky things from the books of stamps. Their jagged edges gunk up every surface, turning black.

They don't come off with a fingernail either. Jeanne goes back to find the Goo Gone. Turns on the radio while she's at it, not that she expects any real news.

It's just "Jingle Bell Rock" again. Of course! Only today it's not only annoying but it feels downright sinister.

*

A snow day is exactly what she needed. A whole day to herself, socked in, alone in her room.

The guests are out skiing, Megan's taking care of the front desk, and there's nothing Sophie has to do right now but practice.

Honey's mom finally put her foot down. She wants this hymn and Sophie will do it. There's no more time to waste.

She plays the opening four chords over and over again, getting nowhere, just trying to make perfect something she committed to.

"Abide with Me" is a little churchy, Dad said. But just think of it metaphorically.

It's a little obvious, too, but don't worry, even Ella Fitzgerald sang it. And sometimes the obvious choices turn out to be the best ones.

In that case it's too bad she can't play the Pachelbel Canon. She's heard it a hundred times at weddings and yet every time it draws up and up on some cord in her. Up and out the top of her head.

She wants to be able to make people feel that when she sings. That's what she was hoping, but probably not with this song, this hymn, the only thing they approved of.

She'll just have to be satisfied with playing competently, singing on key. It's hard enough to do that.

Which is why she needs this snow day. She needs a whole week of snow days.

She's terrified, is the thing. To get up there and sing, all alone.

And yet, if Sophie is terrified of this, what must it be like for Honey? In six months, five now, giving birth, her body ripped apart.

If Honey can live with all that, then Sophie can at least live with the terror of singing in front of people. She has no choice now anyway. She promised.

Everyone will be there, half the town, people from New York. And what will they see? A local girl, one of Honey's friends, how nice that she has such good friends. Talented too. That's what she wants.

She tries again. From the top.

Abide with me . . . fast falls the eventide . . .

What does that have to do with love and marriage?

And now a knock on the door. "Sorry to interrupt, Soph."

It's Mom. What does she want? She must've heard Sophie fumbling around just then, off key. She doesn't want anyone to hear her when she hasn't got it right, not even Mom.

"We need some help," she says. "The state police are here. More are coming. We need to get hot coffee and sandwiches for them. It's a search and rescue."

*

Nell hears a truck, Leonard's truck, and looks out the kitchen window to make sure.

The plow's attached, but he turns off the engine, and Helga bounds to the front door, like a porpoise through waves of snow.

Nell pats down her hair. Takes a quick look around the kitchen. Why is he here now? It's nearly dark, and she was just going to have some bread and cheese and read her book, go to bed early.

She opens the door just as he's about to knock.

"Oh, thank god," he says.

"What?"

"I thought maybe it was you. The search and rescue. Just came to make sure."

"What search and rescue?"

"You haven't seen the guys in the orange vests? The dogs?"

"No, no, I haven't. Is it a hiker? Who is it?"

She tries to think who it might be but can't help turning over instead the fact that Leonard is here, on a Wednesday evening, nearly dark.

"You didn't answer the phone," he says, "so I just came to make sure."

The cold air hovers around him as he stands in the doorway. It had been so peaceful and quiet, with the snow out there and the warmth in here, but that's gone now. Just like that.

It's the words "search and rescue." Park rangers, their jeep racing across those flat expanses at dawn, then stopping where she told them to. At the top of the ravine.

And it's the look on Len's face, not his usual easy smile. It's like he knows, like he sees it too.

Nells tries to run through the people she knows now. Who it might be. Christine's kids back from college. Or maybe one of the LeBeau boys?

"Could be a skier," he says, "caught in the storm early this morning."

"Well, take off your boots and come in," she says. Nell is unsteady now too. She was steady till he came. She had a good day in the snow and cold, and now by the fire.

"Maybe a homeless guy. Maybe like Little Fox," he says.

Nell remembers Little Fox. The rescue two winters ago when he'd gone out camping during a thaw that then dropped 40 degrees overnight.

They found him the next morning badly frostbitten, but alive. Even Christine heard about it, up in Kingsbury, the heroic rescue.

"Who would go out last night? We knew snow was coming."

"It wasn't supposed to come till this afternoon," Len says.

He takes off his hat, and his hair is flat and his forehead shiny with sweat. Helga shakes off the snow, standing next to him, panting.

"Looks like it's snowing again out there," she says. "You can hear the wind picking up."

"Won't be good for the search and rescue." He looks behind him at the snow falling beyond the storm door, still standing in his boots. "I wish I could help."

"Maybe tomorrow you can help."

"Probably be too late. Tomorrow."

Too late. Search and rescue. It gets under your skin. Under Len's skin, too, she can see it.

It's also the dogs. Knowing they're out there sniffing around for a person, hoping to find someone alive in a bank of snow. Or maybe not alive.

Like how they found Laura, just hours after she told the park rangers.

My sister hasn't come back, she said. She went that way. How they searched and then they found her. How the hours yawned wide open with terror.

Someone else is feeling that terror now.

Dogs will find a body. Police will call the family. And there's nothing anyone can do. No way to go back and change that one vital thing. To say, no, don't go. Stay here with me.

"Why don't you take your boots off and sit down a minute," she says. "I was just about to eat something, nothing much."

"It just gives me the chills, when they get the dogs out like that. I thought maybe it was you, up to your tricks again." He laughs a little. "But here you are, in your slippers."

"Yes, here I am, and here you are, so why don't you give me your coat. Dry it off by the stove."

When he came to the door he said, I just had to make sure it wasn't you.

Isn't that what he said? Nell can hardly believe it. Here he is. The terror but also the gladness.

*

David can't fathom it, what's going on.

"So what happened, when did he leave exactly? When did he go? He was supposed to stay."

"He wanted to go back home," Honey says. "He's allergic to the cats, couldn't stay on the couch all night."

David and Ruth turned in early, like always, Ruth awake and listening just long enough to make sure Honey went to bed, which she did, and not too late either.

"It wasn't supposed to snow much till today, this afternoon," Honey says. "It was only just flurries when he left."

She tells them the same thing over and over. He left last night. He said it was the cats, he said he couldn't sleep there.

She says it like she doesn't want them to think it's her fault that he left and she didn't stop him, as if that could possibly matter.

She says it like it's not a big deal, as if by pretending it's fine it will all be fine.

David just needs to know what happened. Where he is. It doesn't make sense.

"He's done it before. He's walked home from here at night before," Honey says.

"Oh, really?" Ruth says, "and when was that?"

"You should know. You're the one turned him away. You didn't even tell me he came!"

None of this matters. Nothing of the past matters. They just need to know where he is right now.

David should have woken Honey immediately when he got up and saw that Will wasn't there on the couch. He just figured he was up early, too, maybe outside walking in the snow.

But he waited, took his time over coffee with Ruth, and when Honey got up and told them he left last night it was already so late.

Honey called the house, and he wasn't there either.

If only they'd known sooner. How could she have let him go like that?

"If he's not home, maybe he went somewhere else," Honey says. She says it like she might really believe it. That's he's gone somewhere else.

There's more than a foot of snow on the ground and no trace of him. Even if he were out there, they wouldn't find him. How could they?

Honey insists on it now: He must have gone somewhere else. Up to Kingsbury to get a suit, he said he didn't like his suit. He's too smart to get lost in the woods, she says. He knows the way.

But even Ruth seems worried now. Worried he's lost and worried it's her own fault.

Neither of them thought much about it first thing this morning. Maybe they were even a little relieved. They never liked the idea of his being there for breakfast anyway.

It didn't even cross his mind that the boy might have left last night. Why would he think that?

If he had, then they would've started looking sooner.

But how could Honey let him go?

And how could Will do this to them—to all of them?

*

Sarah must've fallen asleep for a minute but it's still dark out. Why hasn't Will called? He has to call from somewhere, wherever he is.

Go home, go to bed, they told her and Jim. She was only creating a danger for herself, and for them.

Go home. Home. Is this even home?

Jim sat up with his laptop all night, the two of them on the couch facing the big black window, as if he might appear.

As if Will might send a note, like he did from school. Every day a quick email to Dad.

Jim holds on to that laptop. Refreshing, refreshing, waiting. There was no point in getting into bed, not for either of them.

Once they went to bed it would be another day and if it was another day—she can't even think of it.

The vigil is important. It must be. He could call any minute.

Maybe he got spooked about the wedding. Maybe he's on a bus now, back to Strattenburg. He must be!

He can't be out in the snow.

They would have found him by now. They know the trail he would have taken. The trail near the river back by Honey's house.

He may have gotten lost in the dark, they said, even if he knows the way. Everything's different in the dark.

They asked what Will was wearing. Sarah remembers him putting on boots, a jacket, but that's all she knows for sure.

Thank god she insisted on the boots at least.

And a down jacket, though a thin one. One of Jim's ski hats.

But why is she thinking of this? This can't matter. He can't survive in the woods in a down jacket and hat. Good boots. Can he?

He must be somewhere else.

Escaping the cats. Escaping Ruth, too, maybe. Her disapproval.

He seemed so happy. So happy just to go see her and to marry her even. It's how they got into this mess in the first place.

But maybe he and Honey had a fight.

Sarah knew something wasn't right last night. She could feel it, even with the snow falling in the light off the deck, so peaceful.

Cooking dinner and then anxious, preoccupied sex, though she didn't know why. Maybe because he was calling for them, right at that moment.

Fallen down, lying in the snow, calling out to them but nobody could hear.

No. She can't do that. She can't think that.

All day long today, they called his name, over and over. Stumbling through the snow. As soon as Sarah spoke to Honey. As soon as Honey told her he went home to sleep in his own bed.

They ran outside, to the trail. Neither of them speaking, not knowing which way to go, the snow so deep and impenetrable.

First one police car came to the house. Then another. Two men, four men, so many men.

What was he wearing? they asked. A blue down jacket. Royal blue—it took Sarah a second to remember the exact shade. Thank god they got him a good jacket.

Oh, Willoughby, please. Please call.

But nobody calls, not the police, not Honey, nobody.

The world has grown dark and silent. The wind has died. Just the occasional creak of a tree. The men might still be out there.

Sarah might lose her mind. She has lost her mind already.

You're doing more harm than good, the men said when she and Jim were trying to help, walking this way and that in the woods. Go back inside.

So hard for Jim to hear it, so hard to be useless, but the searchers have snowshoes. Orange vests. They have dogs.

If it hadn't snowed so much it would be easier to pick up his scent. That's what the man said. His scent, he said.

Ma'am, we've seen this kind of thing before. You have to let us handle it.

Yes, people can survive a night out. Depends on the clothing. Depends on whether they find shelter.

Or maybe somebody saw him on the road. Somebody picked him up to rob him, to hurt him maybe. To steal him away.

She can't bear it. No. She doesn't know what's worse. Her boy in the snow or her boy hurt somewhere else.

There was that boy who came to the door with the gun.

Maybe it was him. Maybe he had been lying in wait, watching, waiting for Will to go out the door.

Oh, god, why didn't she think of him before?

That's it. It must've been him, that kid with the gun. One of the LeBeau boys, there are so many of them up here, they never liked her.

Just a prank, they said, we know Eli, and she let it go. She didn't want trouble from anybody.

But it must be him. Any minute that boy will call. He'll want money. A ransom.

Oh, please let him call!

Maybe he was Rudy's own kid, and she'd never hired Rudy, whom Dad always called to open the camp. She never trusted those people.

Jim's eyes are closed, but she knows he's not asleep.

"Jim," she pushes on his arm. "Jim, remember when that kid dropped the rifle out on the deck?"

He opens his eyes.

"He was one of the LeBeaus, from up the road. One of Rudy's bunch."

"Do you think he has something to do with this?"

"Yes," she says. "Call the police again. Call them now."

12

Last night Leonard said he would sleep on the couch. He would not trouble her.

But Nell said no. She said the loft stays warmer, and the bed is big. It's fine, really. You'll be more comfortable.

What happened was that it was dark and had begun snowing harder. She didn't want him to go. She asked him to stay, and he did.

Up in her loft beneath the rafters, beneath the roof covered in snow.

He kissed her this morning when he got up, said he was taking Helga out. Kissed her like a husband as she lay there in her bed.

Last night she was thinking of warmth, thinking of the stranger lost in the snow. And of Laura. She wasn't thinking it would happen like this.

They lay so close. She must have known this was what she wanted, even if she told herself no.

How the body responds even if you don't think it will. They were only going to hold hands, to be a comfort to each other.

But when she turned on her side to get more comfortable, she put her face up against his shoulder.

She put her mouth near his ear, and he turned and kissed her open mouth.

She kissed him back, her body knowing before her mind knew, the way animals know. Both of them so warm under the down comforter, and both of them surprised. Or, Nell was surprised anyway.

All of it just happened, without further thought, without consideration, as if she meant to be with him all along.

And now this morning getting up is easy. There are still some embers in the stove, and the new log she places inside catches immediately.

She makes the tea. Tea for two this time.

He has taken Helga out, said he'd be right back. Kissed her on the cheek. So this is the morning after. This is what it looks like.

She's standing here, on her own feet, and she feels glad. Who cares how long it lasts?

She parts the curtains over the sink, and it's still true. His truck is still there, under a heap of fresh snow.

The sun is bright, the sky a brilliant blue, as if she knew all along that it would be.

*

Sophie can't concentrate on verbs and nouns. She's barely here. How can she be here today, and not out there, searching?

How can the sun be shining?

Preparing for the *bûche de Noël*, like every year. But first they have to sing carols in French.

At lunch they talked about it, the "missing person," like it's the news. Like it's not real.

The fake horror on people's faces in the cafeteria. Sophie can see that, behind their grim faces, they're actually thrilled that something of significance has happened for a change.

She can hear in the way they talk about him as if they knew him. They didn't know him, not the way Sophie does.

How can school still be happening right now, and how can she be here, conjugating? She should not have come today.

And yet Willoughby is not her fiancé. Not even her friend. She has no claim, so why should she be allowed to stay home?

What she feels is nothing compared to what Honey must feel.

Again, it's Honey racing ahead, Honey at the center of it all. The only other person who matters today.

Yet Sophie feels numb, cold, like her whole body is hollowed out. Maybe everybody does. They're thrilled, they're horrified, it's a kind of glee. And yet it can't be.

In life, in death, O Lord abide with me, goes the song Sophie was going to sing for them. In just ten days' time.

The song feels eerie now, prescient. How could they have known?

She will never have the chance to sing for him if he doesn't come back. She was so counting on it, she has practiced so hard. They were going to see her, finally.

How can she be worrying about that? No, she can't think of that now. Her own selfish part.

They're searching the piles of snow that have been plowed in the parking lots. They're searching for a body, Will's body.

So horrible, she can't think of it. It can't be true.

So horrible she can't not think of it.

*

A detective from the state police, the guy said he was. Mom handed Eli the phone and his heart started beating in his mouth as if he was guilty.

His hands all shaky and cold. Like ice.

But then the guy only wanted to know about the missing kid. How the hell should Eli know about Willoughby Calper?

And Mom just handed him over to them like that.

Sure, he's here. Just a minute please, she said.

Mom and Amber outside his room listening the whole time. Wanting in on his business.

He just has to look innocent. He *is* innocent! Even if his heart is beating like crazy.

He figured it was Jason they were calling about. Or Jeff. He knows something about them.

Up to their necks in shit, is what he knows. Some guy didn't get what he paid for and now someone else has to pay for it.

But the cop didn't ask about that. Asked where he was Tuesday night after 8:00 p.m.

We're calling anyone who might have a lead, he said. Sarah Calper mentioned the encounter in October.

The encounter. Is that what they call it when you go to someone's door and they don't answer, don't even offer to help an injured hunter?

Yes, he did go to the Calpers' house that once, he told him. And no, he didn't go inside. Didn't know the kid.

He saw him once in the woods behind the Mitchells', but he didn't talk to him. The kid just ran off. Nothing happened. Not with the lady and not with the kid.

And Tuesday night at 8:00 p.m. he was here, in this house, as anyone could tell them. Didn't even go out till Mom made him shovel out the car the next night, which was Wednesday.

No, the police didn't have anything on Eli.

Or Jason or Jeff either.

Thank you, the guy said. Thanks for your cooperation. That was it. That was all. What a lousy shit detective that guy is.

Eli blows on his hands, which helps a little. It's always so fucking cold in here.

"Eli?" Mom calls. "Eli, are you all right in there?"

He opens the door and Mom wraps him in a hug. Where'd this come from?

"They were just calling about Willoughby Calper," he says. "'Cause I'd met him a couple times."

"It's just so sad about that, isn't it," Mom says, and she keeps hanging on to him. Nearly smothering him.

"I wonder why they didn't call me. I'm the one met him first," Amber says. "Before anyone else, when he moved here this summer."

"Maybe that's why he ran away. To get away from gold diggers like you," Eli says.

But Amber won't even fight back. She actually looks like she cares. Why should she care about Willoughby Calper?

"Everyone only cares about this kid because he's rich," he says. "They wouldn't bother if it was you or me out there."

"Eli, stop it."

But Eli knows. He gets it.

It's why they called in search and rescue from Kingsbury. Probably call in the National Guard too while they're at it.

Call in the president of the United States. Doesn't the president care? Maybe he'll send in Air Force One.

*

Steve's on the late shift tonight, but he should be back by now, after midnight. It was slow even at the bar.

Leila pages through *Food & Beverage*, but she's too tired. She's not sure why they even get this anymore, the magazines just pile up, a whole stack of them next to her on the couch.

She waits up for him, like always. She thought he'd be back a while ago.

The girls finally went to bed at least. It's been a hard week. Sophie says she doesn't know whether to cry. She wants to cry, but is that giving up?

It doesn't matter, she told her, you cry when you feel like it.

Leila feels more upset than she should too. She doesn't know the family well. It's just so close to home—all of it.

The magazines make everything look easy, perfect. You have to stay on trend, but it's hard to care year after year. It's even harder to care today.

How can Steve stay out on a night like this, when she just wants to draw everybody close?

The girls are upstairs, they're fine. She should not be feeling annoyed or angry when someone else has lost their child.

Steve likes to stay for a drink sometimes, when all his work is done. More and more he does that.

Actually, he always he does that. He stays too late and comes home slurring and silly.

Hopefully he's not hanging around with Jenny Rose. He wouldn't do that tonight, would he, with the missing boy?

It's after midnight, but not yet closing time, not yet two.

Finally, there's the door opening in the kitchen. It slams shut. His heavy footsteps.

"Leila!" he calls, and she goes cold. Something is wrong. She knows it immediately.

"Leila," he says more quietly.

She sees him there, leaning on the sink, still in his coat, the black wool brushed with snow.

When he turns around his face is bright red in spots, but also gray. Everything about him seems smudged and blurry.

"What's wrong? What is it, why is your coat covered with snow?"

"I fell down. Right out there. I fell down in the snow."

He's slurring, not even trying to be funny, to distract her with boozy kisses.

"I was just walking home, and then I was on the ground. I might have passed out."

She gets him to a chair.

"I fell down," he says. "Like a drunk. I'm a drunk."

"How long were you out there?"

"Not long, I don't think. Not long. There's that boy out there, and then

I was there too. On the ground. Leila . . ."

She smells the cold off his coat, the hot and sour warmth of his breath.

He's trying so hard to be alert. Desperate to say something. And she waits.

Then his words lurch out with a sob. "I just need you to help me!"

Now he's sobbing, at the kitchen table, in his coat.

She sits down and takes his cold hands. She can't read his face but something else has happened. She feels cold now, too, a creeping in her gut. Something terrible.

"What—was it Jenny Rose?"

"Oh, Jenny Rose LeBeau, la belle dame sans merci," he slurs, tries to smile, but it's not charming. She's not amused. She waits for the rest of it.

"But no, no . . . yes. I don't know. I don't want to be with her. I want to be with you, but she . . ."

"She what?"

"She likes me. She thinks I'm funny."

Here it comes, the confession she's been dreading. But it can't be, can it? He was in the restaurant. Caleb is there, the staff.

"I'm not funny. I just wanted to be funny, charming. I want you to like me. I want everyone to like me."

"But did you . . . did she?"

"No, it was nothing. Nothing . . . but she likes me, she wants to, I don't . . . I just want to be with you. I've only ever wanted to be with you."

Relief washes over her. Warmth.

"And now I'm just a drunk."

She still has his hands, they're at the kitchen table, it's not too late.

"What if I hadn't gotten up?"

"But you did get up. And I would have come for you."

"Randy cut me off. My own bartender. Jenny Rose said one more for the road. I had just one more. It's too much."

His hands are still cold inside hers. His face is slack like his words are slack.

"I'm just an alcoholic. That's all I am. I wanted the girls to be proud of me. I'm so proud of Sophie, and Megan, and you, but . . . I need you to help me."

"I will," Leila says. "It's going to be okay."

She pulls the conviction out from somewhere. She didn't even know she had it, but it feels good.

"I can't do this anymore. I'll die like this."

"I can help you," she says. And she will. Now that she has her orders she knows that she can march.

*

David knows it's good for the trees, for the animals, too, to have snow cover. Good for the birches and maples. But why this year? Why that night?

Honey really should get out of bed, get outside. The sun is rising pink. It's cold as hell out there but it would be good for her.

Last night David went in to say good night, sat on the edge of her bed for a while without either of them talking.

Four days and four nights now he has prayed for Will to return, but last night he only wanted it to be over.

Maybe this is how it happens. You want it to be over, so you stop praying and start wishing another life away.

Then it's set into motion. Some kind of plague. Colony collapse. Like the drugs that are so easy to get ahold of these days, the young ones losing their way.

There's nothing to do but pray, even as you watch and wait for everything to be destroyed.

He can't sit around guessing what the bigger plan is, thinking he knows better. He just has to bear whatever comes his way.

When He has tested me, I will come forth as gold.

He will get Honey up and out, right now. Four days and four nights is long enough to stay inside.

It's Sunday morning, Christmas Eve, she needs her church and her people. Needs to know they're here for her.

David needs it too. People will give them those hangdog looks but nobody will say much. What would they say?

Good luck? God bless? They didn't say much when they found out about the pregnancy and the wedding, and they won't say much now.

He drinks his coffee and looks out the same window as always. A way to say yes to another day. Yes, here I come.

The sun is coming up, making the clouds all rosy. Dark blue, gray, pink.

This is the holiest part of the day, no matter what anyone says.

And Honey needs to be here for this too. Not lying in bed where she'll start feeling sorry for herself. Blaming herself.

He goes quietly, up the stairs, missing precious minutes of sunrise himself. And when he eases open her door, it's all shadows, a closed-in smell.

The smell of grief maybe, and private things.

She's been saying that she's feeling dizzy. Says she can feel the baby crying in there, though she doesn't cry. She just lies in bed letting the hours pass.

"Honey," he says. He sits on the edge of the bed.

He rubs her shoulder. "Come on."

"Why?"

He wants her to hurry but takes it slow, coaxing her out of bed, then leading her down the stairs into the kitchen.

The place hasn't warmed up yet but that's okay. That's part of the morning's character, too, how it wakes you up.

She hasn't been out yet in this beautiful snow. Before she never would have missed the chance to go out in snow like this.

He takes her jacket from the hook, but it looks so small. Just weeks ago she was a little girl who wore this jacket.

"Here, take this," he says. He gives her his own parka instead. Brown and thick with down.

Wraps it around her like a sleeping bag and zips it up. She just stands there, her hands disappearing into the sleeves.

He guides her feet into her boots and kneels to tie them. Ties his own and throws on the barn jacket.

And then there they are, the two of them, on the edge of the white field with the sun casting its light.

"There, Honey," he says.

"Say a prayer," he says. "God is listening for you."

She just stands and stares, but he knows she can't help but see it and feel the cold. The big sky and the pink light on the white field cluttered with hives.

Bees in there, warm and snug for the winter, keeping each other warm just like they should, like they always have.

Hundreds of them will die this winter of natural causes. It's not a plague, just part of the deal.

Which of course doesn't mean the plague won't come. You can't see it. Even if you're watching close, you can miss the important things sometimes.

Snow has drifted among the hives, and it's blue and gray like the sky. A day beginning. Another day and Honey is here in it with him.

This is what you get. This is what God gave you. You must be grateful for it.

And he is. But mostly he's grateful for Honey, right here beside him, her baby, too, so tiny and yet so present.

The baby's there in everything she does. In the way she holds a protective hand against her middle even when she's barely awake. In the new slowness of her movements.

What she's thinking, he has no idea, and it doesn't matter.

All she needs to do right now is stand here. Stand here for another minute in the cold.

And later to go to church with her family.

Today they will find him. They just have to.

*

Nothing helps, not the tears, not the words meant to comfort, not her own mother, come to stay a while.

It's like Sarah is whipped from one thing to the next, from tears to anger to madness, and none of it makes sense. Her mother only makes it worse.

She should be a comfort, but she's not, she just weighs down the passage of time with expectation, watchfulness, judgment even.

When she was a child Sarah must have gone to her mother for hugs, to wipe away tears, but she can't remember that now.

She has taken over the guest room but also the kitchen. She's always in there now.

"Did you eat anything today?" she asks when Sarah comes in for a glass of water.

Sarah shakes her head and leaves without the water she came for. Goes out to the living room with its torturous window that only looks out on bleakness.

Tomorrow is Christmas and then Saturday should be the wedding. She ordered the cake, but she won't cancel it. Not yet.

Jim is no comfort either. He asked her this morning if she'd like him to get a tree.

Why would she want a Christmas tree? For what?

She shouldn't have shouted at him, though. Her mother gave her a look, surprised, it seemed, that Sarah could be so cruel.

Don't take it out on your husband, she said. Mom, who's never been one to stand up for Sarah's husband.

The man from the hippie retreat, she used to call him, and later "the environmentalist," as if it was something he should outgrow.

It seemed she could only really love Sarah when she was still moldable, a small child, cute and under her thumb. It stopped as soon as Sarah grew awkward and ugly and started talking back.

Maybe Sarah did the same to Will. This fall, so angry and disappointed in him.

But she'd always been there for him, hadn't she? She might've wanted him to be more assertive, stand straighter, be more focused, have some genius for something, but she always loved him.

She was a good mother to him, most of the time, enough of the time. He knew she loved him, no matter what.

He only wanted to get away from the cats, from his allergies. He only wanted to come home.

Or else someone has taken him. Pulled him into a car and taken him somewhere. She can't think how or why.

Or he has run back to the city, or back to Strattenburg, on the bus. Why can't anyone find him?

She can hear the chopping, smell the onions filling the house as her mother drops them into the pan. You need to keep your strength up, she says.

Her mother hasn't made anything from scratch in probably decades. Even she is doing her best.

Except for the hours out searching in the snow, Sarah hasn't left the house since Tuesday. She only wants to curl up in a cave and die.

Jim has gone out into the woods again. He's always out there walking, or going somewhere, looking for an errand to do. Sarah knows he's looking for Willoughby.

He drove Mother down to the grocery store earlier for carrots, celery.

There are missing person posters there at the Shaw's now, he said. Everywhere you go you see his face.

She gave the police the photo from their end-of-summer hike up at Mount Jerryfield. She cut Jim out of the picture, cut out herself.

It was her favorite photo, framed on the dresser since the day he went to Strattenburg. But it will always be the missing person face now.

She can't stand it, the smell of onions in oil, the start of the healing soup.

Sarah knows she should go in there and be with her mother, but she can't.

She can't stay here in the living room either. There's nowhere to go. No matter where she goes she's trapped, even in sleep.

She already called the police chief this morning. She calls him every day. What else can she do?

The dogs have been called off, he said. The dogs who know her son's scent from the clothes she gave to them. He's not in the woods. They would have found him.

They've dug through piles of snow plowed from the roads and dumped by the river.

They've had farmers search their fields. Even by air, in helicopters with infrared heat technology.

We won't be able to dredge the river till spring, the chief said. Too cold, too fast, not safe for divers.

Infrared heat. Divers. Dredging. None of this can have anything to do with Will.

If only he would call! She would forgive him anything. If he wanted to get away he should have said so, even after all the plans were made. It would not have been too late.

They would've done anything to get him out of it if that's what he wanted. The number of times they said to him, it doesn't have to be this way. There are other choices.

She and Jim can barely look at each other. He blames her, she is sure.

Just as she blames him. And Ruth. And Honey. And mostly herself, for all the ways she failed to keep him safe.

She prays to the universe, as if one child in the universe might matter.

To the trees, she hears her own voice begging, please. Please let him return. She sees the squirrels out there, running across the snow.

Crows call across the empty sky, an urgent message but not for her. For her only silence.

The loom sits there with its white threads hanging off like a shroud.

That's what it will be for me. I'll finish it and will wear it until he returns.

The sun is out now, and icicles drip from the corner of the woodshed. Blue sky peeking out from behind the clouds.

How dare it. How dare the sun shine down on the world, down into these woods, if my boy isn't here.

Jim leaves his coffee cups in the sink, hasn't changed his clothes, and she doesn't care.

Their bed forever unmade, while Will's remains empty. The blanket folded exactly how he left it. His duffel bag still full of laundry.

He could be anywhere, Mother says. Could have been kidnapped. People around here see you and they only see money.

She wants to hire some professionals from Boston or New York, she says. Not leave it up to these country people who don't know how to look beyond their own backyard.

But a private detective wouldn't know this place. Wouldn't be able to read the icy trails and the blank faces of these locals any better than Sarah can.

*

It's nearly noon, on Saturday the 29th of December, and the kitchen smells like butter and sugar.

By now Sophie would have finished singing and they would all be eating wedding cake in the fellowship hall.

This is the first day Sophie will not practice the song, because today is first day she knows for absolutely certain that the wedding will not happen.

Instead it's just the Saturday after Christmas and she's baking a coffee cake.

It's a small thing, but Mom said it was a good idea. They need to eat. It will feel good to do something

Twenty more minutes in the oven now, and then Amber will be here, and they'll go.

Sophie turns on the oven light so she can see the cake baking inside. She used to love to sit on the floor in front of the oven and watch things bake.

She sits there now, looks into the hazy yellow glow, but it just feels childish.

Maybe this is how you become an adult. All the magic goes away, and not even Christmas can protect you.

Christmas used to be a day so different from every other day, as if cast in a spell. Nothing could touch it.

This year they did everything the same as before, gifts around the tree and music on the stereo all day long, but it still felt just like a day among many.

She would forget about Will for a minute or two, but then it would all come back, breaking over her like cold water.

It's like there's some other, more frightening world right next to hers, she can barely see it, but it's so close it might swallow her up.

Mom told her to call Honey. It's supposed to be her wedding today, why don't you call her?

Sophie was so nervous she had to rehearse over and over what she'd say.

Hello, this is Sophie, may I speak to Honey, please? Or should she say "Dorothy"? Her parents are trying to call her that. Or they were.

Hello, this is Sophie. How are you, Mr. Mitchell? What a question.

Just call her, Mom said. There's no right thing to say right now but you won't be wrong either.

She doesn't want to talk on the phone, Mr. Mitchell said, but it might be nice for her to see you. Yes, why don't you come over.

At least Amber will go with her. Together they can make some kind of conversation.

Not about the wedding, which is canceled, obviously. Not about Will. But about what—school? Christmas?

Maybe Honey will want to talk. Maybe she'll talk and they'll just listen. Sometimes you just have to listen, Mom said.

Sophie could do that. Or more likely Amber will think of something to say.

Amber has a way of just asking the questions everybody has but won't say.

Like, will she still marry him, if he does come back? Won't she be so angry?

They just have to believe there's a chance he'll come back, and yet Sophie can't think how or why.

She feels older today. Like she will be different after this, no matter what happens in the end.

But if Sophie will be older, Honey will be much older still. Honey has already crossed over. It happened last August when she got pregnant.

Sophie wraps her arms around her knees and watches the sugar brown and bubble as the cake rises.

She will not practice that song today, not to herself, not to anyone, but it plays in her mind, over and over.

O thou who changest not, abide with me.

It's the kind of thing that brings people comfort in times like this. But not Sophie.

To her it's just another failure. Her own chance at becoming something new, at being something more than Honey's quiet friend, has been canceled.

And yet it is too selfish to feel sorry for herself, even for a minute.

She'll just sit here in this warmth until Amber arrives, then they'll walk up that long driveway, into Honey's house.

That house was once so familiar, but now it feels both terrifying and unknown. A place Sophie no longer belongs.

*

Cyrus coughs as soon as he takes a breath, it's that cold. Freezes your nose hairs.

But what he really wants is that first draw from the cigarette. Wants it enough to go out in this frigid air that burns your fingers when you take a glove off.

His boots squeak when he walks on the porch, like Styrofoam.

He pushes through the crusty snow toward the sugar shack. You can tell someone's been back there since the first snow, but not for a while now.

It might be a little warmer in there, though probably not.

No wonder people called in sick at the Bowl for tomorrow. Supposed to be cold like this for the whole week.

Sure, yes, of course I'll come in for New Year's Day, he said. If he's going to train to be a snowcat operator, he better get used to it.

The cold, the hours, the holidays. And the holiday pay. He could definitely get used to the holiday pay.

It will be much better than community college. It just takes one safety course and a CDL, then you're free up there, driving over the mountains in a warm cab. As long as there's snow, anyway.

The smoke vanishes as soon as he exhales. It's like the cold just snaps it right up.

Cyrus used to smoke so he had something to do when he took a break at Shaw's. A reason to go outside.

Now it's something he *has* to do. You have to be a real smoker to go out in weather like this.

Dad said in other places people can still smoke inside, even in restaurants. He said it was okay if Cyrus wanted to smoke inside, but that just seems wrong.

And what would be the point, if you just smoked wherever you were, right there with all the other people in the break room jawing away?

The door to the sugar shack is slightly open, a thin layer of snow on the floor. The door's so cold it creaks when he opens it. The floor creaks too.

Someone made a path to the door after the first big snow, but a few more inches fell on top of that by now.

What if that kid came in here? Wouldn't that be something, to find that kid here, frozen in the sugar shack.

It's just empty, though. No dead body. Nothing left of Cyrus's brilliant idea either. Not a trace.

At least nobody died, as far as he knows, from smoking that shit.

It can happen, though. He's heard about people smoking too much Scent they just collapse. Something stops their heart.

If he'd known that he never would've tried. Some people just don't seem to care about that kind of thing.

There's nothing here now but a few empty beer cans, probably left by Eli. He's too much of a slob to even clean up his own beer cans.

The old evaporator still sitting there, too, of course, doing nothing.

The sugar shack fills up quickly with smoke. Cyrus drops the butt into one of the empty cans. Better than dropping butts on the ground that he'll just have to pick up in the spring.

The snow will melt and there they'd be, though it's hard to imagine it'll ever be warm enough to melt all this snow.

Maybe then they'll find that kid.

Emily thinks she's seen him around, up in Kingsbury. She says he looks familiar. He might be hanging out with the homeless people up there, she says.

It's like she wants in on the story. It's like everyone wants in on it.

Everyone says they remember him. Or that they might've seen him. And maybe they did.

Eli better not have anything to do with this.

Though of course if he did they would've found out by now. He leaves his empty cans in the shack, leaves Uncle Rudy's gun.

If it was Cyrus who dropped a rifle up there Rudy would still be giving him shit, would've punished him, made him clean and oil his whole collection.

By now everyone just accepts Eli does his own thing. It basically adds up to nothing so who cares. Even Mom. Dad gave up trying to talk sense into him a long time ago.

Dad barely does anything anymore, though. He used to take on any old job. Now he just says, I've done my work, now it's your turn.

As if there's ever a turn to stop working, stop getting out and doing things.

He won't even go see a doctor. You think I'm going to go there and have someone tell me to stop eating meat, and then pay them five hundred bucks for the favor? I don't think so.

While he's got his boots on Cyrus might as well shovel the rest of the drive. Maybe bring in some wood. Nobody else is going to do it.

Maybe by next year at this time he'll be making good money on the snowcat.

Or he'll be working toward a degree at the community college. But what for? Emily's gone back to Daniel for good now, she says.

13

Jeanne's still shaking like she's seen a ghost or something. The bell's done jingling, Jim's gone, but she needs to sit down for a bit.

She pulls up the wheely chair. She picks up Jim's book, but forget it. She was only reading it 'cause she had a feeling that if she read his book she might somehow help bring his son back.

She sees that kind of thinking now for what it is. Ridiculous. Even worse than the idea of a kidnapper or something. Some kind of sexual predator come to snatch the kid away.

But she wishes she hadn't said that about the river.

It's the only place left, she said. She was trying to change the subject, maybe, after that nonsense about Will possibly being somewhere else.

Why did he have to ask in the first place? Why did he ask her, Jeanne, who doesn't know anything, barely even finished high school?

All of January, they maintained the niceties. He'd come in here, open and close that mailbox, pick up his flyers, his junk mail.

It got so she didn't mind seeing him anymore. Wasn't afraid that all the pain he carried around would rub off on her somehow.

How are you holding up? she'd ask, and he'd say, okay, and they'd talk about other things. Even the weather felt like a minefield with him, all the usual talk of snow, but they'd been doing okay, maneuvering around it.

Got so she just pitied him, like everyone pities them now. People used to just see them as out-of-towners, the type who take the good seasons and leave the rest.

But now they're just the suffering parents, as if that's all they've ever been and all they ever will be.

Today he had a different look about him, though. Haggard, like a man hung out to dry. His face was wet, too, like he was sweating from the effort of being alive.

He walked right up and leaned on the counter.

Why can't they find him, Jeanne? Why in god's name can't anybody find my son? he said.

And she just stood there. Steady. Steady as it goes, Jeanne, she said to herself. And then she said, as gently as she could, like to a child, They're doing everything they can.

She told him about Chief Cadoret going out there every day, even on his days off, and about how they got all the K9 teams across the state working for them. If he was there, they'd find him, she said.

So you think he's just gone somewhere else altogether? That's what Sarah keeps saying, that he's somewhere else altogether.

What do you mean somewhere else—like, he was kidnapped or something? Or like he ran away and forgot to call home?

That's what she said. Forgot to call home.

She regretted it right away, but that's Jeanne, always with her big mouth. And that wasn't the worst of it.

Because after that she said, No, the river's the only place left. You can't search the river till spring. Too fast, too dangerous, what with the ice.

Right, he said. And he looked away. His face still sweating but gone all white. The same person, tall and smart and confident, but not. Now he was someone else.

Thank you, he said. You're right. It doesn't make sense, that he'd be somewhere else. There's no reasonable explanation. And he wouldn't do this to us. That's what I've been thinking, but Sarah . . .

Jeanne tried to backpedal, saying something about how maybe Sarah knows, his mother must know better. Maybe Sarah's right, maybe there's some foul play, what do I know?

No. No, I don't think so, he said. Thank you. For being honest and not just saying things to make me feel better.

She would have, though, she would gladly have said something to make him feel better if she could've thought of something.

And the fact is, she wasn't even being entirely honest.

She didn't say that they usually find a missing person in the first twenty-four hours or not at all.

She didn't say they still haven't found that girl from Upper Glenville who walked off into the woods in what, 1986?

She wasn't honest and she didn't make him feel better either. So what good was she?

And now he's gone, and he left his mail on the counter and she's here alone with herself, shaking. The fact is, his pain is terrifying. She doesn't want it around.

She was okay with him coming and going, clicking open the mailbox, saying, okay, we're holding up okay.

But she never wanted to talk about the river. She never wanted to take his last hope and crush it, far-fetched as it might have been.

Jeanne picks up the book and looks at Jim's picture there again. He looks so put-together, the man who has everything. She puts it down.

What else could she have said? It was true. The only place left is the river.

She opens the front door to see if he's gone. She doesn't see his car, but there are those missing person posters again.

She'll take those down today. She'll take them down now.

It seems so long ago that she hung them up. Back when there were signs for the Christmas pageant, for tree and wreath fundraisers.

Now it's just handyman signs with little tags to tear off, and a faded picture of Willoughby Calper.

She takes the tacks out of the corners, sticks them back in the corkboard, ready for the next thing.

No, we don't need these to remind us. We all have his face memorized by now anyway.

And the people here really are doing all they can. Let your New Yorkers do any better. Sarah's mother hiring the private detectives, as if their own aren't good enough for her.

In New York they wouldn't get the whole town out looking, volunteering, day after day. No, they probably have a missing person every day there, and nobody even notices.

Jim will probably never come back after what she said. His mailbox will fill up with junk, with final notices stamped in red, and soon she'll dump it in the recycling like she does for so many others.

She hopes not. He might not have had much to say, but it was good that he came in, and good for her to be the person who stood here day after day saying, How are you holding up?

That's her job, more than anything. To stand here and listen to whatever anyone wants to say.

They're not talking about the desk clerks when they say that thing about the postal service, how it doesn't stop for snow nor rain nor heat nor gloom, but it's still true.

*

When the weather warms just a little, the bees go out for fresh air. Today the sun is bright, the sky clear and blue. An early February thaw.

Everything's still frozen now, though, the snow crusted and gray where they've walked back and forth to the goat shed, back and forth to the chickens, to the barn.

In this rare bit of sun David should fix that fence finally, where the billy goat kept breaking through last summer. He should shovel the snow from around the foundation so it doesn't leak come spring.

But the warmth won't last anyway, and it's no good working with his hands outside when they're too cold to hold a hammer right.

Just excuses, but that's why it's always been better for him to go some-place warmer in winter, where the work's more urgent and he's always more than ready for it.

It's good to be outside walking around a little, though, checking things out. The dogs follow along as if he might be up to something, as if this is some kind of adventure.

He's been cooped up, having spent most of these past few weeks in the barn.

But why not? There's a good stove in there, and he might as well fix up some of the old supers, give the whole works a good cleaning.

Doesn't hurt that he can listen to hockey out of Canada. Curling even sometimes, when there's nothing else on.

He's been avoiding the house again is the truth of it. It feels like a funeral parlor in there with no lessons going on, none of the usual fighting, none of the laughter.

David hasn't seen February in Vermont in a long time. It's so gray. And all the jobs he doesn't have time for during the summer are breathing down his neck out here—the fence, the foundation.

But it's been too cold, too dark. This year there's been a good old-fashioned freeze.

People are even out fishing on the lake. Driving their trucks over it, setting up their shacks like they haven't been able to in years.

So much for your global warming, Mr. Calper! But he doesn't want to think anything ill against Jim, the poor man, even if he is on the wrong track about some things.

The river's even frozen down along Main Street. It's been a long time since that has happened.

The river used to freeze over for months at a time, and then you could hear it, come spring, breaking up again. A loud groaning and cracking sound sometime in later March or April.

Today's warmth won't be enough to put a dent in that ice. Just enough to get everything dripping. And to coax the bees out of their clusters for a little while.

They're out today, for sure. And no major damage from mice, not that he can see. The electric fence keeps the bears off, but it doesn't do anything for mice.

There are a bunch of dead bees on the ground outside the hives, but that's normal. Bees who for some reason or other left the cluster or didn't make it back in time to maintain their own heat.

Even more of them are out now, buzzing around the opening, pooping on the snow.

"Now's your chance, girls—better get out while you can," he says.

David too could use some kind of cleansing flight right about now.

But the fact is he's not going anywhere until they find out about Will. He'll want to be with Honey and Ruth. Whatever the outcome, it can't be good.

Ruth has been going easy on Honey. Giving her books about babies, *What to Expect When You're Expecting*, giving her a break on the home-school curriculum.

They should probably start it up again soon, though. He doesn't want Honey pining and mooning all day, whether over Will or over her baby.

Plus she'll need at least a high school diploma if she's going to get a job and care for that baby.

That's getting down to brass tacks for sure, and it's hard at a time like this but it's true.

Maybe that's why Honey goes off with Sarah so much. The two of them up there just wringing their hands all day long with nobody to stop them in all their sorrow and lamentation.

It's all right for now, though. It's good for her to get out of the house, and good that she's keeping that poor woman company.

Even Ruth has warmed up some toward the Calpers. Drives Honey up there sometimes, even goes into the house now and then, to offer condolences maybe, to give them a pot of soup.

In just two more months, the baby is due. God bless it, this business with Will better be over by then.

They'll have a baby to deal with either way. A real baby. It would be nice if the baby had a father, of course, but at this point he would settle for knowing one way or the other.

*

The fire is burning low and steady in the dining room for the breakfast guests, up early for skiing.

There's a nice smell, too, with the coffee going in the kitchen, pushing aside the smell of roast chicken from last night.

Leila didn't think they could do without Steve for a couple weeks, but here they are. The staff stepped in without any explanation. They just seemed to know.

He's been back two weeks already today, this Monday, without a drink, without even a complaint.

Leila's up and ready. Jenny Rose is here, too, before her regular job at the school, pitching in so Steve can go to the gym.

He was up at 5:00 a.m., dressing in T-shirt and sweats, while Leila pulled on the wool pants that she hung up last night, getting one more day out of them before cleaning.

The waistband is a little tight. She should probably be going to the gym, too, but there's no time for that.

Of course there was no time for Steve to go either, and yet he's doing it. Every morning now, driving the twenty minutes each way, no matter the weather, no matter the number of guests.

The coffee is especially good today. Hot and dense as she likes it. All the weekend reservations came and went, and just a few more will check out this morning.

Leila is ready for whatever comes. She's stronger than she thought she was.

She also can't help reminding herself that what she has to bear is so much lighter than what others have to deal with.

Not just the victims of hurricanes, of wildfires far away, as always, but others right here in Glenville.

Jenny Rose comes out of the kitchen with the coffee pot and mugs, serving the early risers, who will be heading up the mountain at sunrise.

Leila will be the first to admit how helpful Jenny Rose has been, despite how much she has to handle at home.

I'm happy for a few extra hours in the morning, she said. Saving up for a car for the kids. Jobs, school, rehearsals, you can't believe the logistics of sharing a car with those two!

The new schedule works for everyone else, so it works for Leila. She doesn't mind Jenny Rose nearly as much now that she's set her eyes on Caleb.

And why not? He's divorced, a hardworking guy with a nice laugh. The other night they were out in the parking lot together, kissing maybe, or just standing close enough to make it look that way.

Good for them. Good for everyone, really. They might as well enjoy each other while they can.

Steve will be back in an hour, fresh from the shower, with more energy than he's had since Leila can't remember when.

And he'll leave the inn early, avoiding the bar and keeping Sophie company back at the house while Leila closes the books.

She's working both early and late now, but it's worth every bit of trouble if he'll just stay sober.

They don't talk much about what happened at rehab. I couldn't get out of there fast enough, he said, and I never want to go back.

The food, the roommate, the meetings—he's just glad to be home.

A man in a wool coat makes his way over to the desk now, pulling a suitcase behind him. "Such a beautiful place you have here," he says. "Wish I could stay longer."

"Thank you," Leila says, "glad you enjoyed it."

It's what people nearly always say, oblivious, as they should be, of all they go through to keep it this way.

Oblivious too of the sorrow that hangs around in the woods outside.

"Maybe next time I'll bring the whole family," he says. "My son's looking at colleges up here."

"Definitely come back in the summer or fall," she says. "I expect we'll be here."

She smiles, but she can't help but think of Willoughby again, how he sat right there at that dining table just a couple months back. A kid on his way to college.

Even for Leila all these days of not knowing are unbearable. But she is able to forget at least for a few minutes if not a whole day.

But for Will's parents—how can they live in the anguish of not knowing?

If they knew, they could begin to mourn. Like when Steve finally said it: I'm a drunk. Then they could begin to heal.

The man picks up his suitcase and heads to the parking lot alone.

Before Leila would have felt just a twinge of wishing to go, too, to walk out the door with just one little bag to wherever he is headed.

But she feels held by her life now, wrapped in the threads of what she has maintained and will continue to maintain.

Soon Sophie will be out front, waiting for the bus, the cords of her earbuds dangling beneath her pom-pom hat.

I want to do something important, Sophie said last summer. She thinks she'll be different, and maybe she will be.

But for now Sophie's own small life is enough. The urgency of what to wear to school, how long to spend on that French paper.

She imagines that one day it will be different, grander somehow, but she has no idea how quickly everything can change and how little control she will have.

Leila's not afraid anymore of how terribly she'll miss the girls when they leave home for good. That ache, that loneliness, will be bearable, beautiful even.

Even struggling with Steve, through whatever the next seemingly impossible chapter will be. This is good, it is growth.

What she could not bear is if any of them were to be simply missing.

It really is a beautiful place they have here, and more difficult than it looks to anyone on the outside, but she'll take it.

She'll gladly stand here and smile, her cashmere sweater keeping her warm, the fire burning low, as long as her daughters are not lost in the snow.

There she is now, Sophie out at the bus stop, her hat pulled low over her ears. Just a girl on her way to high school with a bag full of books.

Leila would like to go out and wrap her arms around her, kiss the top of her head. Please don't go. Please be careful. But Sophie doesn't care for hugs anymore.

Whatever Leila can give her she already has. Sophie has what she needs now to face whatever the world is going to give her. Or she doesn't.

*

Jim skis through the woods slowly, following his own tracks. It thawed and froze over again, and more snow fell last night, but he can still find his own tracks cut through the woods. He sweats.

Willoughby looked at these same trees.

In summer when they were thick with leaves but maybe in winter too. Where the trail widens to an old logging road.

Fifty-one days now. Jim repeats that meaningless number over and over as he gets a rhythm with the skis, just as yesterday he repeated fifty.

If he didn't count, the days would just pass, each one like the other, one endless day.

He doesn't know what day of the week it is and doesn't care. It's just day fifty-one.

The days are moving faster for him now, though in fact the sun is making the days longer.

Is it possible he's getting used to this?

Skiing the backwoods to be near his boy. To be far from his wife. To be with himself. Sweating.

Back here it's all about moving forward, about not falling, not hitting a tree or a rock hidden in a drift. Not thinking or remembering.

It's beautiful back here in the woods. The snow on the hemlocks. The snow on the tall, tall pines. The pines don't care. They don't miss one more human being.

His publisher told him to take some time off. You have enough to worry about. I'm so sorry, they all say.

He's not dead, Jim wants to say. He's not dead, he's not dead, he's not dead. *Swish, swish, swish.* If he just keeps moving.

But fifty-one days now since he left. Wherever he went, wherever he could be.

The only place left is the river, Jeanne said.

They've pushed the pub date for *Rising Tides* to May. He can't promote it in the state he's in. Can't go out and do interviews.

By May they'll know. By then this needs to be over.

How many days would that be? He won't count that far. When a new day begins he's sure it will be the day they find him, and yet another day passes.

It seems impossible that he won't come home. But it also seems impossible that he will. He's stuck. Hanging here in an endless poisoned space.

Jim allows himself these woods and no farther, but to Sarah it's a sacrilege to even leave the house.

She's always there, barely eating, always waiting by the phone, by the door, hoping.

If he stops waiting, stops hoping, does that mean Will won't come?

When Jim stops, when he holds still for a moment on the trail, in the woods, he hears only the pulse of blood in his ears and the wind in the treetops. A soft wind today.

He's warm. Even his hands, sweating in his gloves. He's been gone a couple hours. Maybe there will be news when he gets back.

He moves forward again. He knows this trail leads to the river, and that's where he turns around, skis back over his own tracks.

His repetition is no different from Sarah's weaving. Her showing Honey how to weave, too, giving her a turn.

The two of them so quiet up there, with the clacking of the treadle and not much else.

No wonder, no wonder, Sarah says. If I were him, I would've loved her too. And she really loves our Will.

But Jim feels the opposite when he sees her face, her pregnant body, thirty weeks along now, in his house with his wife.

Will he and Sarah be responsible for this baby somehow, or, maybe worse, for the girl?

She's not their child. She stole their own child away from them.

Together Sarah and Honey entertain the wildest theories of where Will may have gone. You just have to believe he'll come back, they say. Don't give up hope.

Maybe that kind of thinking makes sense for a girl like Honey, raised to believe what she can't see, can't understand. Raised on the idea that God always has a plan, when in reality nature is just going to have its way with us.

But not Sarah. Sarah lives in the real world, or she used to.

"Just believe" is what people used to say about Christmas, about Santa Claus. He had a hard time with that even when he was a kid, even when it was about something that didn't matter.

In his heart he knows Will isn't coming back. And he knows there is no god with a plan. He knows it, doesn't he?

What, you think it's like a kidnapping, that kind of thing? Jeanne said.

He needs to start letting go. Or no. He needs to get away from his own head.

He needs his real home, the mountains of home, of Colorado—to just fly down the slopes, consumed by speed.

He can't do it here, not in these stingy icy mountains of Vermont. But at home.

He goes back over his tracks, back toward the house. Round and round, back and forth. Maybe when he gets back there will be news.

*

Leonard won't come today, but that's all right. Nell prefers it. To look out the window, to remember, to know he'll come back soon.

She goes about her day. She sweeps the floor.

It's okay now to wish for something, to be glad of something, of someone.

Nell used to hear his tires on the drive and pretend otherwise, but now a little happiness is allowed. She might as well, for now, just feel it.

Happiness. How long can it last?

She doesn't care about forever to have and to hold. As long as he smiles at her and kisses her face. Lies next to her in the loft and strokes her hair.

To have her hair stroked. To have a body near. And then to have him go.

It is just as good when he leaves, to be free again, and alone. There are no expectations, and nothing to hide.

He has left some of his things here. A toothbrush, an extra pair of binoculars.

Helga's water bowl, which Nell sweeps around now, tipping just a little onto the floor.

He comes twice, even three times a week. She has told him to come whenever he wants. She doesn't lock the door.

Christine looks at her funny. What's going on with Leonard Larocque? she asks.

Ed knows, but he won't say. He knows enough to let Nell have this, just for now, with no explanation.

People are always so glad when others couple up, as if it's the answer to their own loneliness. As if it confirms, somehow, that they're doing the right thing too.

This morning she found one of Leonard's T-shirts pressed between the mattress and the wall. She inhaled its smell of detergent and sweat, a smell she should not like but does.

The smell of him never leaves her bed, not entirely, not even when he does.

And Helga too. Little patches of fur on the rug where she lies all night by the fire. Tufts of fur under the sofa that fly away from the broom.

They leave parts of themselves behind for her.

Leonard was here last night and just three nights before that, though she's not counting, not really.

Or she is counting a little, so that she knows that surely he won't be here tonight. She'll get to be alone tonight, and her aloneness is better now too.

He won't come unless something happens. Like if they find the missing boy.

It's because of that boy that this even began. It was the night he got lost that Leonard drove up here, incautious. He might as well have said it aloud. You matter to me.

It was that fear, the nearness of death, that made her incautious with him too. It could have been anything, but really, it was the missing boy. Willoughby Calper.

He is most likely dead, so young, so fast.

That is what happens. People live, people die, it isn't fair, and there's not always someone to blame.

For thirty years she needed to find someone to blame, and she did her best to take it on herself.

Not today, though. Nell's done with that now.

This morning she woke up without pain, and the sun slanted through the birch trees onto the rusty patches of snow, and she was glad of it.

She wanted to be here and to remember.

Laura was much more than that one endless night and the years of darkness afterward.

Her whole lifetime was short, but it was full of days and hours, so many of them, and Nell can remember those too.

How lucky she was to have a sister like that, with her bell-bottoms and her Dutchman's britches in the woods. With her recklessness and her virginity both.

Willoughby Calper is just an absence right now, a tragedy even, but eventually he will be that ruffle-haired boy again, the one she saw last summer, lying in the sunshine on Mount Jerryfield.

He'll be whatever he was before that, too, not just the emptiness he left behind.

Nell sweeps the hair into the pan, then into the kitchen compost. Later the birds will pull it out for their nests.

It will be good for the birds to have something warm in the spring, a soft place for their eggs.

In spring, Leonard will help her with the garden. He said he could trim back some trees, let in a little more light.

*

You were aiding and abetting, Amber said, when Sophie told her about how she'd walk up to the trailhead with Honey last summer, letting her parents think they were spending the afternoon together.

But Amber was joking, wasn't she? Of course she was. Sophie was only trying to help a friend. Selflessly even. She was on the right side of this.

And yet if she hadn't helped Honey escape on those Sundays, Honey would not have gotten pregnant, and Will would not have gotten lost in the snow.

Still, what Sophie did was not a crime. It was not her fault.

She walks down the sidewalk with this man, who says to call him Rob, the private investigator Will's family called in.

They're tired of waiting. Everyone's tired of waiting. So let him try to figure out what the locals can't. Let him try.

It's not a good sign that he wears brand new Bean boots, like he's put on a costume or disguise. They won't be good on the ice. A detective should know that.

He has a little notebook. A cell phone, too, which won't work out here—he should know that too. She saw him put them in the big pockets of his coat before they left.

"So, you and Dorothy Mitchell are old friends, she tells me." He has his hands in his pockets and they're walking toward the bridge.

Sophie just nods. Friends, yes, they are, have always been, and yet she hasn't seen Honey for almost two months.

"And I hear you play music," he says. "Are you in a band or anything?"

Sophie shakes her head. "No, I just play by myself."

She really should call Honey. Why doesn't she just call her? It's been two whole months.

"Pick up the bass and you'll be the most sought-after musician in town," he says. "But I bet you play guitar, right? Singer-songwriter type thing."

Something about the way he says it makes her know she should be ashamed. And she is. Of all of it. Walking here, saying nothing, letting the Mitchells believe what wasn't true.

"Do a lot of kids come out here, on the trails, in the summer?"

Sophie nods, says, "Yeah, pretty much everyone."

"Why, what do you do there?"

She looks at him. Is this a trap? Does he want her to say something about the drugs people sometimes do up there, the fires, their jumping off the rocks?

"Just swim and hang out," she says. "There's not much else to do around here."

"Except play guitar, I guess," he says, smiling as if he's onto her. "Did Will have any other friends?"

"Not that I know of. He was only here one summer."

He's not looking for someone to blame, he said on the phone, and she told him how they'd walk up here on Sundays. How she'd leave the two of them alone.

And she feels it, the blame, the disapproval. Singer-songwriter type thing. Big-city cop. Her guilty part in this.

The trail past the bridge is slow going. Sophie can't imagine anyone would be able to find their way here in the dark, in a snowstorm. Not even someone who's walked these trails all their life.

This man, this "Rob," just wants to see the place where they would meet, though, so she will walk all the way up there, slipping and breaking through old snow, to show him.

She'll stand where Will stood, the last time she saw him, scratching the ground with a stick, the time she came alone and told him that Honey was sick. She was busy. She wasn't coming.

Of course now she knows why Honey wasn't feeling well, but back then she was too busy worrying about what Will might think about her, Sophie. What he might say to her, finally.

So what if it's embarrassing, and shameful even? She should tell him the truth if it will help.

She'll say, I was maybe in love with him too. But still I helped Honey sneak away with him. That's how good a friend I was.

I let her go so they could have sex, yes, obviously that's what they were doing. I knew that. I still let her go.

I let her parents believe she was spending the day with me, like when we were kids.

And I was going to sing at their wedding. I might even have hoped that he would look at me, and feel regret, just a little bit. Regret that he chose her and not me.

That is the worst of it. That's all she has to confess.

Except also, yes, she's a singer-songwriter type thing. She plays for nobody, with nobody. She was going to sing in front of a church. Her one chance. But that's gone now. She's a closed loop.

And so what? If you lived here, would you do better?

She is scared. This place makes her sick. It's ruined. She'll never come back, even when this is all over.

She is hollowed out by day after day of not knowing.

And at the same time she knows that what she feels is nothing. She is nobody in Will's life, and not in his death either.

"Well, this is the place," Sophie says, when they get to the trailhead. "This is where I left her with him."

"I see," he says, and takes out his notebook. "Is there anything else you can tell me about last summer, anyone else who he might have met out here?"

*

Sarah can feel it. Something has broken today. The sun feels stronger now that it's suddenly March, the patches of snow thinning down to gray.

And when Sarah called into the station this morning, the chief said, We'll call you if we hear anything. Anything at all. I promise.

In other words, don't call us, we'll call you.

In other words, I give up.

But Sarah has to call them every day, first thing. It's what she does, it's how she copes. Can't they see that?

And then, later, Honey wanted to tie off the fringe. No more new sections. She said she was ready to finish.

Honey has to keep weaving the wedding shawl! She can't stop now. Doesn't she understand that?

Yet as she was leaving today, after working an hour at most, Honey said that she wanted to tie off the fringe, it was long enough now.

Why both things at once? And the sunshine too? Don't call us, let's finish this up now. How dare they?

Something has broken. Something else, something more. Like an iceberg. She can feel it, a rupture.

Because what else could Honey mean. What else besides that it's over. She's finished. And the police, too, are finished. They have other things to do.

But Sarah will keep going with all of it until he gets home. She will let the shawl get as long as her waiting is long.

She calls Chief Cadoret, she watches Honey at the loom, she keeps him alive, and she stays alive too.

Are they all finished, all of them? The police, Will's father, and Honey too?

Well, Sarah is not.

Will's still alive, and Sarah is alive only because she has to be here when he gets back. And she will be here, even if she's the only one left.

Such a surprise for her when Honey took over the weaving, that day in January.

When Sarah told her that it was for her, the thing she herself hadn't touched in weeks, Honey said, For me? But it can't be, it's so beautiful!

And she cried, because Sarah told her it was supposed to be a gift, for the wedding. Her tears were such a relief. This girl really does love him, she thought. She finally knew.

I want to help, I want to work on it, Honey said. Can you show me how?

But now she says it's long enough.

Because in the end, a mother's love is deeper than any girl's love, anyway. Any wife's.

Deeper than a father's love, too, it seems.

He invited her to go with him to Colorado for the weekend, says it will make no difference if they are here or there or anywhere else, but she would not go.

She has to be by the phone in case Will calls. And it has to be this phone, here in this house.

She has to be here in case they hear anything at all, not out in the woods, not out in the mountains, not in a car somewhere either.

Are you sure? Sarah asked Honey.

Yes, Honey said. It's the right length now. For our baby, she said.

14

All the ice is gone now, and all the rivers are rushing, all the streams crashing together here at the foot of the mountain.

A whirlpool of sticks and foam gathers at the curve in the riverbank, where it gathers every spring, caught on its way downriver.

Leonard stands downstream in the shadow of a tree, casting his line. He gives a little wave, and Nell waves back.

The ice has broken, and she can walk down to where the river passes by her old house again, can sit on her rock, still cold through her jeans, even in the bright sun.

She has made it through the winter. Not entirely on her own, but she did it without the car.

Ernie let her help out in the store. Which let him help rebuild the footbridge, crushed by a fallen tree.

So in a way she helped fix the bridge. She didn't help much, but it was enough.

Her bones have healed, the ribs, the tibia and fibula. Small bones that tell her when rain is coming, like it came last night.

A great gushing rain to wash away the dirty snow, the last of the ice on the riverbank.

The trail is wet and muddy, so she walks along the road for now. Up and then back.

It is good to smell the leaf mold, the fishy water, and things thawing everywhere. The smell of life, of spring.

The water is high and brown and tumbling. A whole tree, it looks like, is wedged now between the bank and a rock.

A white bucket there, bobbing up and down. And something blue. Maybe a beer can.

But bigger, caught beneath the foam and branches, and less bright.

She stares at it, but she can't see any clearer, can't be any more certain, though of course she knows. Her blood knows, running cold now, running fast.

He was wearing a blue jacket. And that is blue, that shape, caught now by the tree, wedged there and gathering muddy foam around it.

"Leonard," she shouts. "Len!"

She feels the rush, the darkness, the shimmer breaking her vision. Adrenaline, fear, whatever it is, sucking up the last of her breath.

Leonard has turned downstream, and her voice is swallowed by the roar of the river. She can't call again. She's frozen in place, in time.

She has been here before.

She looks from the river to Leonard, his line casting out wave after wave, until finally he turns upstream.

He moves fast, once he see her, as if he knows. He knows that she's found the body of Willoughby Calper, the missing boy.

And she knows it's him, caught in the trees, in the foam.

Her whole body knows, with a suddenness that locks her in place, cell by cell, right there where she stands looking.

Why me? Why must I be the one to see him there? It's like a great wave now, this knowing what she knows and seeing what she sees.

Leonard's here on the rock with her now, and she only needs to point to the flotsam, the foam, for him to see it too.

He lays his heavy hands on her shoulders, holding her in place, not letting her wash away on the wave, in the rush of cold muddy water.

They look, knowing that they can't go back now to not knowing, to not seeing. Knowing that the whole town can stop searching now and that for the girl, Honey, the endless night is over.

The waiting is over, and now will come the blame, the way it came for Nell at the edge of that river out west.

"Come on, Nell," Len says. "We should hurry before the current moves him farther downstream."

*

April's string of warm days gave David a chance to inspect most of the beeyards. Losses aren't too bad, maybe 25 percent, but the mite testing has only just begun.

So much to do but he will stay close today, testing only the hives nearest home.

Yesterday they told Honey that they found Will in the river, and she just nodded. Like, okay. Like she already knew.

They just went into the barn where she was working and told her straight. He must have fallen into the river up near Circle Current. He was under the ice all that time.

He probably didn't suffer, David added, though he had no way of knowing one way or the other.

And Honey just kept working, sticking the labels on the empty jars, not saying a word.

She's in there now again, so David sets up in the field nearby. The weaker hives will need to be requeened but not today. Today is about mites.

And today Honey might—David doesn't know. What will her grief look like when she finally shows it?

They can't let her hurt herself is all. It's just a couple more weeks till the baby's due and she looks more than ready. Could be any time now really.

And now they can finally lay that boy to rest. Lay their hope to rest, too, and focus on this baby.

David lights the smoker to begin. He'll have to kill a few bees, but it's all right. Bees are always willing to sacrifice themselves for the good of the hive, he's just helping them along.

By now the lucky ones are out foraging, hitting up the tree blooms for nectar. A good day for it, already up to the 60s.

He calms them with smoke, then pries open the lid, lifts the frames, one after the other.

"I'm sorry, my friends," he says, like he says every time.

Scraping, killing, counting, over and over. There's no other way.

Easter came and went this year, with still no sign of the boy, but it reminded him how a resurrection can mean more than one thing.

It's the whole rest of the earth just humming with the urge to get going.

And David is glad to see it. He can't help but to feel glad at the natural order of things, all those little miracles even if not the miracle they were all praying for.

He is relieved that they found Will, which doesn't mean he's glad the boy is dead.

They will all shift now, and find a way to live with it, just the way the hive gets a new queen and keeps working. The way it lets him sacrifice a few hundred of them without fighting back.

They say the greatest losses can be a blessing, because they reveal God's love at its most profound.

Still, David would rather not have any of God's love, if it would mean losing his child. Not that he has any say in the matter.

He's just relieved that the waiting is over, and there's so much work to do.

Ruth is relieved too. She has been praying constantly for Will, for his parents, and for Honey, but now she's free to worry about the practical things of here and now.

For Ruth that means preserving her daughter's good name. She really should be considered a widow, she says, given the same respect.

For David it's more about testing and swarming. It's about this hive here, its mite count low, a blessing. The sun is high. Another blessing.

The pollen is scarce now, but soon there will be the full explosion of dandelion. That's when the bees' labor will begin for real.

He likes the sound of it, labor and delivery. That's how it should be, hard work followed by relief. Deliver us from evil.

But he's scared for Honey. For the inevitable, God-given pain of it. He doesn't know if he can take it, not with his own daughter.

But women don't die in childbirth much anymore, do they?

They just sometimes need a little help. Like the lady goat with her babies, penned up over there and licking them clean.

A little rough at the start, but a helping hand was all she needed. And Honey will have Dr. Cranbow, who was there for her own birth. He kept her safe then and will do it again.

I will not cause pain without allowing something new to be born. So says the Lord.

David sees Honey's golden head through the dirty window, sees her moving to fetch another crate, setting down to work.

He can't take away her pain, can barely even imagine it. But there can be no doubt that something new is about to be born.

*

Sophie hasn't been to Honey's house since that Saturday in December. They sat politely eating coffee cake with her parents, while Honey said almost nothing.

Pale, tear-stained, of course she was. Amber kept talking, trying to say reassuring things that only made things worse. Maybe he just got cold feet. He'll be back and he'll be sorry.

But Honey called today, and so Sophie is here. They walk down the driveway with the dogs following, like always, then out onto Chubb Road.

The road is rutted with potholes, which are full of water, and they can't walk a straight line.

Last time she was here the fields were a brilliant white. Now they're just dead and gray, stubs of corn stalks and snow-flattened leaves.

She thought by now Honey would have different friends, other pregnant girls, or maybe the girls from her church eager to be her handmaidens. Why would she call Sophie, after all this time?

Honey walks slowly now, and with a limp. She says it's sciatica, which sounds like something only old people should get.

"They say I have to walk a little every day," she says. "So I like to walk past the house. That one there. That was going to be our house."

It's a small clapboard, with dirty white siding. The grass out front is still brown from winter, and there's a bright plastic play set on the porch. Someone else lives here now, some other child.

"Will wanted to paint it blue. We were going to put in a skylight and make love under the moon."

Oh. Sophie didn't need to hear this. Why is Honey telling her this? To make her jealous again, reclaim the upper hand?

"I wanted to see you all winter," Honey says. "But I didn't think I could be around anyone who didn't think he was coming back. I couldn't be around anyone except Sarah."

"Sarah?"

"Will's mother. We were making something. I'll show you when we get back to the house."

Honey never calls parents by their first names, but now she is friends with this woman from the city who always seemed so aloof, so sophisticated?

What about the girls from her church whom Sophie imagined, assembled around Honey's swollen feet?

No, instead Honey has been making something, with Sarah. Something beautiful probably.

"And then I couldn't see Sarah anymore because I just had a feeling," she says. "Like that I knew in my heart he was dead and couldn't hope with her anymore."

Honey says it with hardly any feeling at all. Matter of fact.

"So I guess I knew a few weeks before they actually found him. Though I suppose you all knew long before that."

Sophie has to stop walking, let her catch up. She is so painfully slow now.

Honey takes her arm. She's huge, waddling, bloated, but her face still has that brightness.

It's in her eyes, maybe, that Sophie can see the little girl whose hair she used to braid, silky like a doll's, until Honey would get impatient and they'd rush off somewhere.

The same girl who waded out into the freezing water that day, calling for them to follow. She's still in there somewhere.

"You're going to leave, you're going to go to college and leave me here. But you have to promise to still be my friend."

"Of course, I'll call you whenever I come back," Sophie says.

How could anyone promise something like that? And why should she?

No. Honey had Willoughby, she was loved, she stood at the center of it all, all winter and spring, and soon she'll have this baby. That's what she gets. She doesn't also get Sophie.

In another year Sophie will be gone, becoming someone else altogether, and Honey will just be a mother, competing with other mothers about when the baby says Mama. Dada. No.

"Please, you have to promise me." Honey stops and looks Sophie in the face, searching her eyes like she knows Sophie doesn't mean it.

"I'm going to need you to help my baby get out of here. You and Sarah will do it. My mother will want to keep me and the baby close. She'll want my baby to be her own, and she'll do it too. She will."

"Okay," Sophie says, but she still isn't sure. What could she possibly do?

"My mother never loved Will. She turned him away. And this baby is his too. We can't let her try to change that."

"I don't see how . . ."

"You'll come back. You'll go away and get some fancy degree, and you'll make a record, but you'll come back. You will, whether you promise or not."

She says it like a warning, like she knows something. Does she know something? Of course not, she's just Honey, and Sophie will only be back for holidays, to visit.

She won't be sitting at that front desk forever, counting up the receipts, like her mother. And she won't be just a pathetic singer-songwriter girl, playing only to herself in her room.

Sophie will have a life in the city, maybe she'll learn to play bass, be a sought-after musician, and then she'll do something significant somehow. She imagines much more for herself.

But so did Honey. And Amber, too, but where is Amber now? She barely even thinks about going away for college anymore.

"Sarah is planning a memorial," Honey says. "She asked if there was anyone else local who might want to say something, and of course I told her you."

"What, why me?"

"I know you loved him too. I always knew it."

"No, I didn't."

"Well, whatever you say, it doesn't matter. I want you to play what you were going to play at the wedding."

"I can't play that. It just makes everyone cry."

"Then play something different. You can't tell me you haven't learned anything else since then. Nothing at all. I've been growing this baby, crying my eyes out, what have you been doing?"

"Well, I've been working on something . . . but . . ."

"Oh, I knew you would!" She pulls Sophie closer, and she can feel Honey's huge stomach against her hip, feel her heat.

"I'll think about it."

"I knew you'd do it! I told Sarah, my friend Sophie has a beautiful voice, she will sing."

"It's not good enough, and it's not finished," Sophie says.

But there it is again, that vision of standing in front of the church, singing, with her guitar, while people see her. Honey off to the side.

Because the fact is there's a song she's been working on. Alone in her room, yes, but it's good. A small part of it, at least, is good.

"When is this happening?"

"Before the baby comes, I hope. She . . . or he . . . we didn't want to know in advance . . ."

And it's back to that again. The baby eclipsing everything, every conversation, from here on out.

But that's okay, because Sophie has this now, too, this vision. Terrifying but true.

She might not know what it's like to have a tiny creature inside, to have been loved like Honey was loved, and to face death the way she has faced death, but she does have this.

She walks with Honey on her arm. Honey who is still her friend, who still wants her in her life and believes she has the power to do something important for her baby.

When they get back to the house Honey hands her a neatly folded package of white tissue. "This is what we made all winter, Sarah and I."

It's a splendid, shimmering thing. Feathery, soft, the lightest silk, with a long, braided fringe.

Sophie takes it in her hands. Tries to imagine a baby, spitting and shitting as babies do, wrapped in something as precious as this.

*

Jim never understood this before, but shock is a kind of protection.

That must be why they are still here after what they saw, what they know now for certain.

Why he's standing here on the deck, solid against the muddy ground. Just standing, looking, not remembering what he just saw.

He can only go forward. Only tend to the immediate, the physical, the facts.

He will hold his wife in his arms, and he will call the family.

They'll all come and stand together right here, on this deck overlooking the trees, overlooking the mountains and the river.

Jim thought maybe they should hold a service in New York, back where they know so many people, where Will grew up, but Sarah has made up her mind.

It has to be here, she said. He was happy here. I want to remember him here.

There's some sense in that, despite the logistical complications. The closest airport is an hour away. And where will everyone stay?

They can't all stay here at the house, that much is clear, with Sarah's mother so long in that guest room it's practically hers now.

How anything is clear when really it is all a horror.

And yet some part of him is pleased to see the sun coming back, to see everything melting, to see the kilowatts pouring back into the meter after a slow winter.

It must be shock, only shock, that allows him to keep going. Now that he has lived through what he never thought he could live through and seen what he never thought he could see.

His mother will call the rest of the family. They will all come out here in a matter of days, as soon as they can.

A part of him has been planning for this since December. As soon as the wedding was called off. One ceremony exchanged for another.

He will say a few words, some of the same words he would have said at the wedding.

He'll stand right here and talk about Willoughby with the only people on this earth who will ever know or remember him.

But not to go there, not to think about that, is the thing. He has more calls to make. They will want to order food. Catering, Sarah says. Maybe from the inn?

Will was always so much like his mother. He might've looked like Jim, but he was his mother's son, right up to the end, even in how they fought.

There were perfect days, like last May, the three of them out here on this deck when they just arrived. Eating the salad and samosas he brought back from the farmers' market.

Those last days in December when Will was bubbling over with happiness and hope and a little fear, too, when they'd finally set a date for the wedding.

They never did get up to Lake Willoughby with him. They always meant to do that, to show him where they first met, where Will was conceived, if not literally.

Sarah seems finally to have awoken from her long winter's trance. She's determined to do one more thing for Willoughby. And she wants to do this right for him.

She has picked up the phone and called the roommate from Strattenburg. She called his friends from New York, who will call other friends from New York.

Sarah wants them all here. She will pay their way, will pay for anything, she says.

Every single room at Birches. Leila will hold the whole place for them.

The Mitchells even said they could hold a service in their church, even though he was not quite a member. He was almost a member, Mitchell said. An honorary member now, he said.

But Jim had to say no. He did it for Sarah as much as for himself. No. A service for Will must be at their house, here in Upper Glenville.

Will did love it here, if briefly.

The clearing around the deck is still too wet for planting, though they have decided to fill it with birch trees as soon as they can.

We'll plant them ourselves, Sarah says. She wants to get her hands dirty, to feel it in her back, her body.

They'll plant a stand of trees which will last longer than any of them, with any luck.

Though birches require cold winters, and snow, and how much longer will this place be cold enough for trees like that?

Maybe also something hardier. Some larch.

He looks out at a few of them now, straggly things turning green at the tips among the budding trees.

Is that right for Will? An ancient tree and a younger one. Larch and birch, they'll have both.

They'll all stand here on the deck and in the great room. They'll open all the doors no matter the weather and have some words and songs.

Honey must be enormous by now. Jim hasn't seen her and he's not sure he wants to, but she'll be here, too, maybe in a black veil. Maybe she'll say something too.

There's so much to do, now that it's done. Now that they found him in the river.

He must have fallen, slipped under the ice. It wouldn't be the first time this happened here in Glenville, Jeanne said.

And that is where Jim has to stop. There are holes in the armor of shock.

He looks now at the sky, the clouds moving quickly past. He has always only believed in the earth, but now he needs something beyond it, past the sky even, past all this.

Why couldn't it have been him first, and then Sarah, or even, my god, Jim's own parents, who are enjoying yet another spring in Arvada, planning another summer in their lake house? He knows any of them would be willing to trade places with Will.

But this is what it is. Later he'll go straight into that darkness and hopefully come out again, but not now. Because now they have plans to make. One last thing to do for Will.

And after that? After that they will leave here. They'll leave all this quiet beauty, this house, even the trees they have planted, and they will go as far away as possible.

Maybe finally they will go together to India, which they always meant to do, and they will go deep, as deep as a person can go.

They will survive that, too, and then they will be on the other side of it.

A ceremony is good. A gathering of family, friends, words, trees, and a view of the mountains. But it won't be enough.

In India they burn the body on a pyre, or bind it and send it down the Ganges, on to the next world.

Maybe that's what Jim needs. Something grand, something old, the great River Ganges. To be scorched in some kind of fire. To be burned to the ground, down to nothing.

This is a good place, Jim thinks, looking around him, the deck so well built. But it's not theirs anymore. It's the place where Will died. It has to belong to somebody else now.

*

Cyrus was right. It's not cancer like you'd expect, in the lungs or something, but cancer in the nodes. Lymphoma, and not an early stage of it either.

He has the heat cranking, but Dad is all huddled up there, under his seat belt.

The heat's not helping Dad but it sure is putting Cyrus to sleep. He better open a window, smoke a cigarette, something.

Though what he really needs is some actual sleep about now. Up at the crack of dawn for these appointments and taking the afternoon shift to close.

It's not going to work, Cyrus driving Dad to appointments like this. But Dad won't go otherwise. He'll just sit home. Cyrus knows it.

He'll sit home and the cancer will spread and he'll die, slow and painful. Not like that kid, who probably died within minutes of falling in the river. Short and sweet, the only good way.

Cyrus always used to think he'd be better off without the old man, but now he's not so sure. Faced with it, with maybe not having him around.

The doctor says he'll live longer if he goes through the treatments. It's that simple.

But for Dad it's a big, big if. For Cyrus and Dad, because that's what it's down to now.

He pushes the lighter in, lets the little round coil get good and red. He'll just keep the window open when he lights it.

"Sorry, Dad," he says. "Got to stay awake."

"Don't worry about it, kid. It's not like I'm worried you'll give me cancer or something."

Ha ha, still always trying to be funny, Dad is. Even when it's life or death.

Cyrus winds the window down a few inches. Another forty minutes down Route 11, he might as well settle in.

Dad too. In a minute he'll be drooling, asleep, until they get stuck behind some shit-spreader or construction site, because it's not the potholes or the speeding, it's the stopping that wakes him up.

It's always something on this road. Which is fine, as long as he's back in time to change, get a shower before work.

People at work are nicer to him now. Carol says, don't worry, we'll cover for you, when he tells her he's taking Dad up to Kingsbury.

Plus everyone's been acting a little nicer to everyone since they found the dead body. It gets you thinking.

Still, it's time now for Cyrus to get serious, because who knows, he might be on his own soon. Really on his own.

The state will take care of most of Dad's treatments, thank god, but medical bills—they're no joke.

Can anyone actually pay for that stuff? It's not even real, the amount for those tests! Every time you step into a doctor's office you owe another couple hundred. Or somebody does.

Better not let Dad see them or he'll just stay home. He's already complaining more about the treatment than he ever complained about being sick.

He even apologizes, which is weird. Sorry to get you up so early, Cy, he says. I know you got a day ahead of you.

Which is true, but not something Dad usually ever says.

When he told Mom, she said she'd help out. Your dad's not such a bad guy, she says, just not someone I should ever've been married to.

She did come up last weekend and clean some things Cyrus had stopped noticing a long time ago. She mopped the kitchen. When's the last time that happened?

Plus, she said she'd help pay for college if that's what he decides to do.

Believe it when I see it, he says. Like Mom always told us, it's the thought that counts.

Maybe once he gets working for Burdette this summer he'll be able to turn in the Shaw's apron for good. He'll be working outside, wearing his own shirts, and he won't have to see Emily anymore.

You're just not my type, she says. She prefers Daniel, even after what he did. And even though Cyrus knows he's better than that.

He'll do excavating in the summer, snowcat in the winter, good enough money to do the classes in the fall and spring.

Johnny Burdette says he'll give Cyrus a chance with the heavy stuff once the ground is dry enough, and if he's good he'll be making twenty an hour, cash, all summer long.

And if he's good Burdette will pay for his CDL training and the test, too, he says.

Maybe he feels sorry for Cyrus now, on account of Dad, and what with Jason in jail six months. Your brother, your cousin, whatever, it ain't easy, he said.

And there it is—he knew it! A shit-spreader up ahead. Tis the season. Mud season, they say, but it's really shit-spreading season.

Manure pits are full, ground is thawed, time to start spreading the joy! At least he's not a dairy farmer. Now those guys, they really have it rough.

They have classes now called Ag Tech for farmer kids. Which he's not taking. He's taking business administration, if anything.

Sounds boring as hell but he might need it. He might have his own business one day. Excavating maybe, if it works out at Burdette's.

Seems so long ago now that he thought he might have a business making Z8. Just last year, he was such a stupid kid.

Besides, the feds are onto it now. Too good to be true, that it was ever legal.

Good thing he didn't waste any more time on that, what with Dad and everything. What with Jason getting locked up and Eli about to graduate.

Believe that when I see it too.

The heat's really cranking now, and Dad's asleep finally. Cyrus still can't feel the toes on his right foot, though, no matter how warm they get.

Too many days out at the lifts, subzero, when nobody else would do it.

Well, he didn't need those toes anyway. You got to make sacrifices if you want to get anywhere in life. That's what Mom always says.

At least his car is still okay. He gives the dashboard a nice pat. It's dusty and has a couple cigarette burns, but it keeps on ticking.

The heat works, too, even if the AC is shot. Hard to imagine the AC will ever matter again, after so many days of cold.

15

Tulips are a little late this year. Still just tight little buds but probably they'll be open in time for the first wedding, the third week of May.

Leila should've put on gloves, but she hadn't meant to get this deep into the weeds. Just meant to trim down some of the dried coneflowers and clean the rest up later.

But she's in it now and it's such a pleasure to see the red tips of peonies poking out of the soil. The curls of green hosta. To smell the moldy earth down there, warming up.

Steve has taken over the desk today without her asking, and she can hear Sophie up on the porch, strumming and singing.

Leila could listen to Sophie all day long and never get tired of it, even if she plays the same song over and over.

As long as it's not "Abide with Me," which has always felt more like a funeral song, especially when Sophie kept practicing it all the way up till the wedding date.

Now that it's warming up Sophie likes playing out on the inn porch. She used to be so secretive, but now she just sits there playing and singing like she doesn't even know you're there.

Which of course she must. Because even though Leila is working where Sophie can't see her, the dead brush rustles as she rakes, the seedpods shaking like rattles.

Leila was so impressed when Sophie played at that memorial service. Just a song I made up for him, she said, as if it were no big deal.

But Leila could see how intent she was, up there in her simple black dress, friends and strangers assembled around her.

Her voice hardly even seemed part of her anymore, so clear and distinct, like some disembodied thing. And Leila could swear she was wreathed in light.

Steve saw it, too, though they know they were just the overly proud parents, a little bit shocked by their daughter's autonomy, how strange it was to them.

Leila carries the debris back to the compost around the shed, but when she listens now the music has stopped.

There's a stroller parked by the step.

It's Honey Mitchell, and she has brought the baby!

She has her hair in two thick stubby braids, and she and Sophie are leaning over the bundle in her lap.

Hard to believe, the two of them, still friends after all that has happened. Or maybe that's why they're still friends, having been through so much together.

She should let them talk, let them alone, but Leila can't resist.

She wipes her hands on her jeans. Not clean enough to touch a new baby or pick her up, but she can at least say hello. See her little face.

"Willoughby," Honey says, "meet Mrs. Pierce, she's Sophie's mama."

"We call her Bee, for short," she says. "Baby Bee."

"She's just beautiful, Honey. Look at those tiny hands!"

And just as she says it, Jenny Rose comes out too. And Nancy from the cleaning staff. Nobody can resist a new baby. Only two weeks old!

"Let me see that little beauty," Jenny Rose says. She's already dressed in her white blouse and black pants.

"You're so lucky you got a girl," she says. "Amber was always so much less trouble than her brothers, even when she was a baby."

Honey holds her baby's head up so they can all see her face. How does that happen, that she goes straight from being a girl to being a mother, just like that?

Steve comes out now, too, to get a look at her. At the two of them, really, because they haven't seen Honey since the service. She was so huge and pitiful up there, her face streaked with tears.

"She looks just like you, Honey," Steve says, though it's not true. It never is true, but it makes the mom happy to hear it.

Steve looks at Leila and doesn't need to say it: How does this happen, when just yesterday they were babies themselves?

Leila misses the evenings she and Steve used to spend out on the porch, sipping their drinks and listening to music, but it has been worth letting go of that to have him back.

And he's the one she has to thank for Sophie's musical gifts, the one whose idea this whole place was in the first place.

It really is a good place most days, even though the paint is peeling again from the gable trim. Even though it's always falling apart in one way or another.

Honey hands Sophie the baby, who starts to cry. "Sorry!" Sophie says and hands her right back.

"Don't worry," Honey says. "She does that with my mother, too, though she always stops crying when Will's mom picks her up."

"Babies are just like that," Jenny Rose says. "I had three and I still could never tell what set them off."

Honey holds her baby close, quieting her with her voice, her touch, whatever it takes. So proud, to be fussing and to be a mother, no matter that she's only a teenager.

And she might go back to school in the fall, she says. 'Cause Mom can't watch the baby *and* teach me math."

"You'd be surprised how much your mother can do all at once," Steve says. "Moms are magical like that."

Leila knows this is his way of praising her. You saved my life, he reminds her again and again, which is an exaggeration but also not.

Leila has lost count of each day of sobriety just as she lost count of the days Will was missing. They were her trials, but also not.

"There's nothing you won't be asked to do as a mother," Jenny Rose says. "Believe me. As a single mother, you've just joined the biggest, most badass club there is."

Leila can hardly keep from rolling her eyes. Leave it to Jenny Rose to make it all about herself.

Well, let her have it. Today Honey is healthy, the baby is strong, and she and Steve are ready to conquer another wedding season together.

*

When people think libraries, they think old ladies in glasses and dusty books, but Jesus god, they have the internet too.

You can get everything here if you just sign up for a half hour on the internet!

Why didn't Eli know this before? He's been living in the dark ages.

Doing homework at school, or not doing it, but now—Bingo!

He's just taking a minute to see what he can find about Willoughby Calper. The police reports, the autopsy reports. If he's going to be a private investigator someday, this stuff is important.

Eli can't believe how many times this kid's name comes up. How many articles. And everything ever written is right here for him to find.

A whole list of who was in on the search. Border patrol. CERT. The fire department. The Maritime Museum?

He thought that was just a bunch of old dudes with wooden boats, but they were in on it too. Divers, from the museum.

Like treasure hunters maybe. Eli could do that, he's good at finding stuff.

And there's some stats from the autopsy, too, a coroner's report. They had to check his dental records to make sure it was him.

The body had his wallet, his ID, even some cash, a MetroCard from the New York City subway. No signs of foul play, it says.

No kidding, Eli says.

Since the guy still had the cash on him, still had his wallet. That would be the first thing anyone would take.

And why the hell would he have a subway card? He must have meant to go back to the city.

Yes, Eli should definitely be an investigator. He knows things before other people do. Sees things they don't see.

He could've told them the Calper kid fell in the river, back there on the trails. He probably didn't see it because of the snow, because of the ice and dark.

Eli could have told them that back in December when they called him.

It says they're still investigating the cause of death and they'll release it when the report is final, but it's obvious. Eli could tell them right now.

The kid fell in the river and drowned. Case closed, he would say.

There were no lacerations, the report says. No head trauma. No damage to the fingernails. Just some snapping turtle bites.

Some fucking turtles were nibbling at his torso!

Eli doesn't care, not much—but to be dead in the river, that's the real deal. And it was nobody's fault but his own.

Except maybe Honey. It was maybe her fault, getting pregnant like that.

But it seems like sometimes Eli just has to want something, and then the universe does it for him.

Like when Jason wouldn't let him work with him. No way, runt, he said. Well—who's in jail now?

Maybe if they'd let him work for them they wouldn't've got caught. He could've showed them a thing or two.

There are transcripts of all the calls with the police. Even Sophie Pierce, who's probably never done anything wrong in her whole life.

And there it is: Eli's own name!

Nothing much except a record of when the cop called him on the phone. But he remembers. The guy asked about "the encounter." And where were you on the evening of Tuesday, December 18?

Now that all the reports are out, you can even find Eli LeBeau on the internet. Not a star witness or anything, but there's his name.

A little kid at the desk next to him is kicking his mom's chair now. Rattling Eli's chair too.

Why anyone wants to have kids is beyond me. Why in hell Honey Mitchell went ahead and had that baby.

She's probably looking for some guy to help her with that baby now, someone to be a daddy.

She'd probably be happy to take Eli now, wouldn't she? Eli's looking pretty good now, compared to Willoughby Calper!

But Eli doesn't want her now. She thought she was too good for any of us, anyone in the whole town, and now look what happens.

Maybe she'll be nicer to Eli now. Maybe her dad will be nicer to him too. Ha!

It's sad, though, the whole thing. He can admit it. Pretty sad to just take a wrong turn and then be dead.

The librarian is coming over now. He must've used up his half hour. He didn't even do any of his homework yet!

"Yeah, yeah, I'm finishing up," he says.

He clicks out of the police report with his name in it, shuts the autopsy, and smiles at her.

"There are other patrons waiting."

"Okay," he says. "But can I sign up for more time? I didn't finish my homework yet. I just need to finish this to graduate."

✷

It amazes her every time. Just a little cardboard box with some holes in it, and a whole flock of chicks can survive a few days in the postal system.

Jeanne peeks in at the little fluffy things bobbing and pecking about. Some grayish, some yellowish, and all so damn cute. But loud!

She leaves them on the counter with the pens and labels, where a nice spot of sunlight is coming in through the plate glass.

Nearly noon and Leonard's not here yet, though she left him a voice-mail a couple hours ago.

Jim was here earlier asking about the noise. That's just one tiny box of chicks making all that racket? Incredible!

He wanted to give her his new book, *Rising Tides*. Said he'd be going away for a while, doing interviews for the book, then taking a trip to India to see some big river there.

Fifteen hundred miles long, he said. Imagine, millions of people live off it, pollute it, worship it. And there's a meditation center he wants to go to with Sarah.

Or, I don't know, he said. Maybe I just need to get away. Get overwhelmed by something.

She can't imagine going that far, but Jeanne doesn't blame him needing to get away. A memorial service can only do so much for a person.

She was glad when Jim invited her, though. You've always made us feel welcome here, he said, which made her feel good.

And it was good to stand up there with all those people, hear nice things about Will from friends and family who came from all over the place. And that song by Sophie Pierce was something special.

Even so, it's going to be hard to get over the death of that boy. For all of them, the whole town, on edge for four months, nearly five, imagining the worst, which finally came true.

Don says they'll get over it soon enough. By summertime kids will be up there swimming in the river. They'll forget all about it.

Jeanne keeps an eye on the chicks across the room while she flips through Jim's new book, which is about where the water will be, ten, twenty years from now. A whole chapter on Alaska. Another on an island way out in the Pacific Ocean, already halfway drowned.

What will happen here in Glenville? Probably no problem with sea-level rise, though people will probably start moving here when places like New York City are flooded.

Jeanne won't be here to see it, but her kids might. Grandkids, if she ever gets any.

It's a relief when the bell jingles, and finally, here's Leonard. He's got mud on his jeans, from gardening maybe, but his beard is trimmed real nice.

"Your special delivery is over there by the window," Jeanne says. "People been asking about them all day. You're lucky I didn't give them away."

"Thanks for keeping an eye on them, Jeanne. Sounds like a lively bunch!" He brings the box over to the counter and opens the lid a little.

"My god, would you look at them! Gray ones must be the Barred Rocks. Supposed by be good layers," he says.

"I'm surprised you're planning to keep chickens now, Len. Didn't think you'd want to be tied down like that."

"They're not for me," he says. "They're a surprise, for a friend."

"Is this the same friend you've been trimming that beard for?" she asks, raising an eyebrow.

He rubs the smooth spot under his chin. "Had to clean up my act sometime," he says. But then he points at Jim's book. "What's that you're reading now?"

"Oh this?" she says. "The latest by our famous neighbor. Fresh off the press, though I guess he finished it before . . . everything. He's going to India next. Some sacred river over there."

"What, our river isn't sacred enough for him?" Len says. "Rivers don't get much nicer than that, if you ask me."

"Nah, this one's important. Millions of people, huge floods, pollution—environmental everything. The kind of thing Jim Calper gets stirred up about."

"Wow. Well. I guess I better get these little buggers home, give them something to drink. First twenty-four hours are crucial, you know."

When the door closes behind him and the baby chicks it's suddenly very quiet. And just like that Jeanne feels a chill again.

First twenty-four hours are crucial. They were for Willoughby Calper, too, out in the weather like that.

Yes, it's going to be a while before she wants to swim in the river again.

She'll get over it eventually, but it's going to take a lot more time, a lot more sunshine, for her to get over the thought of him all alone under that ice.

*

Sarah brings a gift of tea and accepts some honey from the big glass jar.

"Should I go ahead and brew some of this now?" Ruth says, when Sarah sits at the table. "It looks good. I don't think I've had this kind before."

Sarah is trying again. She's withholding judgment on herself and others. That's the plan. Just ignore everyone's pity and listen.

Ruth is not a person she would ever choose to be with. She'd made up her mind quickly, last fall, that she didn't like Ruth.

But if she wants to have any kind of relationship with Will's baby, she'll need at least to be on speaking terms with Honey's parents.

Ruth is busy with the kettle then sits down across from Sarah while it heats. She smooths the tablecloth in front of her. A floral polyblend that's been on the table for a while, by the look of it.

But Sarah isn't judging. Ruth has invited her over and here she is. It's time they get to know each other. The grandmothers.

"How's Bee sleeping these days, is she sleeping through the night?" Sarah asks. She can't bring herself to call the baby Willoughby.

Ruth talks easily about sleeping, eating, and nursing, and Sarah wants to know it, all of it.

But they'll have to find other things to talk about if they're going to get through this together.

When Ruth sits, Sarah says, "Jim wants us to leave here for good now. Now that we've left Will's ashes near the river, and up by Lake Willoughby."

"That's a shame," Ruth says, but what part does she object to—the ashes, or the leaving?

"It would be a shame to leave the baby, of course," Ruth says. "She's your family. I'd never want to live too far from my family."

"Well, Jim's thinking we should sell the house. Go to India. For a pilgrimage of some kind."

"A pilgrimage could be the right thing, I guess. At this time in your life."

"Yes, but I don't want to go."

It's the first time Sarah has said it out loud and now she knows it's true. She won't go. "I want to stay here. This is where I live now."

Ruth pours the tea, a little too soon probably, and Sarah feels it washing over her again, the pure, cold sorrow.

The tears, too, which show up with no warning. She lets them run down her face as the steam rises from their cups.

She knew this would happen. She misses Will. She doesn't want to be here, or anywhere, without him.

Ruth reaches across the table and puts a hand on Sarah's hand. "I'm sorry. This is all so hard."

Sarah doesn't want Jim to leave, but she knows he's going. He has already made up his mind and she's seen his plans, an ashram in Kerala, a brochure on the table.

"Maybe you'd like to come to my ladies' prayer group tonight," Ruth says. "It might help to have fellowship. Between them these women have suffered some real losses. They might be a comfort."

"Thank you. I just don't know. I'm not religious."

"That's all right. I could introduce you and you wouldn't need to say a word. It's tonight at seven. At the church fellowship hall."

Just the sound of it, the fellowship hall, makes Sarah want to run and hide. But she says yes. She says okay.

What will Jim say when she tells him?

He's going to India and she's going to the fellowship hall in Glenville, Vermont, to the church basement, land of AA meetings and bad coffee.

She can tolerate these people, of course, but it would be better, less lonely, if she could understand them.

She'll think of it as a quest, a trip into the unknown, even if it seems too mundane for words.

She drives back up the mountain in a kind of trance. She's been in a trance a lot lately, like she doesn't know where she is or who.

This is me. I am here, she reminds herself. I turn left at the general store. I continue a half mile.

Yes, this is Upper Glenville. This is where I live. It's where Dad used to have his camp.

Will they speak in tongues at this ladies' prayer group? That is what Baptists do, isn't it? They gather together and let the Lord work in mysterious ways. Or maybe that's only in the South.

Sarah really has no idea. Sarah gave up on any kind of church as soon as she went to college. She and Jim both had the same sense of these things.

They were going to go deep together but instead Jim seems only to want to go out.

Sarah has changed, too, though. She has been flattened, made indifferent, small. She is no longer chasing after something but has been cornered and quarried.

She just wants to lie down, to mourn, to die, maybe to pray.

And she wants to see Bee, every day, sucking on the fringe of that silk shawl. To look for traces of Will in her tiny face.

And she wants to see Honey too.

It seems forever ago already, that time she spent with Honey at the loom. In some indescribable way that time was sacred to her. It was such a horror, all of it, but it brought them closer.

Jim has no feeling for the baby, it seems. Or for Honey. He wants to move on.

It's not like him to give up on a place, just like that. To give up on the water-bottling story in Maine, which he was so fired up about. To give up even on *Rising Tides*, which he spent ten years researching and writing.

Jim tells her it's about the Ganges River. It's water, always water, can't you see? he says. And this is the most sacred waterway of all.

But when she thinks of the Ganges Sarah only sees funeral pyres.

No, that's not a place for her. The river here is her river. It's where he died but it is home.

She parks the car along the side of the road and opens the window and listens. The sound of water rushing, of the wind in the trees.

The same sound as that day they stood outside on the deck with all their friends, all their family, and remembered Will.

It was maybe the most beautiful day of her life. All those people up from New York. The roommate from Strattenburg.

Willoughby was such an extraordinary young man.

Or such an average young man, really.

But he was her delight.

And they just planted all those trees. She can't leave the trees. Jim, can't you see, I can't go, I can't leave.

He has to go, he says. He will die otherwise. And she will tell him, yes, you should go. But I won't go with you. I hope you come back.

And she has told Ruth that she will go with her to the fellowship hall.

She will meet these women who have suffered their own losses, though at the moment she's certain not a single one of them can touch her own.

*

Sophie goes to the dining room as soon as she gets home from school, before Jenny Rose, before Caleb, before anyone.

She has to set the scene and set it right. Laying the ground for a conversation with Dad that will change the course of her whole life.

Gabriel sent her an email today. They're playing next weekend and they want her to come down.

Tell your parents my sister will be there too. Tell them we'll meet you at Penn Station.

Sophie unwraps a stack of white tablecloths, fresh from the laundry.

Each table will be perfect before anyone else even shows up. If she sets it perfectly, Dad will say yes.

If she shows how careful she can be, how responsible she always is, Dad will be glad for her, and he'll convince Mom.

He will understand, won't he? This is her chance to play in a band and she will do it. She's going to spend a weekend in New York.

With Gabriel. But it's not about him. It's about music, it's about harmony. It's about the rest of her life.

They sat by the fire here after the memorial and they stayed up too late, Will's friends and Sophie. And Amber for a while, too, till Jenny Rose finished cleaning up and took her home.

The others fell asleep. She and Gabe forgot about them, forgot about the time.

I heard you last night, Dad said the next day. With Amber and those kids from New York. It sounded pretty good.

When she finishes with the tablecloths she gets the burgundy overlays, lines them up. Triangles down the sides, just so.

One after another. Flattens them with her hands. It is calming. She is calm.

Dad, I want to go to New York next weekend. I'll take the train. To play in a band, they're playing a house party.

Just to say it. A house party. She's not even sure what that means.

She grabs a tray of salt and peppers. One set per table.

You have a great voice, you should come down and play with us sometime. Don't you think she should come? Gabe said to the others.

And it's true. They sounded good together, even without Amber and the others, and they know the same songs.

The oil and vinegar are next. Tiny cruets, filled to the top. She places them one by one, her hands a little shaky now.

What will your mother say? Dad will ask, and Sophie will say, Mom will say yes if you do.

She won't say that she's going whether they say yes or not. She'll be getting off the train in Penn Station next Friday, meeting Gabriel, maybe his sister, if he really has one.

She can barely remember Penn Station, just those endless escalators, crowds of people looking up at the board, waiting.

She hardly remembers what Gabriel looks like either. Except tall. A bony neck. Will and I used to play a lot of D&D, he said.

That's Dungeons & Dragons, Dad. How bad can he be? You have to let me go.

They probably should have been more somber after the memorial, not goofing around at the fire, not singing like that. They should have been thinking about Will.

But they've had Will on their minds forever. Sophie will never forget him. How could she, with Honey's baby?

You have to promise, Honey said. You'll help me, and my baby.

No, there's no way Sophie will forget Willoughby, she couldn't ever.

But just this once. Just this once it is about her.

Amber said, Wow, so you're going down to see that guy we were singing with? Kind of a dork, but he's in college, so I guess that's hot.

And that's not what this is about either. Whether he's in college, whether Amber approves. She doesn't understand. Dad will understand.

Sophie gets the oil lamps from the cart. Places them one by one in the center of the tables.

They'll be surprised when they get here and she's done all the work. Nobody even had to ask.

We need you to sing, Gabe said. Our band needs a girl singer. You can play rhythm, too, if you want.

He didn't mean it that way, did he, that they just need a girl, any girl?

She won't light the lamps yet. The days are getting long again.

The days will be long in New York next weekend, too, and the band will start playing around ten. We don't get paid, just free drinks, he said. Not that we'll let you have any.

Come on. You should come. Shouldn't she, guys? They all nodded. Sure, Gabe, sure. Your band needs a girl. What did you say your name was?

They're Will's friends, Dad. He was into D&D. Please!

There's no way she can't do this. She will regret it forever, however long that might be. Maybe only till tomorrow, for all she knows.

She might never do anything great or noble. She won't save the world. She probably won't even do spectacularly on the SATs.

And in ten years, twenty, the bees may all be dead, and a huge cloud of carbon will snuff everything else out.

But she will at least have gone to New York for the weekend and played in a band. Live a little, people say. A girl like you, always working so hard. Isn't this what they mean?

The tables are set. Her hands are trembling.

She'll see if there are any flowers she could put out on the front desk. She wants to make Mom happy tonight, the way Sophie will be happy next weekend, singing in a band.

But now here's Dad. "Wow, looks great in here," he says. "You must've got here early."

"I did. Yeah," she says. But her voice barely comes out.

"Just a few more weeks of school. Are you excited for summer?" He goes to the front desk. Looks at the book. Doesn't seem to have noticed yet that she can hardly breathe.

"Yes, I am excited," she says. Her heart in her throat now. She only has to ask. Or to tell him.

"Waitressing, SAT class, what else do you have going on? Hopefully something fun."

"Yes, hopefully something fun," she says.

And she knows that it's going to happen soon. She's going to cross over, to step into her own life. But first this conversation with Dad.

*

So many times Nell has been down here. When she was a kid, stirring leaves and pebbles into potions, collecting feathers and bits of smoothed-over glass from the muddy banks.

A green heron makes its croaking noise from across the river. She can't see its thick auburn neck, its iridescent back, but she can hear it.

You're kind of a green heron yourself, Len said. He can always see them in the reeds, even when Nell can't. The way they hide without meaning to.

When she was a teenager, she would stand here throwing sticks into the water and watching them pass under the bridge, thinking about what her life might be.

Now she stops on the way to town, her knees aching. A long road ahead still, when you do it on foot.

It has always been her river. But now when she looks over to where the water gathers and swirls, she sees him. Willoughby Calper.

The boy from the photo. The boy with the sun in his eyes.

Will he always be there, in the foam, the eddies? The sadness of his death is like a stone she puts in her pocket and carries around with the others she has collected.

It's not hers. She didn't know him. And yet she keeps it with her.

She watches an empty bottle, bobbing up and down, not leaving its place in the muddy foam.

What gets caught in that eddy seems caught there forever if you stand and watch, but when you come back a week later, it will be gone.

Only the river stays the same, moving all this time, all these years, changing everything around it.

The bucket is gone, the tree they pulled out of there when they pulled him out.

At her old house the gazebo is gone, with half-barrels of impatiens at the edge of the porch now. The garden has given way to grass.

Nell wished for her own life to be reduced to nothing, more than once. As if having it all taken away from her would in some way let her give it all back to Laura.

But Nell's own life gives and continues to give, whether she wants it to or not. Whether she deserves it or not.

Things are given and things are taken away. That's all there is.

Len is not fishing today. He would be standing there downriver, casting under that tree.

He's part of her river now, too, just as that boy is, and Laura, and the birds.

She could just stay here forever, watching the shoreline for herons, and for flycatchers skimming.

She can easily enough make it to the store and back before dark today. It's nearly June, and the sun will be up high and long.

It shines on the surface of the river now, breaking into patterns of darkness and light around each rock, each curve of the bank, as it goes.

Acknowledgments

Thank you to my early readers and friends Elizabeth Monson, Alix Mac-Gowan Calligeros, Meghan Laslocky, Jennifer Bates, Rebekah Irwin, and Antonia Losano. Thank you to Jaclyn Gilbert, Janet Kauffman, and Kathryn Davis, for example and encouragement. Thank you to Leslie Bazzett for her generous and incisive attention to this book's much-longer first draft. Thank you to all the writers who've sent their work to the *New England Review*, both the many we were unable to publish and those I've had the pleasure of working with up-close. Thank you to my editorial colleagues, among them Stephen Donadio, Marcy Pomerance, Elizabeth Sutton, and Leslie Sainz. Thank you to Max Richter, The Weather Station, Wellspring House, and the Middlebury Area Land Trust. Thank you to Monica and Pete Kuebler, my always encouraging mother and my dad who was always reading something good. Thank you to my essential, affirming sisters, Anne O'Brien and Marie Dixson. Thank you to Mike Lindgren, Sofia Demopolos, and the entire lively and dedicated team at Melville House. And thank you, in all weather, to my beloved husband Christopher Ross and our daughter Vivian.

About the Author

Carolyn Kuebler was a co-founder of the literary journal *Rain Taxi* and is now the editor of the award-winning *New England Review*. Her stories and essays have been published in *The Common*, the *Massachusetts Review*, and *Colorado Review*, among others. She lives in Middlebury, Vermont, with her family.